Sim Moy is a London-born author with a well-travelled and diverse background. He has been writing for more than a decade. *A Case of Gravity* is Moy's fourth book. It is a follow-up to his two previous books, *Waters' Edge* and *Sky High*. Their genre is not specific, although they are often described as adventure thrillers laced with a little situation humour. *A Case of Gravity* is set in present-day Cornwall in the south of England. It generally concerns the events of a hapless but affable Foreign Office employee Christian Simpkins. *The Christian Simpkins* series has proved to be an enduring and popular endeavour for Moy's particular take on modern day life.

Sim Moy himself describes this literary contribution as a conceptual novel, woven around a novel concept.

To Birgitte, my ever-patient wife.

Sim Moy

A Case of Gravity

AUSTIN MACAULEY PUBLISHERS™
LONDON • CAMBRIDGE • NEW YORK • SHARJAH

Copyright © Sim Moy 2023

The right of Sim Moy to be identified as author of this work has been asserted by the author in accordance with sections 77 and 78 of the Copyright, Designs and Patents Act 1988.

All rights reserved. No part of this publication may be reproduced, stored in a retrieval system, or transmitted in any form or by any means, electronic, mechanical, photocopying, recording, or otherwise, without the prior permission of the publishers.

Any person who commits any unauthorised act in relation to this publication may be liable to criminal prosecution and civil claims for damages.

This is a work of fiction. Names, characters, businesses, places, events, locales, and incidents are either the products of the author's imagination or used in a fictitious manner. Any resemblance to actual persons, living or dead, or actual events is purely coincidental.

A CIP catalogue record for this title is available from the British Library.

ISBN 9781398467088 (Paperback)
ISBN 9781398467095 (ePub e-book)

www.austinmacauley.com

First Published 2023
Austin Macauley Publishers Ltd®
1 Canada Square
Canary Wharf
London
E14 5AA

Table of Contents

South Wales	9
Cornwall	33
Cars	60
Whitehall, London	76
Sheena Voltaire	92
The Cotswolds	120
Robyn	158
The Rosemount Hotel	182
The Boat	212
Overt to Covert	229
Daves	266
Cleaning House	280
Tsargrin's Prognosis	289
Loose Ends	305
Christmas Cheer	322

South Wales

Christian Simpkins parked up and wound the window down, he had been to this part of Wales several times; it was in the South West, close to the churning waters of the Atlantic and not far from the quaint little town of Llandover. The headland he was on was part of an expanse labelled a place of outstanding beauty and this, here and now in early September, he, Christian, had to agree. It was getting a bit chilly but with the windows down he could still embrace the sounds of nature at its best. Wind, always the whistle of the wind, songbirds, gulls and the roll of the waves. It was a happy moment that he thought he owed to himself after ploughing up the M4 motorway from London. He then had to cross the black mountains and down through to the coast among quaint little villages that he could not pronounce along with road signs that didn't even yet register in English.

This was to be an interesting little appointment, nice almost, if one were to dwell on his previous near-fatal assignments in the Sahara followed by Central America. For some reason, he was still employed by the Whitehall department known as Ancillaries and Procurement. Although, his back-office duties were catastrophically dull, he still got paid and his life didn't have to hang by a thread anymore. In

Central America, he had somehow managed to get himself on TV far too often, Christian did not want to be a celebrity and neither did his mirthless boss, Sir Jeffery Pollock. It was deemed that between the Welsh assignment and his unobtrusive departmental desk there was very little scope for any death-defying adventures and unwanted public attention. Clearly, he was being kept on a very short leash at present. Ancillaries and Procurement was a little-known department to fix or annul problems that often plagued the Foreign Office. One wouldn't think that Wales belonged on the Foreign Office front of things.

There were only a few buildings up upon the headland, a couple of old crofters' cottages and a nest of clean grey Portacabins, and for the latter of these, he headed. He checked his phone, he liked to get people's names right. Robin Reilly was the new site engineer and Christian looked forward to the meeting as the engineer was on loan from Tsargrin's facility in Cornwall. Tsargrin Throtestabler, Christian's old friend, chose his people well and the more tricky aspects of such a project needed the right man in the right place.

A few paces before he arrived, the door to the first Portacabin opened and a girl beckoned him over, he stretched out his hand and she limply took it.

"Hello, I'm Christian Simpkins," he began.

"Yes, I have been expecting you, we have a lot to do. Robyn Reilly, production engineer."

One of the few important talents Christian had was people, it was a skill that he had honed in his previous years in the diplomatic service, speech, emotive understanding and so forth. He scanned her briefly as he entered, but she was quick and raised an enquiring eyebrow.

"Presumably I am not what you were expecting, Mr Simpkins?"

"No, not really—" She cut in before he could continue further.

"What is it? I am a woman, black maybe, something else?"

"No, not at all," Christian countered, "it is because you are so young, but if you have come from Mr Throtestabler's team, I know you are going to be good." Robyn faltered slightly and her voice rose an octave as she edged onto the defensive.

"Oh, er yes, I guess I do look a bit younger than I am, um…so I am told anyway."

To Christian, something was definitely amiss, he decided to politely clam up on the immaterial niceties until the situation eased. There were only two others there, one busy on his computer and the other pacing up and down outside on his mobile. Christian smiled slightly at the latter before turning toward the drawing table. Everything was very neat and tidy and organised as such, the programme chart on the wall pleasantly confirmed that everything was on schedule and the coffee machine looked equally welcoming. He fixed himself an Americano and placed himself down on a seat at a desk opposite where she was sitting.

"Any trouble with the local authority?" he ventured.

"No, none really, they seem more intrigued than anything else. We did have a woman around from the heritage people, but apparently, everything is fine, just routine, it seems." Christian nodded and stroked his lightly bearded chin. He didn't actually like facial hair, but it served its purpose to make him less identifiable and hopefully more intelligent.

"Budget?" he prompted.

"As in my weekly update, slightly over but within our contingency range." Her voice was still a little too clipped but betrayed the trace of a south London accent.

"Yes, your reports are just fine, thorough and easy to read, thank you. How's production? The circular hull must be almost complete by now, any complications?"

"Not that I know of."

"Surveys?"

"Land and seabed complete, nothing to report." Christian sipped his coffee and looked over to her, she immediately averted her gaze.

"The Spanish then, any news?"

"They are not Spanish, Mr Simpkins, they are Catalonians, a principality, somewhat akin to Wales. The Welsh wouldn't take too kindly if you referred to them as English, anyway they are well off the mark and they still doubt what we can achieve here."

"What, regarding the tidal generators?"

"Exactly, however, as I have said, everything is as it should be. Mr Throtestabler's design and calculations are second to none."

"But?" He placed his cup down and studied her, there was a but and he wanted to know what it was.

"Er…but?" she repeated.

"Yes, Robyn, there is a 'but', maybe you should tell me about it?" Slowly she nodded to herself.

"Well, actually there are two, no three of these buts, as you put them. It is probably better if I actually show you the first, come with me to the shoreline, it is easier to explain." She donned a big orange padded safety coat and indicated another for him to wear. Robyn was, in his eyes, a pleasant enough girl; capable and relatively forthcoming. It was a good ten minutes' windy walk to the headland shore side, but to Christian, walking was a good way to venture certain things, little eye contact and a physical gait that would offset any awkwardness.

"You are not overly enthusiastic about me being here, are you, Robyn?"

"Yeah, well spotted."

"You going to enlighten me?"

"Well yes, why not, as you've happened to bloody ask. I know all about you, Christian Simpkins, everybody does, a right little James Bond I hear, I suppose you have your gun with you right now, huh?"

"Nope, carry on…"

"Good I will, thanks for the opening. Mr Throtestabler is one of the cleverest people any of us will ever meet and guess what, he is all alone. Nobody knows anything about him, most people doubt that he even exists, and you, Mr Smart-ass Simpkins, take his grand achievements, put your name to it all and rake in all the credit for yourself and that bastard Sir Jeffery Pollock. In short, it is just a load of chauvinistic shit and I would add, I refuse to have any doings with your games, Christian bloody Simpkins, because it will just not work with me, no way."

"Mmm…okay, I get the message…Feel better?" She stopped for a second and looked across at him.

"Well, yes I do actually, by the way, that was the second but."

"Er, right, okay."

"Well, aren't you even going to argue the point then?"

"Nah, can't be bothered, now, what are you trying to show me?"

"That," she said jabbing out a forefinger. Christian followed her line of sight, just a small pebbly beach and an outcrop of rock reaching out to sea a couple of hundred metres.

"Yes, beautiful isn't it, what am I supposed to be looking at?"

"You just said it, beautiful, well at the moment, anyway. The drill ship has already bored the anchor points, but very soon a huge circular hunk of steel and concrete half the size of a football field will be anchored to it. It will be going up and down with the tide, all twenty feet of it, four times a day. It is going to be one hell of an eyesore in a location designated as a place of natural beauty. I suspect that the heritage people were expecting the more regular wave generators that sit just no higher than wave level or something."

"Hmmm…I get your drift, erm, if you will excuse the pun, however, you may well be right but we would never have the time or the funds for that matter to install wave turbines. We'll have to think of something I suppose."

"We? You and your department you mean."

"It is still less intrusive than the planned windmills though, oscillating heads or not. Anyway, it will be a temporary affair and will provide enough power to construct the windmills and also supply the town of Llandover if needed, or at least until the windmills are in place."

"God, have you any idea as to what you are inferring? I cannot believe what I am hearing." Whatever she was on about was lost on Christian as she stomped off in an act of frustration. He thought back on what had just been said, he just could not fathom out her train of thought. Back inside the warmth of the portacabin, he removed his high-vis coat. For some reason Robyn Reilly looked furious, to Christian, she would look quite pretty if she smiled once in a while. She gave him another withering look.

"Has the penny dropped yet?" Christian stared back at her, his open palms begging for some sort of enlightenment.

"No? Okay, one more time then, sit down and I shall tell you a little story." Christian obliged and sat as he was bid, quietly alert and upright, he felt like a 12-year-old back at school. "Right, are we comfortable?" Christian nodded meekly, he was supposed to be the one in charge but something was brewing and he didn't have a clue as to what it was. Once she was sure that she had his undivided attention, she began.

"Right, we have two quaint principalities participating in a project exchange, both environmentally friendly enough and topical to tick the boxes. Wales has sent a team of specialist miners to the mountains of Catalonia. They are there to promote a less damaging system of ore mining, vertical mining, very clean, minimum waste and so on. A much-favoured ideal to their own particular place of outstanding beauty." Christian began to mouth a response but she jabbed a finger at him to hold his tongue. "In return," she continued, "the Spanish or rather the Catalonians, intend to construct a new type of wind farm on this very headland. They're considerably smaller than usual and have, as I believe you know, oscillating heads, super-efficient, apparently." Christian already knew all this, yet he simply just nodded.

"Good, I think that we are getting somewhere, now, to facilitate all this the Spanish need power, lots of it as they have to set them into the bedrock and assemble them on site. This area is not on the national grid and the whole headland and adjacent areas are classed as organic so big diesel fed generators would be frowned upon, distinctly un-green. The power feed to Llandover town, four miles down the road is at its limit."

"That's it," agreed Christian, "and that is exactly what we are doing, we—"

"Mr Simpkins, will you just listen up for God's sake, please?" Christian swallowed hard and sat back in his seat, the other two members of staff slunk off to somewhere out of sight. With a heavy sigh, he waved a hand at her to continue. To him, he was right and she had got completely mixed up about something or other. Again, re-composing herself, she continued.

"Now listen carefully to the next bit, these special windmills are designed to supply the town of Llandover with clean energy. It is a small fishing port so no need for overly big power and the current arrangement of electricity cabled in from a spur nine miles inland would only need to be used as a top-up when the wind fails, correct?"

Christian lazily nodded his affirmation. "Good, lovely even, if it were not for the fact that Mr Throtestabler's tidal generator would outperform all the windmills three-fold, Mr Simpkins" – she looked at him carefully – "getting it yet?" she asked quietly. He blinked at her a few times, it was like the morning sun rising inside his head.

"Oh my god, of course, shit, the windmills will be pointless won't they?"

"They will be, yes, nice to have you back with us." Christian stood, a little pale and flustered.

"Three-fold you say?"

"Uh ha, except for slack tide, of course. You didn't give Mr Throtestabler the whole picture did you, you asked for cheap, easy power and you got it, right?" Christian just nodded, he really had nothing else to add.

"Um…I think I ought to be heading off I suppose, er…thanks for the heads up." Robyn Reilly just stood, arms crossed shaking her head at him. He felt about six years old now instead of twelve. Something jogged his memory.

"Ah yes, Ms Reilly, you said three 'buts' I think, what is the other?"

"Mmm, not really a 'but', more of a nudge, the Spanish surveyors will be here in a couple of weeks and you are our only Spanish speaker, you will have to be here." She then mouthed the word 'unfortunately'. Christian nodded uncomfortably, turned and left. She stood at the door and watched him leave. To her, Christian Simpkins did not seem to be the hotshot that everyone perceived. Firstly, he was hardly dashing, average build, average height, mousey hair and pale grey eyes. She tutted to herself slightly, she had been pretty mean to him, almost boorish. But, how could such an ordinary man be in such demand? He was neither arrogant nor even the slightest bit pushy. Christian Simpkins was already beginning to intrigue Ms Robyn Reilly.

"Whatever the man has, he hides it well," she said out loud to the emerging figures of her staff.

Christian, for his part, was pottering back down the tiny country lanes. He dammed himself for not grasping the clearly obvious. Something was amiss and he needed to think. A large welcoming pub loomed up, almost on autopilot he pulled into the car park. He got out and grabbed some air, he then grabbed a pint of the local brew, went out into the garden and sat. The Welsh project now had a problem, one of his own making. Strangely, as he sought to rectify it, his mind began to whir. It was not a new feeling, he had experienced it many times before, normally amid times of strife or danger. Only then did he realise that his mind had lapsed into some sort of stagnation. Back-office desk work was the culprit he surmised, but the whirring was back and although somewhat bothersome, it was much welcomed. An urgency now gripped him, he downed his pint and headed purposely back to his car. It was a different Christian that now took to the bends of the Welsh country roads. He found some rock and roll on the radio, shut down his phone and powered his way back to the motorway and eastward to London in an attempt to blow away the cobwebs of eight months of grinding drudgery. By the time he got to his little flat in North London, he had come up with a plan. Christian Simpkins loved a good plan.

He arose early the following morning, an agenda-free Saturday. He fired up his computer and made himself a pint of sweet tea, something he occasionally did, a comfort thing he inherited from Tsargrin Throtestabler. He glanced at his scribbled list, the top of which read, oscillating windmills followed by Pyrenean weather fronts and the standard wind patterns of South Wales and so forth. He was on the scent of something as yet unknown. With the world at his fingertips, he pursued his train of thought with unaccustomed gusto.

Monday morning, 8.30 sharp, he strode into the office of Ancillaries and Procurement in London's Whitehall. At his desk, he placed a scruffy pile of assorted papers in front of him, he picked up the phone and called a rather hapless project manager in Barcelona. Curious co-workers glanced back at him, not because of his prolonged Spanish dialogue but for the verve and purpose in which he delivered it. The esteemed head of the department was one Sir Jeffery Pollock and he was a difficult man at best, a conniving bastion of self-interest in Christian's eyes. He knew Sir Jeffery far better than most and picking the right time to see him was an art in itself. He picked his moment well, just after midday was best, Sir Jeffery was prone to twitch a little if there was a chance that he might miss lunch at his club.

"You can go straight in, Christian," trilled Sir Jeffery's new secretary. Christian nodded his thanks and did a double-take on the young woman, he had seen her before, somewhere else, but couldn't be sure. He knocked and entered, the tall greying figure had his back to him, he was staring out at the park below through a huge Georgian paned window.

"What is it now, Simpkins?" he said without turning.

"It is the Welsh project, sir, we have a problem."

"You mean, you have a problem, Simpkins, you are the project coordinator, are you not?"

"Of course, I am, sir, and you are mine," Christian's response impelled him to slowly turn. Simpkins had long been a thorn in Sir Jeffery's side but the young man that he now faced had some annoying but irreplaceable talents, and in the right state of mind could prove as wily as they come. Sir Jeffery was determined not to get caught on the back foot yet again.

"Explain."

"It is the Spanish, sir, they are way behind schedule, their specialist windmills have been inadvertently earmarked for somewhere else."

"And?"

"Well, I have been researching the findings of the heritage team and I have looked into the wind patterns of the Pyrenees. The oscillating windmills are designed to take into account inclined winds, perfect for big mountains, but in Wales, it would be completely unnecessary. Standard pivot would do and they are made here in the UK. In short, sir, we do not need the Spanish windmills."

"Mmm…And whose particular failing is this Simpkins, our department? I sincerely hope not."

"Not really, sir."

"Not at all! Would sound better."

"It seems to me, based on my research, sir, that the Spanish sales team sold their product overly well. We didn't need it and it now turns out that they are unable to deliver it. Well, currently, anyway."

"So not my department then, fine. What about expenditure so far?"

"Well, it is, as you know, funded by the World Heritage Fund and the Welsh Assembly, and now, if we don't bother with the windmills there will be no excesses. The vertical mining project is covered as will be the work so far undertaken in South Wales. If, sir, we were allowed to continue with the tidal generator scheme we could effectively succeed in the clean power requirement anyway, er…at no extra cost I think."

"You think? Well, that's a fresh idea. But let me take that troublesome task from you." Sir Jeffery paused for thought and drummed his fingers annoyingly upon the leather inlay of his enormous desk. He glanced up at the wall clock and indicated that Christian should sit while he perused the data on his screen. Ten minutes of awkward silence followed before he grunted to himself, glanced back at the clock and addressed a slightly smug and an overtly relaxed Christian Simpkins.

"Right, Simpkins, liaise with the Spanish, cancel the ruddy windmills, with no added cost to us of course, and then hopefully we can put this debacle behind us. I want a full and detailed report on my desk by morning and make sure to include all your research findings. The people of Landrover may not be so happy regarding their subsidised power. Deal with that also, will you?"

"Yes, sir, by the way, the town is called Llandover."

"Whatever, anyway I think you should go now, you have a lot to do and I have some important people to see. File here at 9 am sharp."

"Sir!" Christian brightly retorted as he stood and made his way to the door. He had already liaised with the Spanish and had pretty well compiled the file that Sir Jeffery now demanded. Closing the office door behind him, he smiled at the secretary. She had a Chinese look about her; a bob of short jet-black hair, a broad face and a wide bewitching smile.

"Hello, Christian."

"Ah um…yes you are Mie, right?"

"That is right, you have no idea who I am, huh?"

"I am sorry, no. But you look sort of familiar."

"I am sure I do, maybe it's because we all look the same, don't you think?" Christian grimaced and tried to think of some witty reply. She laughed at his effort, which nicely defused the moment. Sir Jeffery then emerged wearing his coat.

"Ah Simpkins, mmm…right. Mie, I have an appointment, back around three, divert my calls will you." He looked aside at Christian and thought as if to make a remark. He opted not to and left.

"Well, at least he used your first name, that's more than I ever get."

"It is only because he can't pronounce my other name, it's Ng." Christian smiled.

"Are you going to tell me how I know you? Er…please."

"Christian, you don't know me at all, you have my old desk, there is a photo of me in a police uniform. It's above the radiator, I had a hunk of leave to take before I settled into my new posting here. You've been there for ages. I used to be in the police, diplomatic protection, terrible hours, but because I speak Mandarin and a bit of Cantonese they upped my clearance, so here I am in the best job ever."

"Huh, you actually like it here with Sir Jeffery?"

"Of course, he is just so, so interesting."

"Interesting? Well, that is a first. I'm going back to my desk, or rather yours I suppose. I'll check out the photo, I promise that I will like it." Again she laughed, Christian walked off scratching his head.

Robyn Reilly re-read Christian's e-mail and again glossed over the relative attachments. It was late Monday afternoon. What she now read was a complete game-changer. It transpired that the wind turbine project had been called off due to a logistics problem in Spain, something that the project manager in Barcelona was more than happy with after reading Christian's wind prognosis. It seemed that Wales did not need them in the first place, this was something that she had suspected for a good while. She was to continue with the work on the tidal generators and link everything up to the supply transformers in Llandover town when the time came.

Christian had also outlined a wonderful little extra to make the giant mechanism friendlier. In short, it was to have a flat level surface with handrails and four or five clusters of mooring points. After all, the basic construction was akin to one huge weighted tin can that rose up and down more than twenty feet with the tide, twice a day. Every time it went up, it pulled upon a dozen mighty hydraulic pistons that fed the powerful generators within and when it went down it pushed them down, five thousand tons shifting around thus, created an awful amount of joules (useable energy). However, Christian had worked out that the top of the generator would always remain the same level above sea level whatever the tide, therefore a perfect mooring point for small craft, vaguely akin to a floating marina. Robyn was highly enthused by Christian's proposal, for various designs of the structure could be utilised anywhere where there was a suitable tidal range.

"Brilliant," she said to herself, "just brilliant." She sat back and dwelt upon the facts and figures in front of her, then she thought of Christian Simpkins as a person, unassuming to the extreme, had she got him wrong, or did he know all these facts beforehand, before their meeting together. If that was the case, and because of the amount of relative material at hand, plus Sir Jeffery Pollock's input, the Spanish response, and then the wind charts etcetera, she guessed the latter and now felt a little bit foolish, deceived even. It was clear that Christian Simpkins should never be underestimated. She then had another thought, Tsargrin Throtestabler, everyone knew that they were friends, he just ran it all past Mr Throtestabler, who else? She was a lot happier with this latest reasoning and decided to keep with it, for if Throtestabler said it is so, then it is…Brilliant.

The ensuing week turned out to be productive and reasonably stress-free for both Christian and Robyn Reilly. Again on a Monday, the last in September, Robyn received another email from Christian informing her of his arrival in a few days for a meeting with the local authority in Llandover, it would, he thought, be beneficial if she could attend. She was a bit easier with him now, a little less frosty. She still referred to him as Mr Simpkins and sincerely thought that she should tread a bit more carefully with him. Christian had a fair way to travel and such meetings were a huge drag on his time. She though, Robyn, stayed in a pleasant little hotel in a town quaintly called Tyddewl, or, easier on the tongue, St David's. It was the largest town within fifteen miles of the headland. She was there five days a week, at the weekend she was back in South London from whence she hailed. She checked out her calendar and replied to Christian's e-mail that the meeting would be a tad tricky for her as she had another meeting scheduled that afternoon.

Thursday came bright and early, and so did Christian Simpkins. *Clearly a night driver,* Robyn thought as he pulled up in a large saloon. She cocked an eyebrow, for he had an SUV on his previous trip.

"New car?" she questioned as he got out and stretched his limbs a little.

"What, oh…no not at all, it belongs to the department, I have to grab whatever I can. I don't actually possess a car of my own, I'm not so often about you see. Nice to see you, Robyn." He stuck out his hand and she shook it a bit more positively than when they first met.

"Mr Simpkins," she said politely, "come through, unfortunately, I could not rearrange my meeting, it is with the hydraulics people, kind of important."

"No worries, mine is at ten this morning but from experience, it will probably go on through to the afternoon, you can sit in for a while if you wish."

"No thanks, without sounding rude, there will be little I could add or answer considering my field if you know what I mean."

"Granted, oh well, I'll take a little time to update myself if you don't mind."

"Sure, coffee?"

"Love some." *Good,* thought Christian, *a bit mellower now, makes life easier.* While Christian was doing what he did, he looked up at Robyn, tutting at her computer for the third time.

"Problem?"

"Yes, well sort of, I'm trying to contact the facility in Cornwall, the chief engineer, he hasn't responded to any of my requests, he is normally so thorough."

"Do you want me to have a go?"

"Please, if you could, I need some info for my meeting." Christian flipped the lid on his laptop and tried to log into Tsargrin's facility but to no avail. He gave her an encouraging wink and tried to enter via a restricted route, this too, failed. He delved a little deeper and made a call assuming that yet another security lock-down was in progress.

"There you have it, Robyn, I'm afraid that they have a bit of a security scare, I wouldn't read too much into it. It happens, drives Mr Throtestabler potty though, could last the rest of the day."

"How on earth did you manage to get into the restricted system, Mr Simpkins?"

"Category six clearance works every time."

"Right, six, yup, that would do it." She studied Christian for a bit as he got on with his work, glancing sharply away every time he seemed about to look up. Category six was not given away lightly.

Christian arrived with time to spare at his 10 am meeting, it wasn't going to be desperately hard but he just knew that it would be desperately long. Lots of folk on lots of different committees, basically they would all want to know how exactly they would benefit, what to expect and what to do, etcetera. Christian used his time to text Consuela a smiley face, it was their little communication hello. Consuela was lots of things, first and foremost, she was Tsargrin Throtestabler's housekeeper as he lived at the facility, which was really just his house and a couple of rather special 'barns' set in a few acres of Cornish farmland. Consuela was also a C.I.A. agent, a plant, someone to keep a wary eye on the goings-on of one of the UK's most inventive minds. However, Consuela had been there so long and being so outstandingly clever in her own right, she became Mr Throtestabler's right-hand person. Bizarrely, the people that matter, knew that she was C.I.A. and the C.I.A. knew that the British secret service knew that they knew, but it all seemed to work very well. To M.I.6 she had proven her loyalty to Mr Throtestabler on numerous occasions and so had become an extra line of defence by default. Conversely, she filtered through to her operators all sorts of interesting titbits and scientific know-how, and they were most pleased, yet most of the information given was from her own scientific doings at the facility, and anything big was invariably shared with the Americans anyway. A really special, special relationship now operated quite smoothly between the two countries.

Christian's meeting with the local authority in Llandover went as well as could be expected. He managed to put a lot of minds at rest, gained a lot of permissions and undertakings by selling them the prospect of tourism and finally escaped just before 4 pm when their offices closed. He looked dubiously at his watch, the thought of another five hours of driving didn't bode well. There were a few bed-and-breakfast places to be had and they all looked nicely typical, but he knew from experience that they were probably crap. He sat in his car and checked his phone. He was looking for a smiley face from Consuela to confirm that all was well. The lack of response puzzled him a little even if there was a lock-down at the facility. He barely noticed a car pulling up behind him and was doubly startled when someone rapped on his window. It was Robyn Reilly, this was a little unexpected and he clambered out to speak to her.

"Oh…hi," was all he managed to say.

"Hi, sorry to bother you, Mr Simpkins, I was on my way back to St David's. I saw your car, I see what you mean about drawn-out meetings."

"Yes, unfortunately, it was longer than usual and I didn't actually think that was possible, I did manage a lunch break though."

"Look, Mr Simpkins, I think that we need to have a little chat, I still can't get through to the Chief engineer, they still appear to be in lock-down. It really is causing me some bother."

"Okay, Robyn, I'm sure that I can sort something, I was about to head for the pub. I'm blowed if I'm going to head off for London now. Looks like a B&B and an early start I guess." Robyn had to agree, it was a hellish drive if you weren't in the mood. She nodded her assent and they both headed for, the *Golden Leek* public house, across the road. Christian was happy with a nice cold lager and Robyn with a nice, hot cappuccino.

"Yes," he began, "they normally have these things sorted within a day, and if not, they would definitely have comms back on by now."

"Please, Mr Simpkins, give it another go, I've got people waiting, it's getting a bit awkward."

"Okay, I'll make some calls, how about calling me Christian, Chris even? C'mon, we're in a pub now."

"Okay then, Chris, it is."

"Yep, that's good," he said pulling out his phone. No amount of tapping seemed to elicit anything, He took another tack and called Sir Jeffery Pollock. Mie, his secretary picked up the call, happily trilling his name in a breathless response. "Hi, yep Mie, it's me. Listen, could I talk to Sir Jeffery please? Pretty important."

"Sorry Christian, he is not available."

"Yes, he is, bang on his office door for me, please." Robyn looked at him, slightly perplexed, there was a short pause, and then the unmistakable upper-class drawl of Sir Jeffery brought her to her senses.

"Okay, Simpkins, this had better be good. What do you want?"

"Afternoon, sir, I'm trying to get hold of Mr Throtestabler's facility, I'm told they are in shutdown, could you verify this for me please, er…sir?"

"Mmm…haven't heard anything, stay on the line, I'm putting you on hold."

"Wow, Chris, you even have Sir Jeffery running around for you."
"Not really, Robyn, no. He just likes to be in the know, that's all, gives him an edge, you know, a bit of kudos. Ah, here we go."

"Right, Simpkins, it's as I thought, it's all been sanctioned by M.I.5 on executive orders."

"Gosh, Chris, he just hung up without a word, bit brash isn't he?"
"Yes, that is one of his better traits, still, we know where we are, M.I.5 are on the case."
"Ah well, thanks for trying, bit inconvenient though."
"How often do you get to go there, Robyn?"
"Where, Cornwall? Quite a bit, I suppose, but mostly I'm out on designation, here for example. A lot of stuff I do for the facility is quite beyond me, to be honest. About a year ago, I spent the best part of a month plotting the old tennis court there with gravimeter readings, heaven knows why dots and

lines to the millimetre everywhere. Still haven't got a clue why, not an inkling."

"Huh, I know how you feel. I haven't a clue, I have to corner Charlie, I mean Mr Throtestabler, to put it into layman's terms for me."

"Did you just call him Charlie?"

"Oops, guess I did, keep it to yourself though, but that is what the locals around there call him. I reckon that they just can't get to grips with the name Tsargrin, who knows?"

"You like him, don't you?"

"Yes, eccentric genius, socially inept and the most genuine person you could ever meet."

"Consuela gives me the creeps a bit though."

"Ah…Consuela, yes, she is alright once you get to know her. You are so lucky to be working for someone like Tsargrin, I mean it. Do you mind if I give you a couple of pointers, Robyn?"

"Go ahead, I think I can take it."

"Don't speak too soon, he expects a lot from his people, was that ever mentioned to you?"

"Yes, several times, the first, at my first interview, in fact, all three of my interviews."

"Right Robyn, essentially you are a government employee, so anything you produce ends up as the property of some ministry somewhere, right?"

"Well, I suppose so, yes."

"For example, when this project of yours is done and dusted and proven to work…"

"It will."

"Good, positive stuff, well, when it is all complete, they will batch up all your drawings, specifications, calculations and even artist's impressions and these will all be sent to, in all probability, the Shore and Coastal Engineering Department. Now if this design works as we think it will, someone in the ministry will recognise its potential and put the design, your design up for tender with a profit margin in mind. Normal stuff really, now here is the bite. This tender package will have one underlying name upon it Robyn, yours, not mine, not Tsargrin's, not even the ministry's but yours, Robyn Reilly. A name just has to be put to it. Yours, in-perpetuity. I am not saying that you are going to make a lot of money or anything, I am saying that whatever catchy name they give for the tidal generators, your name will be written just after it. How cool is that then." Robyn fell silent, she gulped a couple of times and stared into her empty coffee cup.

"I'm going to be famous then, is that what you are saying?"

"More like someone of some renown Robyn, in the engineering fraternity that is and of course, to the world of grand designs."

"And your name is nowhere, and Mr Throtestabler's too, but it is his design, his idea."

"Won't be there, my name will pop up now and again as an administrator, but to the outside world it will be your baby and I have a gut feeling that these things are going to be big business."

"I think I need a drink."

"Gin and tonic maybe, works wonders for me sometimes." She just nodded and when it came, just stared into it.

"Little me, Chris, this is going to be me?"

"Yep, no doubt about it."

"My God, the greatest day of my life and I nearly missed it. Is this why you have had all those accolades on all those projects?"

"Not exactly, granted that they are all of Tsargrin's designs but my name is not on any of the documents, with me it's plain old media hype. I have a much-unwanted knack of getting myself on TV." For the next fifteen minutes, she sat in silence, oblivious to the chatter of the pub and Christian's attempts of small talk. Eventually, she stood and went around to shake Christian's hand, had a quick change of mind and stooped and gave him a big squeeze, muttered a thank you and left.

Cornwall

Come morning, after an early but lame breakfast, Christian was back on the road. London, though, was not his destination, Tsargrin's facility in Cornwall was. He was sure that everything there was fine; he was already in the West Country, sort of, so why not pay Tsargrin a visit? He had barely driven twenty miles before the weather closed in. High winds, heavy rain, slower and slower he drove on the tiny winding roads. Eventually, he was forced to put in at a rundown garage forecourt. As the crow flies, South Wales was only a hundred miles or so away from Cornwall and its Lizard peninsular, driving though, as he found to his cost, was closer to three hundred miles. He could not believe that a ferry crossing did not exist. In a couple of hours, the storm abated a little and he continued the torturously slow route to Cornwall. As darkness fell, he realised that it was far too late to pay an uninvited visit. There were lots of hotels and inns in and around the Lizard peninsular and he checked into one that he had used before. Come morning and a far better breakfast, he climbed into the big departmental saloon to find that the thing just wouldn't start. Popping the bonnet was a pretty futile action as he knew next to nothing about mechanics. Being a departmental car, it should normally have been well maintained. However, he had a number to call for such an event. The mechanic from the depths of the underground carpool was far from helpful and insisted that Christian should not have been driving it on a Saturday as everyone knew that there would be very few motor staff in. Christian knew quite well that the mechanic was talking bollocks. Again, he made another couple of calls to get someone to lambast the hapless mechanic. Eventually, the man agreed to get a replacement car. This operation took many unnecessary hours but curiously, he too could not work out what was wrong with the vehicle and insinuated that Christian had tampered with it. Christian shrugged negatively and in a very nice way demanded the keys to the said replacement car. As he neared the facility that afternoon, he immediately realised that something was definitely amiss. The roads had been closed off by the police and despite his pleas, there was no way to get through, somewhat forlornly he turned back. His weekend was being eroded into nothing. Tomorrow, being a Sunday should, he hoped, if he spoke to the right people, furnish him with a security code so he could pass the closed roads.

There were cars, security cars and police vehicles everywhere, darkly clad men bearing arms could be seen among the grounds and a gaggle of dark-suited men were out front on the driveway. Christian would have little chance of entry without the correct pass. As the man at the gate was giving him a severe dressing down for even asking to be let in, one of the suited men caught his eye and marched over.

"Christian Simpkins…well, well, how interesting." Christian recognised him instantly, it was the man that he only knew as Norman, a shadowy figure from M.I.6. Christian was surprised to see him as this should be an M.I.5 operation. M.I.6 was for overseas.

"Norman," was all he said, he was never sure if that was his first name or his surname.

"Bit strange you turning up here right now, or did you just happen to be in the area?"

"Yes," said Christian through the steel uprights of the gate. "I heard that something was up, thought I'd check it out. I was in the west country anyway."

"You thought you could help huh, even more interesting, how did you know something was up?" Christian knew this man and he would latch on to anything such as a lie or a hidden motive.

"Oh, I spoke to Sir Jeffery Pollock on Friday, I thought that this would be an M.I.5 op." Norman stared intently at him for a few seconds before giving the gatekeeper the nod to let him through.

"Okay, Simpkins, you are normally full of bright ideas so listen up. It was a bogus M.I.5. team that showed up here, apparently one of our executive officers has either gone rogue or defected. He has now disappeared as has our Mr Throtestabler along with an enormous amount of classified information." Christian stared around him open-mouthed.

"Oh my god, they've taken Tsargrin."

"That is what I just said wasn't it? They were extremely well informed, well-armed and funded. They got away by helicopter."

"What about our security bods?" he said hopefully.

"Didn't stand a chance, the two in the car have been killed, murdered more like. The in-house guy, the one on comms, was out cold with a fractured skull. That is all we are aware of at the moment. Fortunately, the housekeeper worked out that something was wrong, somehow she managed to overpower one of their men and made a break, down through the grounds, clever girl that one, they were using a phone bump."

"A what?"

"Phone bump, it is a meaty looking device that can disrupt most forms of digital communication, nothing special, they are often used. It seemed that she somehow guessed the range of the thing. When she got to the perimeter wall, she fired off a text and chucked the phone into the undergrowth. Strangely enough, Simpkins, she alerted the Americans who then alerted us, bit odd don't you think? Anyway, they recaptured her, not really knowing if she raised the alarm or not. It is more than a bit odd that this woman keeps reappearing on my radar. They knocked her about a bit though." Norman then jabbed a thumb at one of the military ambulances.

"Any idea who they were?"

"At the moment, no, I was hoping that you might have an idea, anything? Initially, Wednesday evening three guys pertaining to be from the security branch arrived all proper and correct. Friday the armed men came and Saturday the helicopter, well organised and very well drilled. As it is we, or rather the police almost surprised them, which probably wasn't for the best as they weren't armed. Once they heard the sirens, they clambered into the helicopter in a bit of a rush and headed southeast. They left one man behind but shot him dead rather than wait the extra half-minute…nice, huh? Right, go and see the housekeeper, er, Consuela isn't it? Also, keep in mind that we will need to speak to each of you." Norman dipped his head slightly to elicit an affirmation from Christian.

Consuela was sitting up in the back of the ambulance, she had been fixed up quite a bit by the medics, with a couple of big plasters, a bandage on her left leg and a purple right eye.

"Bloody hell."

"Ah, hello Christian. I was wondering when you would turn up. Nice of them to allow you to see me." Christian immediately cottoned on that the ambulance was, in all probability bugged. He mouthed an okay and sat on the edge of the trolley.

"Hell, Consuela, they knocked you around more than just a bit."

"Yes, my own fault really, a quick escape, then a sprint down to the North wall. I managed to get a quick text off then it was 'hands up and surrender' pretty sharpish, these guys knew their stuff and would have shot me if they needed to. They gave me a bit of a hiding though, they wanted to know how they gave themselves away."

"Well, I am truly glad that you did, what was it? Their mannerisms, accents maybe, wrong shoes, what?"

"I have no idea actually, Tsargrin recognised that something wasn't quite right and that's normally good enough for me. I understand that he tried to lock himself inside the underground laboratory. That was the last I heard of Tsargrin, I think he evaded one of their men and darted into the laboratory, you need a security code to get in, apparently, the guy just pulled out a slip of paper and entered the code. Poor Tsargrin, I'm getting too old for this housekeeping game you know." Christian grinned slightly. "After that, we were all crammed inside of the house, no-in and no-out until we heard the police sirens."

"Oh yes, Norman says that they need to talk to us, I guess that we have some questions to answer."

"Yes, I suspect that my little housekeeping number is up. A certain colleague of mine is on his way. It's all about Tsargrin now Chris, we, and I suspect mostly you will have to find him, get that strangely tuned brain of yours into gear."

"My brain is not strangely tuned, I'll have you know. Anyway, I'm wondering what they were actually after."

"What do you mean?"

"Well, an operation like this, M.I.5 executives, soldiers, helicopters, it's pretty big isn't it? A lot of money too as well as risk. This M.I.5 guy, pretty high up isn't he? You would have thought that he would be more valuable where he was. Possibly, maybe, I don't know, I'm sure these guys will work it out."

"Yes Chris, I hope so too, I'm desperately worried about Tsargrin, he is not cut out for anything like this, he'll go to pieces as soon as they lock a door on him." Christian nodded, it was well known that Tsargrin had a thing about locked doors, routines too, he needed his routines and about a dozen other little foibles that shouldn't be trifled with.

"Good point," whispered Consuela, Christian gathered that she also may well have a clue of some sort.

Presently after their rather arduous 'talk' with Norman and an obscure American man accompanied by a high-ranking official from GCHQ, Christian and Consuela were allowed to leave. All that had been established was that Consuela was a C.I.A operative who was known to the most senior people of British Intelligence and that her C.I.A.

operators knew that she was known by the intelligence services and that she still maintained a presence at the facility. Nothing that Consuela, Christian, Tsargrin and Norman didn't apparently know already. One thing they really didn't know was the scale of infiltration that M.I.5 had succumbed to. They had far more information at hand regarding Tsargrin's facility, more than the M.I.5 executive committee could know. Presumably, they thought this quality of information could only have come from someone within the facility, somebody on the inside. Both Consuela and Christian were savvy enough to realise that they too would be on the suspect list. There was a lot of probing around, investigative postulations and old-fashioned ground searches. The only clue left behind was the man that didn't make it to the helicopter and paid for his tardiness with his life, he carried nothing that could incriminate anyone, except his fingerprints and face. By late evening, theorised conclusions were being mooted and a plan of action, or rather, in-action, in Christian's eyes, had been assembled. Most of Tsargrin's staff had now been dismissed for the day under strict orders of confidentiality. Five remained, Consuela, the chief engineer, a boffin named Clive and a couple of bemused technicians, enthusiastically accompanied by twenty or so security bods. It seemed that they all had one thing in common. They were all part of a particular project, a project that was deemed important enough to provide a motive for the murderous raid on Tsargrin's facility. Norman was to chair a meeting to get across the enormity of the unfolding situation. Christian tentatively asked if he could sit in on the meeting, Norman, for once, was in agreement without the normal barrage of 'why's' that he tended to inflict on people.

Despite the lateness of the day, Norman insisted that the people involved should be made aware of the probable cause for the raid, he or others had clearly isolated the most viable explanation.

"We have," Norman began, "after quite a bit of deliberation, come up with a scenario that fits the bill, the only 'something' we think would elicit such a raid. Everyone here had a part to play in this project, except of course, myself and Mr Simpkins here. This probable cause is, in Mr Throtestabler's terminology, called the 'Fridge' project. Apparently, it is called this because this particular device looks like one. Now I understand that several of you will know of this project. About seven months ago, you may also remember some irate Royal Air force types logging a complaint." Christian noted a few slight nods from the boffin and the chief engineer, he flicked his glance over to Consuela, she was poker-faced and nothing could be read in her deep-set eyes. Norman continued. "The people that did so had every right to register a complaint, for this device, this fridge, was photographed by a scrambled RAF interceptor at a height of 43,000 thousand feet. So no ordinary fridge then. It caused quite a bit of a stir at the time as there were no heat emissions, wings or other means of propulsion. The object was described as a UFO. Correctly too, as far as I'm concerned. Mr Throtestabler, was, by dint of his location, the immediate suspect. To this he vaguely apologised for not notifying the air force, suggesting that it was a, and I quote, 'a little bit of a mistake'." Christian bit his lip to stifle a snort of laughter as it was so like Tsargrin to trivialise such an event. "Before I hand you over to Clive here, I would like to add that this flying fridge thing was too slow for a missile and much too fast for a balloon. About 120 mph straight up, ceilinged out at a bit over 60,000 feet before plummeting back down in a semi-controlled fashion that ended up as a free-fall straight into the Irish Sea. Needless to say, the Ufologists and Conspiracy theorists had a field day."

Norman then nodded to Clive a white-coated boffin, to continue. To Christian, he looked like a type-cast school teacher, with a greying goatee beard, a pair of dusty corduroys and comfortable sandals with woolly socks, everything he said he had to emphasise with his hands. He barely got started on the ins and outs of the Fridge project before Christian got lost in the tech talk. One particular statement did stick in Christian's mind, when Clive the boffin suggested that Tsargrin had very possibly managed to describe gravity, more than a few people including Consuela drew an intake of breath. Christian logged this moment out of ignorance and then it all lapsed back into the world of unintelligible tech talk. One more item did strike a chord and this was the obscure plotting of the tennis court with an array of gravimeters. To Christian, this was highly significant as it now embroiled Robyn Reilly in the strange affair. There was something about a gravitational benchmark and then Clive the boffin faltered and stated that it was as far as he could go. Christian eyed the wall clock; it was now nearing midnight, his life had just been cut short by nearly two hours of unintelligible science-speak. He made a mental note to find someone to interpret the aforementioned for him.

The Chief Engineer then stood and paced around Tsargrin's living room whilst trying to explain the workings of the gravity compensator. Although, in all probability an expert in his field, he also had some difficulty in expressing things to others outside his profession. Christian tried hard to take in what was being said but capitulated when he could feel one of his nosebleeds taking hold. Norman then rescued the situation and put the Chief Engineer at his ease.

"Well, thank you for that, and to you, Clive, for summarising the Fridge project. It should be noted that the prototype of the fridge had been taken by the raiders and to be honest, we believe that only Mr Throtestabler has the know-how to operate it or to construct another. What I am saying is, that our Mr Throtestabler is very much alive as we speak, they need him, so they will look after him. Christian, your input please?" Christian started, his mind was whirring away as it should, but as yet nothing very coherent had surfaced.

"Er…excuse me?"

"You asked to be here, Christian, so what do you think? What's going on in that head of yours?"

"Oh yes, right, well I am still assimilating what has been said I guess. So not much is really there erm…yet. However, the importance of such a device, a gravity-defying device is I'm afraid, global. Whoever has that knowledge and takes full advantage of it would wield astonishing powers of leverage. Everything that currently flies would soon become obsolete. Quite catastrophic to very many industries, you cannot put a cost to this thing, especially its military potential, it really is a game-changer to whoever has it, including us."

"Yes Christian, a game-changer it is, now, know this. The Americans recovered the remains of the Fridge from the bottom of the Irish sea several months ago after some sort of tip-off." He looked over at Consuela, she squirmed slightly and gave an awkward smile. "The Fridge was damaged beyond any chance of repair. However, they tried hard to replicate it, the graphite discs, the compensator and all the various balancing tubes. This replica should, by their reckoning, do something, yet it does not. They have the engineering but not the science, Mr Throtestabler's calculations are the key. Now, as a matter of national importance, we must also construct another, a replica of the one that propelled itself high into the Cornish sky. All other experiments and projects are to be put on hold from this day forward. This Fridge thing will be of the highest priority, and in this case, and this case only you will receive unlimited funding. Okay, you are all dismissed for now and should return here early Monday week, so a good few days off. You have all been kept here overly long and unfortunately, against your will, support will be at hand if needed. Every little thing is strictly confidential, you will all be monitored by our security services, so be very careful, for they are not the gentlest of souls at the best of times."

Before the Chief Engineer departed, Christian approached him. "What about Robyn Reilly?" The engineer was a bit startled by the question.

"Yes," continued Christian, "she was in on the project as well I thought, she was trying to get hold of you to okay something or other?"

"Robyn, of course, where is she?" Christian picked up on his eagerness and despite the proximity of Norman, he lied.

"Oh, she is in South London for a few days, bit of catching up to do."

"Oh…of course, thanks," he replied as Christian opened the door for him. Norman took him aside and waited for all the others to leave, including Consuela.

"What are you doing, Simpkins?" He noted that the nicety of first names had again disappeared.

"Regarding what?"

"You know quite well that Robyn Reilly will be back at her site in Wales in a few hours?"

"Simple really, if I know where she is, and you also, then why doesn't he? The Chief Engineer. She is one of his people, and I may add, I know she has worked on the Fridge project too." Norman studied him intently, this always unsettled Christian a little bit, he then released his gaze and nodded that he should leave.

It was now nearing 2 am and his flat in North London was just too far. Because of the facility's seclusion, there were several rooms in the roof space of Tsargrin's rambling farmhouse that were available if needed, guest rooms, small but very clean. After a couple of polite enquiries, Christian managed to secure one, the last. He knew his way around the farmhouse and to some extent; the grounds and the two huge barn-like structures that housed the workings of the facility, yet this was the first time that he had actually overnighted there. The room was small and basic and reasonably comfortable. His mind was beginning to slow down now and he hoped that it would continue thus and so allow him some much-needed sleep. One of his final thoughts, before he drifted off, was that if Consuela aka, 'the housekeeper' was so enrapt with the project side of things, then who actually kept the house in such fine fettle. Everyone near Christian's orbit now seemed to be suspect.

6 am, barely light, something was happening, a sound maybe, possibly a voice. He swept aside the covers and swung

a leg out then the door slipped open, there was no lock, Tsargrin couldn't abide locked doors.

"Morning, Christian," said a female voice, Christian emitted a tiny girl-like squeak and clambered back under the covers. It was Consuela with, presumably, a big mug of tea.

"Consuela! It's you, I er—"

"Yes, it is, tea?"

"But it is six o'clock in the morning!"

"I know, but we need to have a little chat, the earlier the better." Christian sat up and accepted the brew. Consuela planted herself down at the end of the bed. "Bit of a mess, isn't it?" Christian nodded and took a big slug of his tea in an effort to wake his senses.

"Yes, it bloody is, I don't know who to trust, it has to be someone inside, it just has to be, even the chief engineer seemed a bit dodgy to me. So does the comms security guy, the one with the cracked skull, been here for years, he knows everything."

"Yes Christian, good point. Everybody who works here, 22 in number, goes through a vigorous vetting regime."

"Yes, but by M.I.5. a hunk of which has been compromised."

"True, however, M.I.5 normally keep a tight house, they will get to grips with this, incidentally Norman is handing the investigations back to them. He is M.I.6, remember, overseas stuff?" Christian pinched the bridge of his nose and breathed a deep, thoughtful breath.

"Tell me, Consuela, if that is actually your real name. If you are supposedly here as a housekeeper but are clearly doing everything else, then who is actually doing the housekeeping? Look at this room, clean, not a speck of dust."

"Ah…So I am on your list as well, Christian. Okay then, Consuela is my real name, and my surname 'Smith' was given to me by my husband, as for the housework, it is done by the, shall we say, maid."

"Maid, I have never seen a maid here, who is she?"

"She is a he, a charming young man by the name of Christoph, he has been vetted too, am I in the clear now?" Christian placed his mug on the bedside table and glanced at his watch.

"Sorry…" he said sheepishly.

"No, that's fine, Christian, keep on analysing, something may hit home."

"Yeah, I guess, I'm really worried about Tsargrin though."

"Yes, aren't we all, his little quirks won't wear well with his captors. He tried hard, the laboratory should have been the perfect safe-room, it's built like a bunker, but they even knew the access code on the keypad, they knew everything, they just dragged him back out and stuck him in the helicopter."

"Oh god, poor man, did you see all that?"

"Nah, too busy licking my wounds. We are still trying to fill in the missing bits."

"How are you anyway, apart from the black eye, swelling is down a bit I see. You had a few stitches as well?"

"Yes, nothing major, it will heal."

"What happens now, Consuela?"

"Well, as for me, I am sort of under house arrest, I'm not permitted to go anywhere and I'm to be kept incommunicado. Effectively, Christian, I have been put away. But I did have some input in the Fridge project, so presumably, they will keep me busy for a little while. Now, I know that you have a fair bit on your plate at the moment so you have to get Sir Jeffery Pollock to free you up somehow. We are going to need you. You are independent and so you are not tied to the various machinations in operation at the moment. To the raiders, and their operators, you are an unknown quantity, so watch your back. As for the people currently here, don't expend too much thought, they will be carefully monitored. They are not front-line people Christian, unlike myself, Norman and occasionally you. They will never have seen death up-front, been in the proximity of gunfire or even had so much as a slap. They are scientists, boffins, people of learning, what we have here now is not their world. Easily traumatised."

"Ah...a bit like Tsargrin, then?"

"Unfortunately, so now I suggest that you get back up to Wales today, find Robyn Reilly and get her back here, right here is now easily the safest place to be. Do not give her too much information. Oh yes, don't leave before nine. The new M.I.5 guy will want to interview you, his name is Rutherford apparently. Norman will be here for the rest of the day. I know you two do not really get on, but he knows his stuff, he is very good at what he does. So if he gives you a nudge, listen, okay?"

"Righty-ho, shame that you are out of the picture though."

"Not entirely, Christian dear, not entirely." He watched her leave, wondering what exactly she meant. Quickly he called her back, she stuck her head back around the door and arched those jet-black eyebrows.

"One more thing, I know that I've been briefed already, but how long were the gunmen here exactly?"

"Hard to say, they just came in through the gates, on Friday, kitted out the same as M.I.5, same weaponry, same M.O…the three guys who arrived late Wednesday let them through. We had no idea that our security bods in the car had been taken out. To us it was just the security boys doing their stuff, they confined most of us to the house as they undertook their 'search' as they said. Saturday morning, everyone was getting a bit restless, then sometime before the helicopter came, the security guys turned their guns toward us. That is it, very professional I had to admit. Soon enough the police turned up, but bless them, they were so out-gunned they couldn't do a thing until the Special Ops team turned up and that was too late, the bird, as it were, had flown. What is on your mind Christian?" she said hopefully.

"Fuck all at the moment, Consuela, just trying to cram it all together."

"Good man, and good hunting. Don't forget about Rutherford this morning." Christian gave her the thumbs-up and slunk back under the covers.

Christian grabbed a rather dusty looking bacon roll for breakfast at the canteen at the far end of the main 'barn' and ambled around a little, being careful not to touch anything. At the large metal door to Tsargrin's laboratory, Christian gave it a tug and it swung open. He checked out the keypad, six-digit input, nothing special. On entering, he came immediately to another similar door and this wouldn't give an inch when he tried to open it. He shook his head in personal despair, emitted a little 'tut' and closed the outer door and then opened the inner. It was an airlock entry, something used for chemical hazards, Christian already knew this, plus, it said

'Air-Lock' in big yellow letters inside and out. The inside door could not be opened unless the outer door was closed and conversely the other way around. Through the inner door, there was a narrow steel spiral stairway and a small lift between it going down slightly beyond one level. Opting for the stairs, he came across the workings of Tsargrin's special laboratory, the place where the dangerous stuff was carried out. Someone had found the time to have a rummage around the place, Christian was doubly cautious about touching anything. It wasn't a very big place; just a couple of rooms, thirty feet down, concrete walls, low ceilings and no natural light, just like a bunker, as Consuela had suggested. Christian was keen not to catch anything and swiftly made his way back to the stairs, pausing briefly to appraise a promotional poster of an overly curvy woman with an unnatural pout. He recognised her charms as one Ms Sheena Voltaire, an 'A-list' celebrity from the nineties. Shaking his head at Tsargrin's choice of interior decor, he exited the laboratory and negotiated his way back through the air-lock with no difficulty, in doing so, he noted a couple of slight boot prints upon the inner door, something, in all probability, caused by the scuffle it would have taken for someone to manhandle Tsargrin's portly frame through the opening. They were clearly in some haste to get Tsargrin into the helicopter, blue lights and sirens shortly after probably helped that dash.

Come 9 am exactly, Christian was introduced to the M.I.5 section head, Mr Rutherford. They were now back in Tsargrin's living room and the man called Rutherford actually seemed glad to see him, which was a first considering Christian's history with the security services.

"Christian Simpkins, at last, I have been looking forward to meeting you."

"Er…you have?" responded Christian shaking the proffered outstretched hand.

"Yes, I have been following your field career quite a bit, Manzania in Western Sahara first off. Freshwater to the desert, magnificent stuff, then the Skyship thing in Belize, genius pure genius. So what have you found here? Was it you that exposed the American spy?"

"No not at all, it isn't what it seems, Mr Rutherford, as our security has been compromised, we are not really sure who is who and who isn't who if you get my drift." Rutherford eyed him carefully, he was a very different animal to the cagey Norman. A bit too much bluster, but Christian's intuitive gut suggested that he was more than just okay. He looked fit and able, sported a headful of auburn curls and had a handshake like iron. Christian liked his energy, he was well versed in difficult situations and soon had a good command of what should be done. "There is one thing though," ventured Christian, "do we have any idea of who our newfound enemy actually is?"

"Good point, but as yet we really do not know, it has only been a couple of days. The helicopter was found abandoned just outside Southampton. Ex-French military job, very vague purchaser records, but we are still on the case. Although, just to dump a bit of kit like that tells us that they are ludicrously well funded."

"Anything interesting found?"

"Sorry Christian, very little, nothing to show that Mr Throtestabler was there, they had booby-trapped it, but this was spotted and made safe. I am aware of your friendship with

Mr Throtestabler, please try not to let that influence your actions. There is very little you can do here now, we would very much appreciate it if you could round up Robyn Reilly and bring her here."

"Sure," said Christian getting to his feet, "erm…do you have a first name, surnames tend to smack of the services."

"Of course I do, but just call me Bill."

"I'm guessing then 'Bill' isn't really it?"

"No, you are absolutely correct, for your information only, Christian, my first name is Ivan."

"Right, okay-dokey, 'Bill' it is." Ivan Rutherford laughed, reminded him to stay in touch and bade him farewell.

Christian sat in his car, a big blue Ford saloon, similar to everyone else's. He was pondering over his next move, he had to get Sir Jeffery Pollock to free up some time for him, which meant Whitehall in London plus he had to get Robyn back from Wales and to the facility. He needed to ring her and get her to come here probably under some false pretence. He also knew that every phone would be bugged somewhere along the line and every car, tagged with a locator of some sort. He drove maybe ten miles westward and made a call at one of the few public call boxes left. He looked carefully around. Maybe he hadn't been followed but then again, why should they? They could just see his car or maybe his phone on a screen somewhere.

After a couple of rings, Robyn answered, she sounded a little vexed.

"Hello Robyn, Christian Simpkins here."

"Oh…at last, Mr Simpkins, I've been trying to get hold of you, er…where are you? Strange number on my screen."

"Oh…public phone, bad signal here, look I was going to come back up to Wales—" Robyn cut in before he had a chance to finish.

"If you could, it would really help me, I've just had a call from a neighbour. I think that my flat has been broken into. I need to get back, this is so frustrating."

"Okay Robyn, I hear what you are saying, I'll phone you back very shortly."

Before she could utter any response, he cut off the call and phoned Rutherford from the same line. "Hello Bill, er…Mr Rutherford, Chris Simpkins here, I've only managed to get about ten miles down the road, just received some information from Robyn Reilly, her flat has been broken into, South London, Streatham, I think."

"Right, Reilly R, okay, I'm on it, you are on a payphone right, good man, stay where you are and I'll get back to you. Half hour maybe"

Christian got back into his car and rolled the window down so that he could hear the phone if it rang. He did not really like the way things were panning out. He was in a pretty little village quite typical of the area, agriculture and tourism were the main links to any form of commerce. There was a pub, a church, a good few tiny shops and a little bus station, outside of which he was now parked up. Christian smiled at the sight of the pub, Tsargrin loved a nice pint or two and took great pains to secrete himself out of the facility to visit one. The *Smugglers Inn*, was one of his favourites and Christian and he had often connived together to meet up for a pint and a pasty when they could. He used to escape via the rear entrance on his bike, his portly frame peddling like fury to avoid the timing of the security car that patrolled the perimeters. Tsargrin Throtestabler was far too valuable to the government to be allowed out without authorised company and good reason. The authorities' answer to cater for this particular foible was to stock a fridge with beer. To Tsargrin it was the wrong beer, the wrong service and the wrong place, he never touched it. Before Christian could lapse into more fond memories of his friend, the payphone rang, with a bit of nifty footwork, he got to it before a curious villager did.

"Simpkins," was all he said, he recognised Rutherford's voice.

"Okay Christian, listen up, Robyn Reilly's flat has been broken into. The lock has been snapped, no other damage, been turned over a bit, but can't identify much missing."

"Wow, you guys work fast, okay I will inform Robyn."

"Yes, she should be here, one other thing, your flat has been done too."

"Oh bollocks, really?"

"'Fraid so, same M.O. lock had been snapped, professionally too, we don't think there is much missing either. Your computer is still there, minus the hard-drive though. I have placed both properties under observation, we will sort the locks."

"Well, thanks for that anyway, I'll speak to Robyn."

"Oh hang on, Christian, Norman here wants a word."

Christian's heart sank a little, why couldn't Norman just hand the operation over to Rutherford and take a hike?

"Hello Norman," he said in a very matter-of-fact way.

"Yes Simpkins, glad you called, I just need to clarify a few points with you. Tell you what, I'll pop down and see you, I'm done here anyway."

"Er, okay, it's not like I've gone very far, do you want me to come back?"

"No, don't bother, you are on my way, see you shortly, 15 minutes or so, okay?"

Christian grunted some sort of affirmation as he replaced the handset. He shook his head slightly, for he hadn't even told Norman where he was. He called Robyn back.

"Hi Robyn, sorry to have kept you, I am about ten miles away from the facility. I have had some checks done and you are right, someone has broken into your flat. The place is under observation and the lock will be fixed, not much damage I am told plus they don't think much is missing."

"How the hell do they know what is missing or not, also, Mr Simpkins, who the hell is 'they'?"

"The 'they' is M.I.5 Robyn. There is a big security storm brewing and it is really best to avoid it if you can."

"This is crap, who are you to judge what I should do, and come to think about it, who are you to go bandying my affairs

about with your damn low-life security buddies? My flat, my home has been invaded and I am having none of it."

"My flat in North London has been hit as well and I am not best pleased either. You are wanted here at the facility, Robyn, you were working on the Fridge project and that is what all the fuss was about."

"Fridge project? Now, what the hell are you talking about?"

"Okay, remember when you told me about some of the weirder jobs you did for Mr Throtestabler…In particular, the one with the gravimeters?"

"Aah…yes?"

"Well, that was an integral part of the project."

"And what is the bloody Fridge project then Mr Christian Simpkins, what is it, tell me that?" Christian was momentarily stumped, he thought back to the briefing and found the most innocuous thing he could remember.
"Robyn, it seems that our Mr Throtestabler has found a way to describe gravity." There was a lull on the line, Christian prepared himself for some more overly pointed dialogue.

"Oh my god, he understands gravity, oh my god, god. Okay, Mr Simpkins, I mean Christian, I am leaving for the facility now. Oh my god, this just can't be true." After a few

more 'oh my gods'. Christian hung up, he really didn't understand the fuss. But whatever it meant, it got the job done. Back in the car, he drummed his fingers upon the steering wheel. Too much was happening far too quickly. He reached for his phone and popped out the sim card to ensure that one bugging device was sorted out. The car should be next but that would take some help. It turned out to be a long 15 minutes or so, eventually, a car, very similar to his own, pulled up behind. It was Norman, but he wasn't ready to leave the car at the moment as he was on his phone. Presently, he emerged and sat in the passenger seat.

"Okay Simpkins, sorry about the delay, I was waiting for something." He tapped on what appeared to be a box file on his lap. "This is important, keep it with you." Christian received it and weighed it gently in his hand before placing it on the floor of the rear seat. He eyed it and Norman quite carefully.

"Look Norman, this is all getting a bit beyond me, I don't quite know who to trust and to be honest I am really worried about Tsargrin. I am not all that bothered about the Fridge thing, we are re-making it, the Americans have reconstructed the salvaged one and the bad guys have the prototype and all the information, so why are they bothering with Tsargrin?"

"I think you have realised that the Fridge is the common denominator in all this. Throtestabler is a very valuable asset, just depriving us of him has a huge value." Another car pulled alongside, a slightly battered old Ford Focus. Norman glanced up.

"Mmm…it's Rutherford, he is just doing what he does, I'd do the same, to be honest." The rear door opened and he joined them.

"Welcome to my new office, Bill," said Christian.

"Yes, an excellent little ruse, I must say," Norman grunted his agreement.

"Yes, textbook stuff, drove out of the range of the tech sensors, disabled his mobile and here we are ten miles from the nearest eavesdropper and right next to a pay-phone. Not only that Norman, he has also blocked the car tracker, neat trick, I can't easily do that. I had to use the pay-phone number to find him."

"Mmm, I used his mobile's last position before he shut it down." Norman turned and gave Christian a thoughtful look.

"Yes, we must have a chat one day." Christian nodded slightly, he didn't want to just tell these two master spooks that he had to change his car because it wouldn't start.

"Anyway," continued Norman, "Christian here has a fair bit of motoring to do, he has made his calls to whoever, anything to add, Rutherford?"

"Not really, I am presuming that the file you just gave him is the hard copy of the various meeting minutes."

"It is, same one as you have, he needs to ingest it, then burn it, still safer than anything digital I think."

"At the present time, yes, Norman. Now I want to swap cars with him, these big blue saloons stick out a mile if you know what I mean?" Norman grunted his approval, and Christian peered over at the crappy looking Focus.

"Aw, c'mon, really?"

"Afraid so, old boy," said Bill Rutherford through a wide grin. "That car, my own car as it happens, is supposed to look as it does, but it is very special, it drives more like a Porsche, they race these things around the circuit at Brands Hatch you know." Christian peered at it dubiously, he really wasn't yet convinced. "Also, it is clean, no trackers or bugs and if the police check it, they will find it logged as one of their own surveillance vehicles. It is completely outside of the security services, So Christian, I am going to take this pile of polished shit off of you and give you that." He reached forward and dangled some keys, Christian reluctantly accepted them.

"Okay, I think I'm done here now." Norman made to get out.

"Ahh Norman, couple of questions, won't take long." Norman twisted around to face Rutherford, Christian stared into the rear-view mirror, when he had their undivided attention, Rutherford began.

"Christian, when you turned up out of the blue early on Monday, how did you know something was up, historically you normally stay away when there is a security scare?"

"Simple, as I said, I asked Sir Jeffery Pollock, and he made a call. The facility had been in lockdown for a few days, a lot longer than normal to be honest. It was the weekend and I was in the West Country. I often arrive just to say 'hi' or whatever."

"Yes, we are very aware of your relationship with Mr Throtestabler and his housekeeper, the covert American, I may add." Christian just nodded. "Now my problem is this, I have checked our records with G.C.H.Q and no relative calls were made or exchanged, everything including our little chit-chat is logged, so, who did he speak to Christian?"

"I am afraid that I have no idea, but his departmental calls are recorded anyway."

"Nothing there either, I've checked, so, when you get back to Whitehall, find out and let me know. It is important."

Christian turned to Norman, as he knew Sir Jeffery and his ways quite well.

"He is right, Simpkins, all these avenues have to be checked out, especially for something like this. Maybe you could sound out his secretaries, they should be a good bet as they all tend to hate him." To this, Christian readily agreed. Norman then exited the car without a further word, not even a 'goodbye'. Bill Rutherford smiled knowingly and also removed himself from Christian's car. Christian then proceeded to collect up his belongings and the all-important file, Bill popped open the hatch to the Ford Focus and grabbed a weighty holdall, *presumably, his belongings*, thought Christian. In passing, Bill mentioned that there was some money and a debit card in the glove box.

"The number is 1234, make sure you keep the receipts."

"So much for security." Christian opined quietly.

Cars

Once in the Ford, he took a deep breath and familiarised himself with the interior; It was a manual, so at first, he wasn't too impressed. Norman drove off without a second look and Bill left with a toot and a little wave. Christian found that he loved to drive Rutherford's hotted-up Ford Focus, it was responsive, fast and seemed to be on rails when he took a corner. He was heading back to London; it was a workday, he will have missed Monday, but that was not what was bothering him most, Sir Jeffery and his precious department could wait. Tsargrin was at the forefront of his mind, he needed a little more time to assimilate what was actually happening and in what order. His phone was made safe, the car he now drove was untraceable and he was happy to be off the radar, so to speak, he pulled off the A38 trunk road for an early lunch. It was a nice little town situated at the base of Dartmoor, however; it was very touristy and even in late September; it was a busy place. It was also the last place worth stopping before the relentless motorway journey to London. He found a good-sized car park; the car was perfect, it didn't attract a second glance. After a bit of café food and a decent mug of tea, he decided to say hello to the world again, intrepidly he powered up his phone. He blinked a few times at the amount of alerts he had collected, four calls he should have picked up were diverted to voicemail, they were all from Robyn Reilly who should be heading her way en-route to the facility. The last call was about twenty minutes ago, the message was a little incoherent, so he called her, instantly, she answered.

"Simpkins?"

"Yep, what's up?"

"Where have you been, you cannot do this to me…"

"Do what, Robyn?"

"A car has sort of been following me."

"Sort of…what do you mean?"

"Well, about an hour ago, this side of Wales I kept seeing something, a car, on the bigger roads mainly, sometimes behind me sometimes in front, now it is three cars behind, when I slow down, it does also. I do hope that this is just another of your silly security measures, er…is it?"

"No Robyn, nothing to do with me, where are you now?"

"Just crossed the river Severn."

"Right when you pick up the M5 southbound, stop at the first services you come to, I shall see you there. Park up in the busiest spot and head for the canteen, it should be really busy. I'll find you, promise."

"Who are these people?"

"I have no idea as yet, can you describe the car?"

"Yes, it's a black seven-seater, tinted windows, it looks quite new."

"Any chance of getting the registration?"

"Don't know, I'll try, I'm not feeling great about this."

"Me neither, see you at the services, okay."

"Yes, suppose so, okay I guess."

Christian checked the time, and seeing that he had some to spare, he retrieved Norman's file from the boot; he needed some advice from Rutherford, but his phone wasn't secure, hopefully, there was another contact method. Files were one of those necessary 'musts' but generally really boring, he picked up the top bundle and then put it to one side very slowly. In the bottom of the box file, there was a cellophane packet; it was a gun, a small Walther automatic, 32 calibre. He recognised it instantly, it was of the same type that he carried both in Western Sahara and Belize. He quickly closed the file and looked furtively around before opening it again. He unwrapped it and turned it over in his hand. It was loaded, one full magazine, ten shots, but no spare. It came with a hip holster, the type that he preferred. A couple of official-looking plastic cards accompanied the gun, he studied them carefully. One card was a firearm release order complete with a ten-digit number and a bar code, the other displayed his picture and the details of his permit to carry.

Bloody hell, was all that came to his mind, it was all he could think of to think! He was well used to carrying such a weapon, the Walther 32, compared with other sidearms, was tiny in comparison. He preferred to have it sitting just above his right buttock, less obtrusive and still easy to reach. Christian didn't actually like guns and had the unnerving habit of closing his eyes every time it made a bang. He did though, recognise its presence, sometimes it was more effective just to wave it around a little than to actually fire the thing. His experiences with firearms weren't very good, most confrontations normally ended up with someone taking it from him. He did like its comfort though, just knowing it was there helped a lot. The only time that he actually shot someone was his American air force friend, Dan Lewinski in Belize, a year or so ago, fortunately, he made a full recovery. Somehow though, like Chinese whispers, he was reckoned to be quite deadly with the little 32 and escapades abounded with feats of his prowess. Even getting the clearance to carry one was a bit of a cock-up, but manage it, he somehow did a few years back. He knew this type of gun very well and he knew that the skinny belt currently holding up his suit trousers would be unable to support the weight despite its size.

He needed a new belt, a thick wide leather job, taking a quick whiff of his armpit he also realised that he needed a clean shirt and a shower, the latter could wait and he went in search of a suitable belt. It was a smallish town and there was not much to choose from, eventually, in one of the souvenir shops. He managed to source something that would do him in the interim. The belt was just wide enough to fit the loops, although it was of good quality plastic, it was overlaid with some stitched-on webbing which gave it added strength to suit the heavy buckle, unfortunately, it was also adorned with colourful local scenes of South Devon, sailing boats, Dartmoor ponies and garish surfers riding waves and so forth. It would only be a temporary affair and with his jacket buttoned up, it was barely visible, although it must be said that Christian's sense of style was always lacking that special 'something'.

He was on a quest now, heading North up the M5, he hoped to liaise with Robyn at the busy motorway services. He had to keep his phone on so that he could keep in touch with her progress, thus, slightly painfully, he was aware that he was now digitally visible again. As he approached the services he realised that he had messed up, there was no bridge over the motorway so he would have to go several miles beyond and turn back on the southbound M5 to meet up with her. Fortunately, the Ford Focus did its stuff by wasting the 70-mph limit to allow him to arrive almost simultaneously as she did. He had just parked up when he recognised her car as it pulled in about ten spaces away. He stayed in his car and waited, Robyn did the right thing, as soon as she was out, she was striding quickly toward the interior and the canteen. Christian eased himself out of the Ford as another car approached, a black multi-seater with tinted windows. Three men emerged, casually dressed, heavyset and decidedly grim. One approached Robyn's car and the other two entered the building, Christian followed them in, like most motorway services, it was big, bright and brash, it would be full of cameras and have its own security people.

Christian felt quite safe in such surroundings, he passed the two men without incident and planted himself down at Robyn's table, she looked quite ashen, if that was physically possible.

"Hi Robyn, well done, how are you doing?"

"At last! Frightened, confused and mad as hell if you don't mind me saying."

"Yeah, well I can understand that."

"No, you damn well don't, you know nothing about me Mr bloody Simpkins, since I first met you in Wales, until now we have only met twice, just twice, and my life has been turned upside down."

"Look Robyn, none of this is my doing, I am just rolling along with it the best I can. There has been one almighty security breach and people are running around like headless chickens trying to fix it. I'm going to get you back to the facility, currently, it is by far the safest place. Now, the third table down, the two men there are from the car that has been following you." She carefully looked around and quickly snapped her head back to face him.

"Oh god, they have seen me looking."

"Don't worry, this place is full of cameras, they can't do much, I'm going to have a little word with them."

"What, no, you're crazy, please Mr er…I mean Christian, just stay here until they go, please."

"Sorry Robyn, I need to put them off track a bit, back in a jiffy." Christian did not possess many wonderful talents but he was good with people, always had been and on top of this was his term with the diplomatic service which stood him well. Body language, facial expressions, speech tones and situation adjustment all add up, he would prove to be an excellent poker player if he ever bothered to try it.

As he approached the two men, one donned a pair of dark glasses and the other pulled down the peak of his baseball cap. Christian stopped just short of them. The one with the glasses, burly, with a military look about him, slowly stood and faced him.

"Hello, I'm Christian," he said lightly, "you guys are proving to be a bit of a pain, I would strongly suggest that you go on your way." The man scowled deeply and made to approach closer, Christian popped the button of his jacket, and he begrudgingly halted in his tracks and sat back down. "Don't do this guys, I am going to make a couple of calls…understand?" The men said nothing but stared angrily at the floor. Christian returned to Robyn.

"Okay then, shall we go?"

"Yes, yes, I think we should, I'll just follow you huh!"

"Nope, you will come with me, they would have disabled your car by now."

"Really, but I've locked it."

"Yes, you probably have, but they can easily take a tyre out, although I should imagine they would have stuck something up the exhaust, an old trick, you would get about a mile down the road then the car would give up and 'bingo' you are all theirs." Robyn gulped at the very thought.

"Where are you parked?"

"Ten cars down from you, let's go." Robyn eyed the Ford Focus dubiously, it reminded her of one of the old wrecks that her brothers used to drive.

"Really?" was all she said.

"Yes, really, get in, lock your door and buckle up, we are out of here." As they pulled away, the driver of the black multi-seater reversed erratically into their path, Christian hit the brakes and made quick use of an empty space to the side, almost immediately they were back on the motorway heading South, Christian worked the car hard for a few good miles before settling down to a comfortable 70 mph, Robyn began to breathe again.

"God," she said, "this car is not normal is it?"

"Nope, far from it." Christian could feel her studying him, trying to guess him.

"You were quite impressive back there, I mean, that guy, the big one, he didn't want anything to do with you."

"Huh…" laughed Christian, "if he'd got hold of me, he would kill me, but it was a busy place and people like him answer to other people, normally bad people so he wouldn't act without checking. It is a nice fault to play on."

"Play, 'Jesus Christ', er…is it okay if I call you Christian?"

"Yes, I very much prefer it."

"Good God, Christian, what the hell am I getting myself into here? I have read all about you, as much as I could. You don't come across as I thought."

"No, hope not. Media hype and all that, actually I'm normally a bag of nerves when things like this happen."

"What! I mean, how often do these things happen then?"

"Too often, I seem to be continually plunged into the deep end of things and mostly armed with dodgy info. Must be some kind of conspiracy or something. Keep an eye out for that black multi-seater, just in case."

"What, yes of course."

"We are going to take an alternative route, just to be sure, okay?"

"You're in charge, Christian."

"Oops, that's a bit worrying." He gave her a quick wink and she broke into a smile, the first he'd seen.

They both soon began to relax as it seemed apparent that they were no longer being followed, they were less than an hour from their destination, Tsargrin's facility on the Lizard peninsular in deepest Cornwall. It wasn't quite dark yet, they had been driving for a fair while and Christian was determined to do the journey without a stop. Rounding a bend, they came across a man in a hi-vis jacket waving at him to reduce his speed. Christian dutifully slowed down, more men in hi-vis waved the cars in front of him past, a vehicle slewed across the road and a man held up his hands for him to stop, something wasn't right, Robyn sensed it too. Now almost at a crawl Christian gunned the engine, the slewed car began to lurch into his path and a couple of men raced toward them, in an instant, they both backed off. Robyn turned to Christian, he was holding a gun in his left hand at eye level whilst steering with his right to manoeuvre around the obstruction and back to the open road at a decent turn of speed. Robyn swallowed hard and looked behind her, she began to feel a little sick.

"You have a gun!"

"Yes, only a little one, pay no mind to it. My phone is off, this car is clean, they must have a track on your phone, Robyn."

Robyn uttered a plaintive 'yelp' and delved into her bag, shaking hands clawing at the device until eventually, it was off.

"Sorry, sorry," she gasped.

"Not your fault, Robyn, I forgot to tell you." Christian could now feel the familiar judder of his knees, his nerves had decided to play up, but it was the last thing he wanted Robyn to be aware of. "Music," he said dryly, twisting the sound up, he placed his Walther automatic down on the central console and Robyn just stared at it to the sound of Dusty Springfield. Dusty did the trick and his nerves managed to hold out until they passed through the gates of the facility.

Consuela took Robyn somewhere for a bit of consultative care, Christian stretched his dodgy legs, reached back into the car and stuffed his gun and holster under the seat and out of sight. He then went in search of someone to report to. Unfortunately, Bill Rutherford was not there but another very capable-looking man introduced himself and Christian brought him up to spec regarding what had happened. For some reason, he chose not to mention his gun. Its issue was via M.I.6 and clearly, when Norman gave it to him, it was for his eyes only, possibly, maybe.

There were very few rooms left available in the old farmhouse. The security bods had secured the barn's day-room with a dormitory of camp beds, Consuela was using Tsargrin's own bed and Christian, last in the queue after Robyn, managed to get one of the little attic rooms, the same one as before. He would head back to London in the morning, check out his flat and then make some overtures to Sir Jeffery Pollock in Ancillaries and Procurement regarding the unfolding events. Consuela and Christian had a good prolonged talk with each other that evening. She also thought that it was a bit odd that Christian had been cleared to carry a gun in the UK, he had never really been trained how to even use one, there were plenty of highly trained fire-arm experts at their disposal. She too was desperately worried about Tsargrin and his whereabouts. He was a delicate creature, a bit of an oddball as it were. He hated locked doors and in all probability, he was behind one at that very moment, plus in all likelihood, he would be deprived of his precious odd pint of real ale. For once Consuela was stumped, she was fed up and unsure of what direction she should take. This was a first for Christian, he was sad to see her keen mind frustrated. Christian needed to get her out of there, he needed to give her a chance of using her skills and her renowned intuition.

In the morning at daybreak, his door swung open.

"Oh, hi Consuela," he said through bleary eyes.

"Er…it's me," said a very wide-eyed Robyn.

"Ah, oh, yes of course, sorry Robyn, um…good morning, bit early?"

"Yesss…" she said falteringly, "I er…can come back later if you want," she said, peering behind the door.

"No, now is fine, it must be important I guess."

"Well sort of, I think anyway."

"Okay take a seat, it's probably best if I stay in bed." She looked around, there was no seat, so she as Consuela had, perched herself at the end of his bed.

"Okay Christian, I know it is early but I have a workday tomorrow here, and you are off to London, I need to talk."

"Okay Robyn, fire away, what is bothering you, apart from the bloody obvious, that is?"

"It is Mr Throtestabler, he has gone, hasn't he? Consuela hinted at it. Well, do you remember when you said that he could describe gravity? You really did not quite understand, did you?" Christian shook his head.

"Well, nobody yet has ever achieved that feat. I have also studied physics to a degree, and the gravity conundrum is the holy grail of quantum physics, I don't think it's the fridge thing they are after."

"Well, unfortunately, they already have that."

"Yes but, what they are really after is Mr Throtestabler's calculations, they need the maths that proves it all. And here is the nasty bit, when they have it, then Mr Throtestabler is history. I am sure of this, positive, it is what these people are after, must be."

"Mmm…pass me that file on the dresser please, I need to check the wording." Robyn duly passed over the file, the one he received from Norman. He flicked through a number of pages and handed it over to her, she read very slowly and then once again.

"Oh, it says 'in all probability' in that case, he hasn't passed over the calculations for someone else to reaffirm, so they are not underwritten yet. That is it, that's what they are after, the calculations, nothing could be more important."

"Yes, see what you mean, they are definitely searching for something, God only knows what other avenues are being explored. I'll have to ask Consuela to forensically search his office for it, his den too I think."

"Den! I didn't know he had one. Clive the physicist should do that, or maybe me, Consuela won't know what to look for."

"Yes, she will, if it's there she will find it, she is also one of the few people in the world that can read his writing." Robyn opened her palms wide.

"What is going on here? You are telling me that the housekeeper can make head or tails out of four-field quantum mechanics?"

"Yep, strange place isn't it?"

"It is, it was attractively strange when I joined the team two years ago, now it is just getting weirder and weirder."

"Yes, welcome to the world of Tsargrin Throtestabler, bless him, wherever he is." Almost in slow motion, Robyn brought her knees up to her chin and lolled to one side in a sort of loose foetal position.

"I just shouldn't be here, Christian," she said quietly, "I'm just a little girl from South London trying to better herself, that is all."

"How old are you, Robyn?"

"Huh, 27, a small sensitive 27, that's all, people have been killed here haven't they?"

"Yes, nasty stuff, our two security men and one of their own."

"Oh god, what happened? They all have families, mums, dads, brothers, maybe kids even, it doesn't bear thinking about."

"Robyn, to get as far as you have, you must be really special, as I have said, Tsargrin demands a lot from his people and rewards them well."

"Yes, I couldn't believe it then, but now it is just horrible." Christian gave her a little time to dwell on things, he could do little else, he had no pyjamas and so couldn't even leave the bed. Scrunched up as she was, she looked so tiny, so vulnerable but he sensed that there was a lot more to this girl than meets the eye.

"You know Robyn, this is a bit of a first for me, well, in this country anyway. Too many people I know, old histories, it is not very nice, but it is what it is and we must deal with it. By the way, don't worry about your car, it will be checked and brought back here, just leave the keys with security okay?"

"Oh, fuck the car."

"Robyn, do you have someone, you know, someone you can talk to. There is a landline here, I can get you some time on it, I'm afraid that all the mobile stuff is monitored."

"I suppose you mean a boyfriend or something, well no I don't. Most of the guys I meet are just posturing idiots or just wet as hell."

"Ah…sorry, I didn't mean to pry."

"What about you then, hot-shot? I've read the stories."

"Me, god, I am overseas so often, love doesn't get a chance."

"Well, at least you are man enough to use the L-word." Christian forced a little laugh.

"Huh, I don't recall ever having chosen the way I have to live. Circumstance appears to rule my life I'm afraid."

"What do you think of me? I was pretty sour toward you when we first met."

"Huh, I'm used to folk being sour to me. I'm not really one to mentally profile people if you know what I mean, unless they deserve it I suppose, I guess I sort of just take people as they are initially. I think I took you for a teenager at first."

"God, I know, I have to take photo I.D everywhere. How will all this end, Christian?"

"Well, gradually as the security bods…"

"Bods?"

"Yeah 'bods' security bodies, slang I guess. Once they have exhausted all their enquiries and searches, they will hand it all over to a branch of the police. A couple of weeks, a month maybe. Tsargrin is the biggest worry for me, we just have to find him."

"Yes, I guess, you don't even know where to start huh…"

"Too true, can't give up though." At that moment, Consuela came gliding in wearing a fetching white dressing gown. Robyn emitted a little squeak and sat bolt upright.

"Mmm…good morning, sorry to disturb you, shall I come back later?"

"No, it's okay, me and Robyn here were having a little chat."

"Course you were," said Consuela with a mischievous grin. Robyn stood and straightened out her pyjamas.

"Anyway, I must go," she said awkwardly as she side-stepped Consuela and headed for the door.

"Anything worthwhile on the news front, Christian?"

"No nothing really, all I know is 'they' whoever 'they' are, are searching for something, Robyn is convinced that they are after the calculations to the gravity conundrum, she explained just how important it is, at the time when I was told, I just didn't get it, you did though, I could tell."

"Robyn is quite correct, whoever can mathematically isolate gravity as a force has a pretty good chance of kicking off another tech revolution. Personally, I think that they are after the whole set. When Tsargrin's Fridge device hit the 40,000 feet mark, it disturbed an awful lot of people, powerful state-funded people. I am stuck here, Christian, I can't operate. You can come and go at the moment, so try hard to find a way for me to get out of here, please." Christian just nodded, he didn't really know what to say or do.

"Keep searching for the calcs, Consuela, it's all you can do."

"Yes, it'll keep me busy, I've checked the office and the den as a routine search, bit weird, but nothing grabbed my attention. I could do with checking out the laboratory, but they have changed the code. Anyway, once they realise that I have nothing new to contribute to the project they'll whisk me off to some type of detention and then it will be back to the States with little or no dignity for what it is worth."

"God, what a mess, I am seeing Sir Jeffery tomorrow, might be a pointer there maybe, he likes to stick his nose into other people's affairs." Consuela sighed and nodded her head slightly in a sign of hope.

Over the years, when the going got tough, she was upfront and in charge, and he, Christian, was the ball of confusion in the background. Then and there he decided that the best thing possible for Tsargrin's salvation was the release of Consuela, and this, he now made it his priority.

Driving back to London in Rutherford's Ford Focus, Christian was in the mood to stir things up a little, he needed some sort of reaction, something he could act upon. He purposely left his phone on to see what, if anything, it would provoke, he had his gun, a wicked car and a journey full of purpose.

Whitehall, London

In his Whitehall office in London, Sir Jeffery Pollock was overly pensive. He was pacing back and forth from his big leather inlaid desk to the huge window that overlooked the park. He wasn't used to being unsettled and if he was, then he wasn't in the driving seat. Something was up, for there was a sense of urgency and foreboding affecting several high-profile departments. He was normally surprisingly well connected and now to make things worse; he had a meeting with Christian Simpkins, a wily young man who singularly possessed the knack of contacting him spontaneously. This alone disturbed him somewhat, he liked to have researched responses and an outline of what was to come before it came regarding both phone calls and meetings, like the one he now had to expect within the hour.

For once, Christian wanted to be open and plainly visible and this time he made for the main and rather impressive entrance to this particular building in Whitehall. Generally, he would take the far more unobtrusive side entrance. He wanted to be seen and to attract attention, something he normally avoided at all costs. He had cropped and styled his little beard, donned his snazziest grey suit and shined his shoes, unfortunately, he hadn't replaced his ornate belt from Devon, but wore it nevertheless, along with the hip holster. Christian had never been a master of style. He had the sense not to bring the gun and instead stuck his phone into the handy holster on his hip. To an initiated man-of-arms he would seem to be carrying a weapon of sorts, for it was relatively well known that a man used to bearing arms could spot another even though it was concealed. It slightly altered a man's gait and gave a tiny bounce to his confidence, easily spottable to some. He hoped that his little gambit would elicit some sort of response, hopefully from some of the spooks that covertly abounded the corridors of power.

As he entered a well-meaning doorman dipped his head as he passed, a couple of polite 'hello, Mr Simpkins' followed by a 'nice to see you back, Chris' which prompted a cautious nod followed by one particular greeting that did warrant a little action, a female voice, sharp and twangy.

"Yoo-hoo! Christian?" He looked quickly to his left, Mie Ng, Sir Jeffery's secretary, was there with a couple of her friends.

"Hi Mie," he responded in his best Roger Moore voice, "just going up to see the old man."

"Okay Christian, look, I am done here, I'll come up with you." Five paces away, he could hear her friends giggling. It was only three stories up in the lift, it was busy, they didn't talk but he could feel her beaming away at him. Along the corridor Mie chatted happily, when they got to Procurement and Ancillaries, she darted through Sir Jeffery's office suite and plonked herself down at her desk as Christian, politely bemused, followed.

"Good morning, Mr Simpkins," she sang, "take a seat, I'll let Sir Jeffery know that you are here." Christian scratched his mousy hair and did a double-take at her enormous smile before dutifully sitting down. She pressed a button on her desk phone.

"Mr Simpkins is here for your eleven o'clock, sir."

"Send him in, Mie, thank you."

"Good morning, Sir Jeffery," said Christian upon entering the office.

"I can't see what is good about it, Simpkins, you have pushed hard for this meeting, so it had better be worth it." Christian walked over to the big desk, Sir Jeffery indicated that he should sit.

"Yes, sir, I believe it is. Firstly, I must apologise for my absence the last couple of days."

"Really, I hadn't noticed, go on…"

"Well sir, you may well know, or possibly suspect that all is not well in a few departments of Whitehall. Well, to clarify, there has been one almighty security breach, in M.I.5. in the main, amongst other things it has compromised Mr Throtestabler's facility in Cornwall."

"Mmm…So that is where you have been, I would remind you that you work for my department and not, I repeat, 'not' for Throtestabler's bunch of weirdos. Presumably, this explains your phone call regarding the authenticity of the security alert, does it not?"

"Yes, it does, sir, and thank you for that, I need to know who you spoke to, sir, who it was that gave you that information er…sir."

"What is this, Simpkins? Have you lost your ruddy mind or something, is this some sort of farcical investigation you have dreamt up?"

"Yes sir, I suppose it is, somehow I inadvertently got myself involved when I was in Wales with Mr Throtestabler's engineer. You see sir, if I were not here, now, then somebody else would, M.I.5. most likely. You see sir, and this is of course confidential, the facility has been raided by a bogus M.I.5. security team, three people dead, sir." This last statement was like a bolt out of the blue to Sir Jeffery, like Christian he suddenly realised that he too would soon be involved. He reached for his desk phone and told Mie to divert all calls and to ensure that they would not be disturbed.

"Three people you say, this is news to me, who were they?"

"Two security men, sir and one of the raiders. It seems that Mr Throtestabler has made a startling discovery of some unknown sort that would change the defence strategies of any that possessed it. Even the Americans are involved."

"Hell Simpkins, I answer your one stupid call and now I am going to be dragged into this mess."

"Yes sir, ditto," said Christian eyeing the glare of disdain across from him. "Who did you speak to, sir? No calls are logged anywhere."

"George Willoughby, Simpkins, private line, I know this man very well and would vouch for him in every quarter, I mean, we used to swap summer houses on occasion, he has or maybe had a villa in Spain, a lot warmer than the Cotswolds. I don't think he'll verify my call though, he has been asked to take some leave I hear, must catch up with him."

"Thank you, sir, I can now tick that box. It is all a bit unfortunate but it is just procedural measures, sir."

"So Simpkins, if you are not currently answering to me, then whom?" Christian was a little caught out on this one, was it Norman or Rutherford, thinking on his feet he plucked an unaffiliated source of control from the back of his mind.

"G.C.H.Q. sir, a man came to see me in Cornwall, I've met him before, sir, in Belize."

"Does he have a Name?"

"Yes sir, but I will have to check back to see If I can tell you. They are trying to weed out the origin of the infiltrators, nobody is sure of who is who."

"Hmm…That explains G.C.H.Q.'s involvement then, serious stuff. Do you know anything of this discovery that Mr Throtestabler came up with?"

"Yes, sir, and that is part of the problem and it really shouldn't be divulged. I must say though, sir, you are normally exceedingly well informed, I'm surprised that you didn't get wind of this sad affair already."

"You have no idea of what I am aware of, Simpkins, and you never shall be. However, it is in my interest to be kept updated on all matters where possible if you get my drift."

"Yes, sir, I understand completely. I will get in touch, I mean, if M.I.5 or 6 can't get to the bottom of this and Ancillaries can, well…who knows." Christian arose. "Well, sir, I have kept you long enough so if you will excuse me…" Sir Jeffery looked up at the young man and scowled.

"Are you carrying that damn gun again, Simpkins?"

"Course not, sir," he said truthfully as he headed for the door.

"Liar," muttered Sir Jeffery as he exited.

Outside in reception, Christian was confronted by the wide and permanent smile of Mie. She stood up and walked around her desk to him, she came up close, slightly too close and whispered something in his ear and then patted his holster through his jacket.

"Can I call you?" he said quietly, she nodded and inferred that she would text him her number. Out in the corridor, Christian was prepared as he passed the second door, two men emerged and walked behind him, at the fifth door he was grabbed and manhandled into an empty office. Christian politely obliged without question or comment.

"Okay Simpkins, I'm not sure who you think you are, striding around the place carrying?"

"Carrying what, exactly?"

"A firearm, you idiot." Christian reached behind him for his holster.

"Oh, no you don't, what the fuck do you take us for." Quite roughly they banged him up against the wall and reached to where his gun should be. "A phone, you've got a fucking phone in a gun holster, you playing games or what?"

"Well, sort of I guess, just trying to find what response I get, getting a little tricky around here huh, I notice that both of you seem to be armed, shoulder holsters, huh? If you check my wallet, you will see my clearance." They duly inspected his credentials and scanned the barcode with a smartphone. "Happy?"

"No, we are not, we are on high alert, and we nor anybody else needs this shit, I mean, what is this, some kind of test or something?"

"Yes," said Christian, to add some sparks to the situation, one man shrugged his shoulders and looked at the other.

"You are in Ancillaries though aren't you?"

"Generally yes, but I have been seconded to G.C.H.Q. you can check with Sir Jeffery Pollock if you like, his office is just up the hall you know."

"G.C.H.Q. you say, but your clearance is from M.I.6, anyway, G.C.H.Q doesn't carry field officers."

"Exactly, that is why they need to second some, it will be interesting to find out what your particular remit is in all this."

"Look Simpkins, no need to make a fuss out of all this, we all know who you are, everyone does, but we still need to ask the bloody questions, anyway between you and us, I hope you get to the bottom of this shit, the word is that you are possibly a good bet at the moment, M.I.5 is on the verge of self-destruction if you ask me." After sowing his particular seeds of doubt, Christian exited the building via the side entrance.

Back in his little flat in Camden, North London, he again checked around for anything missing or out of place. He was used to his rooms being turned over in various other escapades, he had learnt to keep the 'vitals' well hidden. His little stash of stuff, passport, cards, bank details and a little book of a myriad of passwords, usernames and log-in codes were still in his possession, cunningly secreted under the kitchen plinth. This little hidey-hole now held his little gun. Despite being in his home, he had learnt the ropes, he withdrew the gun and kept it near him at all times. He really was hopeless with the thing, but by relying on his embellished media reputation, he was painted as a master of arms, a great put off to any would-be raiders.

He had two alerts on his phone, the first was a nameless phone number but the kiss at the end of it led him to correctly believe it was from Mie Ng. The second was a cleverly worded text from Robyn inferring that they needed to talk.

Before he could action either of these Christian had an impulse to investigate Sir Jeffery's old buddy, one George Willoughby. By dissecting Sir Jeffery's rhetoric, he assumed that Willoughby must hold some reasonable rank in M.I.5. to be able to even discuss security measures, and as they were long-time friends, then one should assume that they were of a similar age. He would be far too old for operations, long in service and of the same peer group as Sir Jeffery, therefore in all probability one of M.I.5.'s executives. Also, it would seem bit mad, amongst all the current goings-on to give anyone a leave of absence. Willoughby was the only real hook he had at the moment and some deft research was now needed. Bill Rutherford would be the man to ask, but how, he really only had a couple of phone numbers, but he couldn't tell if one or any was secure. Instead, he just sent a text 'Willoughby' was all it said, almost immediately a response came through, it just read 'clever boy', followed by a link and an access time. Christian studied the response, the reply was too instant to be tampered with and the link appeared to be some kind of photo-share app.

Later on that day at the aforesaid time, Christian accessed the link on his laptop, it was a beautifully easy form of correspondence. One had to simply tap out what needed to be said, then rather than press send, photograph it with the phone and send it to photos via the app. It was brilliantly simple, unfortunately, the content was far from that. George Willoughby, chief departmental executive, M.I.5. proved to be the source of the security breach by all accounts. He had not taken leave but had seemingly fled, along with his wife and dog, his relatives had all taken extended holidays somewhere abroad. Willoughby had vanished and a full police manhunt was in hand. A series of incidentals followed along with a rather dumbed down public appeal yet to be released. Christian studied the data, to him or possibly his intuition, something didn't ring true. As an afterthought, Christian checked his phone and swiped to find the camera, to his annoyance the photographed document self-deleted, five seconds too late, he reckoned. Although he now had some of the information he sought, it did not rest easily with him. Sir Jeffery, pompous as ever, stated that this man, one of his oldest friends, a friend he would vouch for, was a man that could be trusted. Willoughby was an executive officer with many years of experience behind him, clearly a clever man, so why would he not plan his escape more professionally? Why would he put his family at risk? Something had gone wrong but what? In fact, why would he want to leave in the first place? He would have been well-to-do if he moved in the same circles as Sir Jeffery, he would have been approaching retirement, and why would he take his dog of all things? Christian retraced his thoughts and settled for the most unlikely word 'dog'. The man has a dog, without all the jabs, without the special dog passport it would be a nightmare to take it abroad, far too much bother, to Christian, George Willoughby was somewhere in the UK, he was in hiding, he was not defecting, nor absconding, not even seeking a better life, he was hiding.

A thought struck Christian, just a small something that Sir Jeffery had mentioned, he and George Willoughby borrowed each other's country retreats, 'holiday homes' to the common man, George's was in Spain and Sir Jeffery's somewhere in the Cotswolds. Willoughby would have known it, Sir Jeffery was in Whitehall, so he wouldn't be there. It was the perfect place if you hadn't really planned anything, remote and low key. At last, Christian possibly had a plan, the summer house was worth some attention but where amongst the rolling hills and the clusters of quaint villages was it?

Christian felt obliged to call Mie, and quickly realised that she could do a bit of snooping for him, perhaps?

"Hi Christian." Her voice was bright and breezy, and somewhat refreshing to him.

"Yes Mie, thanks for the contact number, are you still at work?"

"Of course, I finish at five, you know that?" Christian winced and shook his head.

"Course it is, sorry time has run away with me. Thanks for the tip regarding those heavies, I was quite prepared, they weren't too pleased."

"Not surprising really, can't be that many folks strolling around here wearing a gun, huh?"

"Actually, I didn't have a gun, my phone was in the holster."

"My God, that's hilarious."

"Mmm…they didn't think so, erm…Mie, I need a little favour, if you could?"

"Me, really, then it has to do with Sir Jeffery then, not sure I want to do that, whatever it is."

"Sir Jeffery won't be in trouble."

"Then why don't you just ask him?"
"It is tricky, can we meet up?"

"Of course, you can buy me dinner."

"Ah, dinner, yes good, of course, when is best?"

"Well, today is Wednesday, I am okay for Wednesdays, but it will have to be near home."

"Sure, no problem."

"I am out in the sticks I'm afraid, Barnet, High Barnet."

"Huh, Barnet is just fine, I'll book us somewhere, 7 pm?"

"Yup, that's cool, okay, text me where please, by the way, I really love Italian food."

"Yes, don't we all, see you tonight, should I pick you up?"

"No, no, don't worry, you pick a place and I'll be there."

Almost subconsciously, he hung up and walked to the front door and locked it. He was two floors up and therefore could not go anywhere anyway, unlike Tsargrin he quite liked a well-locked door.

That evening, driving up to High Barnet at the northernmost periphery of London, something else was now on his mind, he had experienced this feeling before and it always bothered him a little if he couldn't identify it.

He met up with Mie outside the restaurant and escorted her in. She was still her overly smiley self and looked comfortably at ease out of her office gear. Christian had, in an attempt to make an effort wore a fresh grey suit virtually identical to the one he wore earlier. Mie was easy to be with and no real awkwardness was shown by any, after a few pleasantries and a bout of menu translation, Christian tried to ease the conversation toward his needs.

"Mie, just how long have you been working for Sir Jeffery now?"

"Oh, not long, five or six months, why?"

"Well. I know that he can be a bit difficult at times, just seeing how you are bearing up, that's all."

"Me, oh, I'm just fine, he is okay, just a bit quirky here and there."

"Quirky! Not dangerously conniving then?"

"No, he's fine, okay, just a bit misunderstood that is all."

"I see, maybe it is me then, maybe I am missing something, you were in the police though, before that?"

"Of course, your desk used to be mine, I quit the police about two years ago, when the twins started school."

"Twins…wow, bit of a handful, huh?"

"Of course, but Kimmy and Lea are just wonderful, wouldn't have them any other way. Police shift work is just impossible, eventually got a posting here in Sir Jeffery's department, Mum does the school runs, and on Wednesdays she feeds them, helps me out so much."

"Glad that everything is working out for you, Mie, I'm really not here to compromise any of that, you are a happy-looking girl, so just say 'no' if you want."

"'No' to what Christian? You haven't asked me anything yet, at heart I'm still a copper, always will be I guess. I like studying people, profiling them even. You, though, Christian Simpkins, are a bit of an original." Christian creased his brow as if hurt. "No, no, don't get me wrong, original, is a good thing, I have read your file, I have even googled you, put it all together and it reads like an Ian Fleming novel."

"Yeah, a lot of people do that, too many, don't believe everything you read, Mie."

"But I must, it is so fun, you have to write your memoirs one day, a book even, write a book."

"Not a chance, I don't think I measure up to this particular Simpkins, whoever he is."

"Ahh…modesty, so, so sweet." Christian slumped back into his seat, he didn't need all this and he could feel his cheeks filling up with warm blood, he knew what was coming next.

"Christian, you are blushing, I've embarrassed you."

"Sorry, I can't help it." She focused on him, her big dark oriental eyes probing his pale greys as they flicked up and down from the tabletop to her steady gaze. The moment was rescued by the delivery of their starter. Between courses, Christian composed himself. His body often did things his mind didn't want, he'd blush always at the wrong moment and his nerves would often let him down at the most crucial of times. He was neither big, strong nor handsome, in his own eyes, looking in a mirror, he was just painfully plain and yet the journalists that hunted him down after certain events over-coloured him to excess.

"Mie, Sir Jeffery has, I believe, a summerhouse in the Cotswolds, I just need the address, that's all, hopefully, it will come to nothing, but I have to tick that box somehow, that's all I need."

"Oh, is that all, shouldn't be too hard, he has a picture of it, I think, on his office wall, it must be very pretty. Sir Jeffery won't get into trouble because of me, will he?"

"Not at all, Mie, just ticking boxes that's all, it is just procedural stuff, but it must be done." Very soon the mains arrived and Christian was amazed at how she ate it all with so much gusto. If this girl ever had a weakness, it was Italian Pasta. After the meal, Christian offered to take her home. For some reason, she declined, she saw his puzzled look and explained.

"You see Christian, I live with my mum and dad, two younger brothers and the twins, I have done this since my breakup. I am a bit of a burden to them already so I don't want to mix things up, anyway, it's a short walk. I have got your email, so I will let you know what I find." She stood up on her toes, gave him a peck on the cheek and went happily on her way.

Christian thought that Sir Jeffery's summer house was worth checking out, it was his only lead and even that was just a hunch. The M.I.5 officer could possibly well be there, but all he could do was talk to him, see if he knew anything helpful on the grounds that, if he were there, then it was for a reason, which is why he didn't want to be found. He ambled over to the car park still pondering over his next move. Out of habit, one honed from many misadventures, he paused and checked around for cars, dark saloons with tinted windows were often on his mind but also for engines still running or condensation build-ups. There was nothing there to arouse any suspicions, he relaxed a little and looked around, a large neon advert featuring a blank-looking girl with the curves of a racing car caught his eye, he smiled back at the flouncy haired model and shook his head, he recognised her as some sort of professional celebrity from some obscure reality show, Tsargrin tended to refer to such images as vacuous and empty. Christian smiled slightly as he got into the car remembering his friend. There was a host of tumbling thoughts in his head as he started the car, and then like some almighty rising sun it dawned on him. Tsargrin's laboratory…It was built to his specific design about ten years ago after he inadvertently blew up the previous one, the new one was sunk deep into the ground lest it should happen again. He recalled the airlock where the inner door could only be opened if the outer was closed, he remembered seeing the slight boot prints on the inner steel door. Tsargrin managed to get inside, that he knew, but the raiders knew the code and opened the door, but in their hurry, they forgot about the airlock just as Christian had, at that time they would have been in great haste, police sirens, blue flashing lights and the revving up of the helicopter, their only way out. Eventually, when they worked it out, Tsargrin could well have made his escape, this was the possibility that stirred his mind. Why on earth would Tsargrin sport a nicely framed picture of the girl known then as Sheena Voltaire, a pouting vixen dressed in red leather? The phrase repeated itself, vacuous and empty. Tsargrin thought on a different plane, it was possibly a clue to the whereabouts of an escape hatch to his laboratory, he designed the place, he was the one that couldn't abide locked doors.

Christian was now so certain, that with no further thought he headed for the motorway, just a couple of miles north, he was off to Cornwall and a hard night's drive. It was now that he realised that he needed Consuela, yet he could not phone her, everything was still wrapped up under the ever-present security blanket. It dawned on him, that if there was an unknown means of escape, Tsargrin may have had a chance to use it, depending on where it came out, this line of thought meant that it could also be Consuela's way out, for at present she was forbidden to leave the curtilage of the building without an escort. There was still an insider on the loose, that was clear. He needed to speak to Bill Rutherford or even Norman, but the more he thought about his prognosis the more he doubted himself. He was moving fast now and began to doubt whom he could trust at the facility one-to-one. Eventually, this circuitous route took him back to Consuela. A plan was beginning to assemble itself in his jumbled-up mind, he liked a good plan, but the 'good' bit was slightly lacking at present. As he didn't really know why he was heading off to Cornwall in such a dash.

Sheena Voltaire

In his car, or rather Bill Rutherford's car, he had his little gun, hidden out of sight under the passenger seat, and by chance, a small holdall with a change of clothes, by chance, really meant that in case he got lucky with Mie somewhere along the line. He was now zooming up the M4, westbound, he really needed to find a payphone and made a point of performing a pit-stop at the next available services. Presently the service station rolled into view, he grabbed a coffee and located the array of payphones, thought for a bit, and then took a walk. Quite soon his whirring mind came up with a rather novel solution, he knew that all the phones at the facility were monitored, both land-line and cellular, he would contact Consuela direct and deliver her a seemingly dirty phone call, an asinine habit that some creepy men appeared to get a kick out of. Christian was pleased with his effort. Back at the payphone, he dialled the number and delivered his sordid message, he didn't need her to speak.

"Hello my Sheena, you're a low down woman, vacuous and empty, labour on this tasty bosomy image and rid yourself of this flight of fancy, when you are done, come and drink with me in heaven. The grey man. Xx."

Christian replaced the handset and grinned to himself, a beetroot faced woman at the adjacent phone glowered at him, he emitted a rather pathetic little laugh and headed back to the car park. He just hoped she got it. Within another couple of fast hours, he was on the last leg of his journey. Fifteen maybe twenty minutes to the Lizard peninsular, his phone pinged, a quick glance registered a smiley face, nothing more, it was Consuela, she did, after all, interpret the bizarre message, he hoped that she would act upon it with some haste for she still had the key code to deal with but Christian reckoned that it would not slow her down too much. It occurred to Christian that it was now approaching 1:00 am, he hadn't taken into account the dire logic of time. It wouldn't do to just turn up at the facility and demand a bed, just the mention of the word 'bed' reminded him of how tired he actually was. With a stirring mix of stamina and need he navigated himself about dozen miles beyond the facility to the tiny little town that housed the pub named the Mariner's Angel, the meeting place for Consuela, (drink with me in heaven). Finding himself a secluded parking space, he thought to stretch his legs, despite the rain, prior to an uncomfortable night in the car, he hoped that during the night or the following morning Consuela may have found a way to spirit herself out of the facility. Although well past the hour of midnight, there were still a few cars around and the dim glow of several lights in the pub, the Mariners Angel was tucked away from the main road and offered a cosy retreat for the locals of the area. Christian suspected that it was some sort of after-hours bash in the pub. A voice behind him raised his senses as he turned.

"You never fail to surprise me, dear." He knew the voice, it was Consuela. She was wearing an all-encompassing

Kagool and hood. Christian was elated, his guess, a calculated guess must have worked, then he did something that he never had the will to do before, he pulled her close and gave her the biggest hug ever, he knew that she wasn't a huggy person, but he was and he wanted one.

"My God, Consuela, you don't waste any time do you?"

"No, I am cold, I'm wet, desperately hungry and happier than I have been for ages, now, give me the car keys."

"Huh?"

"Please, I will be back in ten minutes, honest." Christian knew better not to argue. "Oh yes, don't liven up your phone, there seems to be some sort of event in the pub, see if you can get in, I'll catch up with you." Suddenly, he was carless, unarmed, offline and now quite damp. There turned out to be no event at the pub; it was just a good old-fashioned lock-in, lots of drunk people having fun out of hours. Quite a common West Country trait. By the time Consuela arrived back, somewhat wetter than when she left, Christian was well into his second pint whilst listening to a nice elderly man talking absolute gibberish.

"Hi Consuela, want a drink?" She looked around at the scene before her.

"What the hell!" was all she could utter.

"It is a lock-in, Consuela, that is all, happens quite a bit, now, do you want a drink?"

"Well, actually I damn do, a big gin and tonic, make it a double, and get crisps, peanuts, whatever, but lots of them." Christian obliged, "by the way your car is a mile or so down the road, outside a country hotel, don't want us tracked."

"That car, you shouldn't have bothered, it's clean."

"Idiot, get the gin and I'll tell you something that may help you live a bit longer." They found a quietish corner and turned their minds away from the drunken babble. "First off, Christian dear, marvellous bit of detective work. Where on earth did you grab onto the notion that there was secondary access to the underground lab? It was built maybe ten years ago, well before your time and a bit before mine as well, you even located it."

"Well, I remember a conversation with Tsar…Charlie a couple of years back, he mentioned, more in passing than anything specific, that he managed to blow up the previous laboratory, taking the best part of the barn with it. He was promptly built another with the dangerous stuff being deep underground, most of which was designed by him. Charlie hates locks, not even the bathrooms in his farmhouse have them. Logically then, he wouldn't want one in the lab, but because of the airlock system he was bound by it, so he simply built in another but kept it a bit quiet. As for its whereabouts, there are a few pictures there but the one on the stair landing is out of place, an arty picture of Sheena Voltaire, a professional celeb from ten or fifteen years back, with lots of pouting, fluffy hair and cleavage."

"Of course, he doesn't understand the concept of a professional celebrity, so in his eyes, vacuous and empty. Clever, so obvious, so simple but brilliant as nobody would ever investigate it unless there was some big problem or other. Well done, Christian, can't thank you enough, I won't be missed until breakfast time."

"Yeah, should give you a head start, how did you suss out the key code?"

"Good fortune, really, yesterday I persuaded one of the security guys to give me access as I was on the lookout for Charlie's calculations, as with everything, he had to accompany me, I just looked over his shoulder, he had the code scribbled down on a piece of paper as he entered it, I just read that, idiot."

"Consuela, what if Tsargrin managed to escape? I mean could he have, where did the escape come out?"

"The bike shed, through a standard-looking manhole cover, the escape hatch, for want of a better word was behind the picture as you said, you just had to slide it upward, it's a circular concrete pipe sealed at each end, so also an air-lock of sorts, you have to crawl westward for ten metres or so and then upward to the exit. I had already worked out the patrol timings, the biggest gap is a little less than five minutes, but as it is downhill to the perimeter wall, it is an easy sprint on a bike."

"The wall, though, that is loaded with gadgetry."

"That, oldest trick in the book, just climb a tree and drop down from an overhanging branch, you see, the whole thing is designed to keep people out, not in."

"So, Charlie could have done the same then?"

"Nope, not a chance, he could do the bike bit but not the tree I'm afraid, if Tsargrin didn't get taken, he would be there right now." Sadly Christian had to agree, normally when he made his escape to the pub the long-serving security man on the rear gate just turned a blind eye as he pedalled through the gate. Not so, with the bad guys, of course.

"Well Consuela, I really am glad that you are free and able, what are you going to do now?"

"Well, I'm off to London and the American embassy, of course."

"Really, oh…I thought maybe you'd stick around for a bit, you know, a bit of direction, that type of thing."

"Have some faith, Christian dear, that's all, bit of invisibility can go a long way, talking of being invisible, in my business, if I gave someone a car, it would be very trackable, no matter what Rutherford told you, that car of his will be loaded. You really are a red dot on a screen somewhere, that is why it is now parked up in a country hotel a couple of miles down the road."

"Oops, I think Bill Rutherford is okay, though."

"Yes, oops, M.I.5. hasn't finished cleaning house yet. There is still a lot of dissent at the facility, it is difficult for the staff to operate properly with some suits continually peering over their shoulder. I think that Robyn might have latched onto something though, she has become very cagey."

"Yes, I think so too, she sent a rather cryptic message to me, she needs to talk."

"Good, but be careful, they are completely stuck on the Fridge Project at this point in time, something is missing, all I was permitted to do was to verify things, the security presence is stifling, I would have thought that M.I.5 would be more subtle than they are, they are well respected in this field generally." Christian was still smarting over Rutherford's car, yet he still managed to take in what had been said, as for the car, it was so very obvious in hindsight, a complete novice could have worked that one out. But not him.

"Right, yes, one more thing, I may have found something worth looking into. Sir Jeffery has a summerhouse in the Cotswolds, years ago he used to loan it to George Willoughby, they are or maybe were, pretty close friends, might be worth a look."

"Willoughby! The alleged defector, definitely yes, but keep it to yourself at present, he has completely disappeared from the radar, so he could well be of some consequence, something is very wrong somewhere, I'm sure."

"Yeah, my feeling too, it just doesn't fit."

"Take your time, Christian, work out where it is, study it from afar and be very, very careful."

"I will, thanks for the tip, what now? It's 2 am and this place is emptying, guess we have to go as well I suppose."

"Agreed, I'm off to London, I have taken the cash from the glove box, your gun is still under the seat, think of somewhere better for it will you, Christian. Bang on the hotel door with some tale of misery, they might find a room for you, offer them double if you have to, give it a go."

"Okay, Consuela I'll do just that, I need a bed, something better than a car seat but what are you going to do?"

"Huh, easy, most people are out of their brains here, I'll just help myself to one of their cars, one of the older ones, easier you see." Christian looked at her dumbfounded, everything just seemed so easy for her. They both stood, she hooked an arm through his and they left the pub and entered the perpetual drizzle, Christian just had one short question.

"Consuela, if you become invisible, as it were, how do I contact you?"

"Good point, I will contact you. Get yourself a pay-as-you-go phone if you can. Turn on your smartphone on the hour, every hour for a couple of minutes, say, between noon and 6 pm, check for alerts, and don't open anything. Right, off with you now, and stay safe."

"Thanks, Consuela, take care." She smiled and did that little finger wave she does before disappearing into the shadows.

Christian managed to blag a room at the little hotel, he told a sad story of an injured puppy and promised them double money. He didn't get up until mid-morning, but having a good sleep, an invigorating shower and a decent full English, settled him for whatever lay ahead. He took the highly bugged Ford Focus and headed off for Tsargrin's facility. There was definitely something astir when he arrived, his car was searched, his phone was checked over and the security administrator wanted to know what he was doing there. He simply responded that he had an appointment with Robyn Reilly, almost a truth for once. Rather than let him into the facility, they fetched Robyn out after a short while.

"God, Christian, you didn't have to tell the whole world that we had a meeting, this is going to be impossible."

"It's okay Robyn, I have a plan, let's do lunch."

"Lunch! But it is barely after midday, what kind of plan is that? I have been cooped up here, virtually against my will for almost a week and I am going to go home tomorrow whatever they say. These security, what do you call them, 'bods' yes, that's it, they are driving me insane and all you want to do is take me for fucking lunch!"

"No Robyn, you wanted to talk, and I have come a long way to make that happen, now c'mon." Robyn seemed both furious and frightened at the same time, a rather conflicting bout of emotions which left her quite speechless, this was good as far as Christian was concerned as they headed for the car. The pub, Tsargrin's local, was only five minutes down the road, Christian knew the layout fairly well as they pulled into the little cobbled car park.

"Okay Robyn," he said quietly while cutting the engine. "You are going to be my girlfriend for an hour or so."

"Your girlfriend?" She looked over at him and uttered a meaningless 'eew' Christian flinched slightly and held out his hand, she faltered a bit and then took it.

"Good, we are probably being watched so play the part please." She nodded meekly and prayed that there was nobody there that would recognise her alongside the styleless, grey-suited man with the funny belt. Once inside Christian led her to the rear snug bar, small and cosy and hard to eavesdrop upon, one of the staff recognised Christian and gave him a friendly nod.

"What would you like?" Christian asked, she looked around the poorly lit heavy beamed recess and acidly replied.

"Er…to get back out?"

"Umm, nope, I mean to eat and drink."

"Oh right, er…isn't there a menu or something?"

"Only what is on the blackboard I'm afraid, Gastro hasn't quite reached this part of England yet."

"Alrighty, in for a penny, in for a pound, I will have what you are having then."

"Good choice, I'm having a pint of 'Proper', a local beer from St Austell and a Cornish pasty."

"Cornish pasty? What's that, cheese or something?" Christian had to think hard about the contents of a pasty, but Robyn surrendered to his lack of knowledge and decided on the same. Christian fetched the beer and she eyed the dark amber brew suspiciously.

"It's local ale, it is what Tsargrin drinks."

"Tsargrin, huh...oh well." She took the tiniest of sips, looked around and voiced her dire concerns quietly, just above the invasive murmur of the pub. "First of all, Mr Simpkins..."

"Mmm, I think 'Christian' would be more apt at the moment, huh?"

"What! Yes, yes 'Christian'. Well, it's that American woman, Consuela, she has gone missing, that is what all that hullaballoo was about back there. The security admin man is going bananas, don't know how she did it, she escaped from number one barn somehow, impossible, I would have thought, especially with all those security bods about."

"Er...Good Lord," was all Christian could add, he nodded for her to continue and took a good slug of his pint, she did the same and grimaced.

"Well, remember me saying that I spent a lot of time setting gravimeter readings around the old tennis court and how pointless it all seemed, well I had to replicate it on a much larger scale elsewhere, Salisbury Plain actually, a few miles up from Stonehenge. Well, when I took the readings back to Mr Throtestabler, he was over the moon, I'd mapped out the exact positions. He then sent me back out there, maybe three months later, with the box he called the compensator. I had to place it in a set position and re-enter all the previous readings, it didn't take too much time at all, unlike the positions before which took me two days. When I'd finished, I had to bring back the compensator still running and had to avoid turning it off, Mr Throtestabler was very adamant about this. Anyway Christian, here's the thing, there is no record of my trips to Salisbury Plain, nothing, I have checked everywhere, it is like it has been erased, you know, long ago. I haven't mentioned this to anyone…except, erm, you now. I think it is crucial to the project. So Christian, advise me, should I tell them or not, c'mon, help me with this…please?"

"Mmm…Tricky, how long ago, at a guess?"

"Few months, three maybe. Long before the security break, I can find out exactly if you want because I had to take some time out from the Welsh project. It will be on my planner, my computer."

"In that case, we must assume that it was Tsargrin himself, so, if it was, I strongly suggest that you, now me, keep it erased for the foreseeable future." She looked at him almost benignly and whispered 'thanks' before resting her hand on his.

"We are being watched I think." At that moment a bell pinged at the bar, Christian arose, glanced deftly around and picked up the two plates with the pasties, he grabbed the brown sauce and brought them back to the table. Robyn had downed her pint and looked up at him with watery eyes. "This beer doesn't taste normal?"

"Wrong, this is real beer, ale," said Christian sitting back down, "the lager rubbish in London isn't normal, do you like it?"

"I'm not sure, can I have another one to go with this thing?" she gave the pasty a tentative jab with the fork and looked at him questionably. Christian obliged, necking the remainder of his and returned back to the table with two more.

"Robyn," he began quietly. "Something you said makes a lot of sense, you know, the Americans have got wind of the Fridge Project, and they have re-constructed the original."

"Yes, thanks to that American woman, Consuela, whoever she really is."

"Perhaps, although the one they have, was found in the Irish Sea, whatever, they still can't make it work."

"Maybe they just do not understand Gravity in the way that Mr Throtestabler does."

"True, I guess, but it is also my guess that the raiders who took away the original prototype, can't get it to work either."

"Everyone seems to be searching for something or maybe someone," cut in Robyn through a mouthful of pasty. Christian fell quiet, for Robyn had a point, it could well be someone. Both of their flats had been broken into, but very little was taken or disturbed, what they were looking for must have been quite big, a second prototype fridge or, more likely, a person and that person could only be Tsargrin.

"Well, that pasty thing certainly hit the spot, what did you say was in it?"

"I don't think I did, but I believe it is onions, potatoes and some kind of mince and stuff."

"Mince, 'yuk' I don't normally do mince," so saying Robyn downed another huge slug of beer to presumably wash the mince away. They sat and talked a while longer, Robyn emitted a loud hiccup and took another large slurp to make it go away. Her hand resting upon his had now turned into a touchy-feely caress.

"Got to play the part," she said a bit too loudly whilst attempting a poorly timed wink.

"I think it is time to go." Opined Christian politely, heading back to the car, she hung onto his arm and leaned closely into him. This was a good thing, not because he quite liked Robyn, but because the watching security bods would interpret it all as petty courtship. At the facility, Robyn very much overplayed the 'playing the part stuff'. Christian needed to speak to the security admin man, he directed Robyn toward the stairs of the farmhouse and went to find him, looking a touch dishevelled, Christian approached the security man and suggested that they have a little chat. The man gave Christian a knowing smirk and ushered him aside.

"Okay Christian, we are quite safe here, you wanted to talk, something pertinent I sincerely hope."

"It is, I think, I believe you lost something today?"

"Yes, that blasted American woman, heaven knows how."

"Interesting, I think that we may be on a similar page, I think Mr Throtestabler may have disappeared too."

"What the hell is new about that?"

"Well, if Consuela could escape, then maybe Mr Throtestabler could have also. There are boot marks on the inner door of the laboratory's airlock when all the sirens went off, I think that Mr Throtestabler may have locked himself in his lab, or at least pretended to, er…maybe. You see if you open the outer door of the airlock, the inner one locks and vice-versa, has to."

"Carry on, it kind of fits into what we know, I am intrigued, what else have you got?"

"Not a lot really, I need to examine the boundary wall, this side of it."

"That has already been done by my people when they secured it."

"Possibly, yes, but I think I am looking for something else."

"You think? Huh, oh well, I shall indulge you, our investigating officer doesn't have much to do." He pulled out his phone, a weird-looking device, he spoke briefly and turned to Christian. "Hang on here, five minutes okay?"

"Sure, by the way, where is Rutherford, I would have thought he would be up to his neck in all this?"

"If I know Bill then he probably is, I keep thinking it is him every time I see that car."

The investigating officer was introduced to Christian; his name happened to be 'Holmes', Mr S Holmes. Christian cracked a wry smile at this disclosure.

"The 'S' stands for Sean, not Sherlock," he retorted laconically, having probably been down this route many times. Christian explained that he wanted a tour of the perimeter wall and added that he didn't really have a clue as to what he was looking for until he found it. Mr Holmes, 'Sean', seemed to get Christian's contrary drift and readily agreed.

The wall was actually not that high, eight feet at the highest. It was built many years ago as the manor farm's boundary, a string of wires and sensors were affixed to the top for the sake of added security. Christian knew the layout reasonably well. Following it from the inside going westward, they came to the rear gate, a galvanised modern steel affair that opened up into the tiny lane beyond.

"This," Mr Holmes stated, "is linked to the comms room in the house, it only opens from there, you have to ring the bell and look up to the camera." Christian didn't know this, for every time Tsargrin wanted to sneak off to the pub he would take this route.

"Mr Throtestabler often took this route when he wanted to escape sometimes. Never really knew how he did it."

"Yes, so we have heard, simple really, the guy at the comms desk had been there for many, many years, he knows Mr Throtestabler, when he sees him, he just presses a little button and lets him through, Simple." It was simple, he, Christian always just assumed that Tsargrin possessed some sort of cunning device that could open the lock.

"He is the guy with the cracked skull isn't he, is he going to be okay?"

"Yeah, he'll be fine, poor old bloke didn't stand a chance, they just walloped him."

"Yes, what was the point of that, anyway, the raiders had the comms desk then and you have it now, so nobody could really go through here without it being known."

"Exactly, Mr Throtestabler included."

"And the American woman, Mr Holmes?"

"Well, I must admit that is a bit of a mystery, how she even escaped from the building itself is puzzling enough, every camera has been checked and no alarms had been triggered."

"Mmm…Clever, huh."

"Annoying, to say the least, Rutherford went ballistic when he found out and I still have yet to tell him that I don't know how."

"Well, I sort of know the layout, been here many times, I bet those big oaks will give us a clue."

"How so?"

"C'mon, I'll show you." They walked maybe fifty yards eastward, with Christian keeping his eye on the base of the wall as they went. He selected the oak with the biggest bough overhang. "I'll wager that this is your mystery escape route, Mr Holmes, up the tree along the bough, then drop down onto the path on the other side. All this electronic gadgetry is to stop people from getting in, not out." Mr Holmes stroked his chin and headed back to the steel gate, he got the comms desk to open it for him by staring into the camera lens, then along with Christian in tow, they approached the oak tree from the other side. A short examination of the grass verge revealed two deep parallel footprints and a small indent from possibly a hand.

"Well done, Christian, spot-on, this has to be the American woman, all too fresh, can't see any other prints though?"

"I'm afraid that Mr Throtestabler, even if he got this far, would never be able to scale that tree let alone drop out of it. Ah well, just a thought."

"Yes, quite a leap isn't it? But well done anyway, we'll head back and see if we can follow the trail from the other side." Mr Holmes took a few photos of both the verge and the tree, and they returned to the inner side, starting from the base of the tree. A nearby path snaked up the hill to the farmhouse, skirting the disused tennis court and branching off to accommodate a dilapidated walled hut known as the bike shed.

"You see Mr Simpkins, it's pretty open ground and these paths are constantly patrolled, our people too I may add, they are alert and they know what they are doing. You would have to be an Olympic sprinter to cover that distance in the time given, must be 150 yards easily, silent too."

"Not so, Mr Holmes, I think we should check out the hut, it's where the bikes are kept."

"Of course, a bike, my god, Christian I think we may be onto something."

"Hopefully, yes, but first I just want to continue around the wall a bit more if I may."

"Sure, I'll have to come with you just in case one of my men gets a bit over-enthusiastic if you know what I mean. Presumably, you are looking for the bike."

"Yes, or rather, maybe, not sure." It wasn't long before Christian's mind settled upon an old tree stump no more than four feet high. "You see, this would be another way up, you could walk along the top of the wall to get to the big oak."

"Yes, could be, well this explains the woman, except for the barn escape that is, except there is nothing to indicate that Mr Throtestabler came this way at all."

"No, unless he flew over in his fridge."

"Excuse me, you can't be…er, are you?"

"Nope, but he is insanely clever though, he doesn't see problems in the same light as you and me."

"No, I've heard. Let's head back up the path now." Christian agreed, a bit before the farmhouse they veered off to the bike shed. There were several bikes there but Tsargrin's bike was missing, his was easy to identify as his bike was the only one sporting mirrors.

"Any missing?"

"Difficult to tell, Mr Throtestabler's has definitely gone though. It was his way of getting to the pub, if you go across at an angle you go straight to the gate, see." Mr Homes followed his line of sight, it was a well-worn path indicated by its usage. Christian was elated, for If Tsargrin's bike had gone then so had Tsargrin, but which bike did Consuela use. He hoped that his missing friend was in hiding somewhere, but how did he get beyond the wall, bike as well? Most of Christian's investigative observations were based on Consuela's recount of what had happened. To Mr Holmes,

Christian was clearly an investigative whiz, plus he now had something to dilute Bill Rutherford's ire when he arrived.

Christian was quite pleased with himself, he had needed to check out the bike shed and the wall, something he couldn't have done if it were not for Sean Holmes escorting him. He had some very valuable information now, but with whom should he share it with besides Rutherford? He began to doubt that Tsargrin had been taken. Whoever the raiders were, they were looking for him, preferably to take him and if not, they would undoubtedly kill him. In that little lane beyond the wall, he could have been picked up by anyone.

It was now late Thursday afternoon. Security had decided that it was fair and reasonable to allow the people to go home if they wished. By the time he had got back to the main driveway a lot of the cars had gone, someone was peering into his car, the deceptive Ford Focus, increasing his stride he reached it in a few seconds, a face emerged from over the roof and smiled, it was Bill Rutherford.

"Ahha…there you are Christian, still alive and kicking, that's good, heard you had a few scrapes."

"Yes, own fault really, left my mobile on I guess." For some reason, he didn't think that it was necessary to let him know that the car was not tech-clean, it would only lead to more questions that he wouldn't be able to answer.

"Ha…yes, smart-phones, they'll do it every time. I am looking for Robyn Reilly, we think that she may be of help, any idea of her whereabouts, Christian?" He didn't really want to put her in the frame just yet, not until he had a chance to have a one-on-one conversation with Bill Rutherford, also in all probability, she was still having some sort of extended post-lunch siesta, dangerous stuff, real Cornish ale, apparently. He looked over at the remaining cars.

"Well Bill, her car is not here, probably left early, she was a bit miffed at being kept here." Rutherford nodded disappointedly.

"Mmm…from what I understand Christian, I am sure that you will see her first, get her to call me, it's important."

"Sure, no problem, can you give me a clue as to what it is about?"

"No, sorry, afraid not, confidential stuff, you know how it is." Christian just nodded and shrugged his shoulders.

"Bill, I think I have something though, I think that Mr Throtestabler avoided capture and is hiding somewhere."

"Explain?"

"As far as I can work out, he pretended to lock himself in the laboratory, escaped to the bike shed and propelled himself to the perimeter wall."

"Evidence, Christian, what do you have?" Christian was not quite ready to play his full hand, something still irked him.

"Well Bill, we have boot marks to the airlock door, the inner one, likely an act of frustration as they couldn't get in. The perimeter wall defences are there to keep people in, not out. The American woman that escaped…"

"Just call her Consuela, we all know her name."

"Okay, Consuela escaped the confines of barn number one, somehow, with a bit of deft timing, she cycled down the path I think, threw the bike over the fence, then climbed along an overhanging tree bough and dropped to the other side, the prints are there, Sean Holmes went over it with me. In short, I think that Mr Throtestabler did something similar, his bike has gone. I think that he is alive and well and in hiding, he is a local figure Bill, lots of people would help him. However, although he is extremely clever, he is not so good at looking after himself. It is my guess that someone picked him up on the lane."

"Yes, I see where you are going with this, but we still cannot discount the possibility that he has been taken, or even killed. What is your next move?"

"Not sure really, things are brewing in my head, George Willoughby was your exec, wasn't he, well what has become of him?"

"I don't think the mechanics of M.I.5. are anything to do with you, all I can say is that he has gone, his house is empty, his wife and dog cannot be found and his immediate family have all taken impromptu holidays abroad. That's all I have to say on the matter. Now Christian, if you come up with anything, let me know pretty damn quick. By the way, I hear you are now tied in with G.C.H.Q.?" Christian was now thinking on his feet, something was up, it was as if Bill was holding back on something.

"Well yes, I suppose I am, Procurement and Ancillaries work in mysterious ways sometimes."

"Nothing new there then, who do you report to?"

"Sir Jeffery Pollock in the first instance." Christian felt quite safe with that response as Sir Jeffery was notoriously difficult to contact at the best of times.

"Right, Pollock eh, I ought to give him a call in the very near future. You are armed as well, I believe, Christian?"

"Not at the moment, it is tucked away with the spare wheel, marvellous car by the way." He added, in an attempt to steer the conversation elsewhere.

"How on earth did you manage to get category six clearance, you know, firearms and all that?"

"The Belize project, Lieutenant Colonel Teddington, pulled a few strings, the gun came in pretty handy, to be honest."

"Yes, we have all heard about your ability with the thing, little .32 Walther, ten shot mag?"

"That's the one, you are pretty well informed."

"Yes Christian, that's my job. Now I have heaps to do, call me as soon as you have located Robyn Reilly."

"Of course, will do." He watched Bill Rutherford stride off toward the farmhouse full of purpose. Sitting in the car, he checked the time, it was a few minutes before 5 pm. On the hour, every hour in the time given he had been turning on his smartphone to check for alerts, as yet nothing that merited any interest, he had missed a couple of hours due to various distractions, this time though he had received an alert, the one that he had awaited, it was a phone number, no name nor link. Instinctively he suspected that it was Consuela, he made a mental note of the number, deleted it and shut his phone back down, he hadn't as yet gotten hold of a pay-as-you-go phone and until then a payphone would have to do.

Robyn Reilly was now his immediate concern, although her car was not on the drive, it was parked up a little way up the road. He assumed that Bill Rutherford did not know what car she drove, or maybe he did but was now playing a different game.

Robyn, he correctly guessed, was up in one of the overnight rooms, Christian didn't realise just how strong a true pint of Cornish ale actually was, something about 5.5% clicked in his memory which made him wince slightly as two of those would have put him over the drive limit. It now appeared to him that some of the security bods were spending far too much time and attention on the science of the project than the actual investigation. The only thing that Robyn knows that they do not, were her two trips to Salisbury Plain and the resetting of the compensator, the term re-setting, somehow stuck with him. It was as if the Fridge project relied on the settings to work, he didn't even know what a gravimeter actually was, but if Tsargrin erased it so long ago then he, Christian, surmised that it must be crucial. He had amassed quite a bit of anecdotal knowledge but trying to link it all together just gave him a headache. Suddenly he glanced up, he had lapsed into some sort of mental stupor. It was now 5.30 pm and he made the snap decision to go and find Robyn, he found her in one of the attic rooms, thoroughly fed up and seemingly furious.

"God, it's you, what do you want now? It may have escaped your notice that I had some sort of reaction to that damn pasty. I came over all weak and had to take some time out, so embarrassing I was supposed to be working."

"Er…Sorry about that Robyn, um…I've never really had any problems with Cornish pasties."

"I want to go home, I just need some good coffee first."

"Okay, I'll sort the coffee, listen Rutherford wants to have a word or rather an interview with you and if I know him (which he didn't) he'll keep you here for hours. Your car is out on the street, if you want, you should leave sooner rather than later, he doesn't realise that you are here. I think he is in one of the barns at the moment."

"Really, well sod the coffee then, I'm off."

"Right, fair enough, do you want me to come with you?"

"What for?"

"Just in case."

"What the hell are you inferring now, are we to pretend that we are fucking engaged or something?"

"No, no, er, sorry." She brushed past him pulled on her coat and stomped loudly down the stairs. Christian watched her through the tiny dormer widow as she briskly strode down the drive. Christian then realised that she hadn't had time to sign out, a routine that all staff and visitors had to do. *Couldn't be better*, he mused with a wry smile. He would give her 15 minutes to clear the vicinity then he too would also go under the all-seeing umbrella of electronic scrutiny.

When he left, Christian didn't go so far, ten miles or so out he stopped near the hotel where he overnighted, he then walked down into the little town, the one he met Consuela in. He noticed then that it had a quaint old-fashioned red telephone box near to the road. Cautious now, as he ever was, he walked past it and a little way beyond before strutting purposely toward it, he now had his little gun loaded and holstered, although truthfully he had no idea why. The call was made and after an overly long ring period, Consuela spoke to him.

"Hello Christian dear, call box huh, well that will do but please grab yourself a dumb phone when you can."

"Wow Consuela, good to talk to you properly, I can't get a pay-as-you-go phone because you took all of my cash, you wouldn't want me to use a card would you, now, where are you headed?"

"Well, ideally the Cotswolds when I can, Sir Jeffery's summerhouse, waiting for more information, though. You mentioned something about George Willoughby?"

"I did, I feel sure that I am right though, he took his wife and dog with him and all of his immediate family have taken impromptu holidays abroad, thing is, if he has taken his dog then he should be in the UK, dogs are insanely hard to take abroad without prior arrangements."

"Good thinking, Christian, yes, when you get your info, brief me please. You can use this number whenever, as long as the connection is clean."

"Are you still in the American embassy?"

"Nope, I entered it via the main entrance as plain old me, everything is monitored in London these days, I spent a little time collecting a few stupid visa forms then went to the loo, stuck a blonde wig on and a quick change of attire and exited via the side entrance along with a gaggle of people also clutching visa forms, then straight into a cab and away I was. I am hoping that M.I.5 will assume that I need some American comfort of some kind. They will make a diplomatic plea to have me handed over, my people will insist that I am not in their care and the British security services will of course not believe them and so on, a great time-wasting exercise, perfect."

"Yes, 'perfect'. Now I am pretty certain that Tsargrin has not been taken, I haven't mentioned anything about the secondary escape in the laboratory, I just suggested he gave them the slip when the police along with all the sirens arrived. His bike has gone Consuela, I have checked, but which bike did you use, mine?"

"Yes, I think so, there were several bikes, the remaining few are bust. So if his has gone then you could well be right."

"In that case, he has probably gone off to a pub, everyone knows him, he was born and bred in this part of Cornwall. Apparently, his great grandfather was a nineteenth-century shipwreck survivor, I'm told, from somewhere in the Baltic at a guess."

"Yep, fingers crossed he's in good hands, I reckon we ought to try and find him then before anyone else does. Although logically, he is probably best off where he is, if we don't know where he is, then they sure damn well don't. At the moment, if you are right, wherever he is right now, is in all probability the safest, agreed?"

"Agreed, okay Consuela, this is where I am, the security people seem to spend an awful lot of attention on anything to do with the Fridge project rather, as you would put it, cleaning house. They have their eye on Robyn Reilly at the moment, they or rather Bill Rutherford seems to think that she is a crucial part, and to be honest, I think he is right and what she said to me verifies it. She made two trips to Salisbury Plain, the most recent, barely six months ago, but that information was erased from the records about ten weeks ago. I think she is pivotal so I thought I would catch up with her in London.

You know, park up the car and tube it to her place, problem is I don't actually know where she lives."

"Aw c'mon, Christian, really, Tsargrin will have her address on file, plus you have her car registration number, pay the right people and they'll give you an address pretty quick."

"Well, very nice to know, but I don't have access to Tsargrin's files and I don't know any of these 'right' people, as it were."

"Fair enough, Christian, but you will think of something, you normally do, however bizarre. Right, call me the moment you get an address for Pollock's summer house. I would also suggest that you race up the motorway a bit, London bound, you have the car, so you might just get a visual on Robyn and then follow her home if you can, once off the motorway, you will never find her."

"Aah, good point, I guess I ought to be going then."

"Yep, call me when you get a phone, okay?"

"Okay, yes, phone, yes, bye." Suddenly Christian was on a mission, he needed to locate Robyn's car, it wasn't an overly distinctive SUV, but it wasn't black or silver, which cut down the odds considerably, he couldn't quite place the colour except that it was sort of light and beigey. He had wasted a good half hour or so, he had a fair bit of catching up to do.

Fate was sort of with him on the motorway, he had just passed the turnoff for Swindon when he flashed past the right make of car and of a similar colour, poodling along behind a coach. The problem was that he needed to follow her, however, he unfortunately now got the opposite. He nestled in with a couple of cars in front of the coach in the hope that she got bored and decided to over-take. This didn't happen but the good old M4 ground to a halt as it approached London, Christian manoeuvred himself into the centre lane and crept along with everyone else. The inside lane crept a fraction faster than Christian's and he soon found himself to be directly adjacent to Robyn's SUV, a very cringeworthy predicament began to unfold. She was bopping away to some kind of hip-hop when she glanced sideways as if sensing Christian's stare. Recognising the car and then Christian she almost leapt out of her seat. She lowered her window, as he had, and lambasted his presence.

"Jesus, Christian fucking Simpkins, this is fucking ridiculous, how long have you been following me, there has to be some kind of law against this type of shit, what is wrong with you?"

"Erm…you are overtaking me, so I couldn't be following, circumstance I reckon."

"Circumstance? Bollocks."

"Okay, okay, I left about the same time as you, didn't I, and we are both taking the same route back to London, we both need this motorway, when I did pass you, I pulled into the inside lane in front of the coach."

"And why on earth did you do that, Mr Simpkins?"

"Give you a tip," he yelled above the roar of countless engines.

"Tip? Tip? What do you mean a tip? Do you think I'm off to the bloody races or something?" Christian ignored the remark.

"Rutherford, or rather one of his people will be waiting for you to arrive, they need to interview you and they will."

"Well, they can just fuck off as well, I am sick of this damn thing, I am sick of everything, well M.I.5 has a surprise coming because I am going to stay with one of my brothers, let's see them argue the toss with our Malcolm, that should be fun." Christian's lane now began to move faster than hers, he just grinned and shouted.

"Good girl, you tell 'em." Five minutes later they were level again, Christian just shrugged, she closed her window and turned up the music. Then, of course, her lane quickened again, and in another five minutes they were again adjacent to each other, he held out his palms in a gesture of surrender and rolled his eyes upward and in response, she just stuck her tongue out at him, and so it was until he pulled off at the next motorway northward while she headed south. The car following procedure was pointless now.

The Cotswolds

It was past 9 pm by the time he reached his flat in North London, he carefully checked his locks before entering, then gun drawn, he crept around the place to ensure that it was empty, he caught sight of himself in the bedroom mirror and sighed in despair. It had been a desperately long week and his body now decided to remind him of that fact. Without a dinner, a beverage of sorts or anything, he collapsed onto his bed half-dressed and awoke that way some ten hours later. Propped up in his bed with a huge mug of tea and his laptop, he attempted to catch up with his life a little. Within the usual influx of emails, he came across one from Sir Jeffery's secretary, Mie, she had come up with a photo of the picture on Sir Jeffery's office wall including the name of the village, no postcode or street name. It was quite a small summer house but beautifully distinct, with a nice dry stone wall encompassing it. *Presumably, then*, he thought, *If I got to the village, I should be able to identify it*, the makings of yet another plan began to take shape in his addled head.

A little later, he ventured out to the local phone shop, in his hand he held his old trusty Nokia 3310 and now sought a sim card for it, this, he achieved without too much fuss, as it seemed his old phone was making some sort of comeback 'bizarrely enough'. As soon as he got it going, he pinged his new number to Consuela, he then made his way toward a particularly favoured café for a fry-up. Just as he finished eating, he received the expected call from Consuela.

"Hi," he said happily, just talking to her made him feel safer.

"Yes Christian, about time you got back online."

"I know, easier said than done, but I'm here."

"Yes, I know, how's the sausages?" Christian froze and looked around him and strangely enough down to the floor and up at the ceiling.

"What? Where are you?" A punkish looking woman with nose rings and long unkempt hair plonked herself down upon the chair opposite.

"Well, what do you think?" Christian took in the apparition opposite him. The eyes gave her away, it was definitely Consuela but she looked like one of those maddish, cosmic looking women that most people would politely avoid.

"Bloody hell," was all that he could say.

"Yes, quite pleased with transformation myself, had to lose most of my hair though."

"Excuse me, but aren't those tattoos?"

"Course, not Christian dear, don't be silly, they are transfers, quite expensive but they last for weeks, now pay up, let's take a walk."

They discussed what they could and outlined various strategies, hers were pretty good and his, a tad lame. It was decided that on Saturday they would head for the Cotswolds and a tiny village called Little Spudding. Christian spent the rest of the day loading up with as much cash as he could muster, he bought himself a decent pair of second-hand binoculars and a set of clothes that he thought would blend in with the Cotswold hiking set. He emailed his eternal thanks to Mie and was pleased to receive an email from Robyn Reilly, which he thought was nice as she referred to him as 'Christian'.

A good early morning start was made on Saturday, the Cotswolds were not really that far from London, up to Oxford and then veer North West, the traffic was light, a slight detour to pick up Consuela and within two hours they stood high on a hill experiencing the delights of a region classified as a place of outstanding beauty. To Christian and the punky looking Consuela, it did indeed look appealing, but they had other thoughts, slightly darker, on their minds. A strong October breeze caused the temperature to plummet, Christian adjusted his bright orange and yellow anorak and tweaked his red woollen hat, Consuela looked dubiously at him and flipped the hood up on her deep NATO green parker. They had yet to identify the house and had left the car, Rutherford's car, in a different village a couple of miles behind them. They probably had another mile to hike before reaching Little Spudding. They made a strange couple, a man with bright, brand new everything and a slovenly looking woman that you would cross the road to avoid, clearly their planning strategy didn't cover the finer aspects of an up-and-coming adventure.

Most, if not all, the villages were sitting in little valleys or dales. Now looking down upon the village of Little Spudding with the aid of the binoculars they could make out most of the buildings. Sir Jeffery's house though did not reveal itself. Consuela pointed out a tiny hamlet slightly uphill from the village.

"Bingo!" exclaimed Christian, he pulled out the printed photo and compared it, it was undoubtedly the house pictured on the office wall.

"Okay Christian, here is what you must do, walk down and through the village to the hamlet, walk a while beyond it and then return by a slightly different route if you can. You are looking for signs of life, it is quite cold now so the heating is maybe on, check for the boiler exhaust, draped windows, cars, type and make, take your time, don't hurry, you are a tourist remember, look at a map."

"Me…shouldn't it be you doing this? You know professional stuff and all that."

"God, it is one damn house, you have the outfit, I am going to filter down to it across the country, get the rear elevation, now, off you go and don't get caught…" Without a second thought, Christian signalled his assent and then handed his little gun over to her. She checked it out in an instant.

"One clip?"

"I know, it was all I was given, mind you I have another old one that I found in my drawer, a memento from the Western Sahara I believe." Consuela nodded and snapped her fingers before holding out her palm, Christian rummaged around in the bottom of his brand-new orange rucksack and came up with the ten-shot magazine, and without a word he placed it in her hand.

He strutted quite purposely toward the village of Little Spudding, had a good look around as he thought a genuine tourist would do and then continued his walk up toward the hamlet. His nerves were behaving wonderfully for once, possibly because he wasn't actually doing anything wrong, plus he was in rural England and also because he had an armed and dangerous C.I.A operative on his side.

As he approached the house, he didn't have to look hard to see if it was occupied. There was a muddy black Labrador lounging around near the front door, wood smoke was coming out of the chimney and an oldish looking Volvo was parked to one side. He passed the house and went upward and onward for a while before texting Consuela, sneaking around as she does, it wouldn't do to ring her. He then retraced his steps back toward the house, he had established that there was someone there, now it was to find out who, which was tricky as neither of them knew what George Willoughby actually looked like, if it was him at all. A silver-haired woman appeared from around the corner of the house carrying a bag of something, Christian nodded a cheery hello as he passed, this was returned with a menacing scowl. He then continued in an ambling tourist type of way back down to Little Spudding. It was a delightful little village, with half a dozen overly clean shops, a church set within a manicured graveyard and of course a pub. There seemed to be a couple of bed-and-breakfasts or guesthouses and curiously enough a small stone bridge under which no water ran. It was over this he exited the village, aside from some farm tracks, it was simply one road in and one out. He waited awhile at the prearranged place that they should meet until he received a text to return to the car a couple of miles away at the other village. An hour or so later Consuela appeared, somewhat damp and muddied.

"You okay?" he asked.

"Aside from being sodden, I'm fine, I still don't have a clear I.D on the man, but whoever he is, he knows the trade."

"Well, that helps, I have the car registration, they have a dog, a black lab, and the woman would be the right age I think, they don't seem to be hiding though, none of the curtains were drawn."

"No, worst thing to do, it attracts attention, net curtains are easily the best. He is quite a tall chap, quite thin, maybe late fifties at a guess, he is taking pains not to get too close to the windows. Oh yes, he is also left-handed."

"Wow, did you get that close?"

"Not really, he stood near the rear doorway and gave a 180-degree binocular sweep, his watch was on his right hand. I think we have found Willoughby Christian. Everyone is hunting for him but you got here first, so for once we can call the shots, er…figuratively speaking of course."

"So, what do we do, do we approach him or what?"

"Hell no, we'd lose our advantage, we need it to be known that you, Christian, and you alone have found him and then we see who or what turns up, there is only one road to monitor, also I would add, Willoughby would be armed and with his background very dangerous, he would only have a side-arm mind, so we keep our distance."

"So, Consuela, who should I call 'Rutherford'?"

"Not sure yet, we have to explore our options, Rutherford will know we are in the Cotswolds so he might add it all up anyway despite being a few miles out from Little Spudding, depending on who he would send. Now I need to get out of these wet clothes, pop the boot will you? A quick change is needed. Christian squirmed a bit as Consuela changed against the blind side of the car, he knew her well enough to know that she didn't possess the embarrassment gene which in turn made her quite brazen. He knew he would be able to see her in the rear-view mirror but with a sterling piece of willpower, he studied the contents of the glove box. Her change of clothes now made her almost presentable."

"Fancy some breakfast?" she said pointing along the road to a gingham clothed tea room.

"Sure, it is more like brunch though, almost midday." Brunch turned out to be tiny cups of tea augmented with buttered scones and a selection of biscuits. Christian leaned over to her, Consuela always sat with her back to the wall.

"Look, what should I call you?" he said quietly. "I mean a different name, you know?"

"Yes, you are perfectly right, think of something?"

"Oh, okay how about 'Sheena' then?"

"You've already used that, try a bit harder."

"Okay, what about Beyoncé then, that sounds nice."

"You serious?"

"Mmm…Sigourney then, how about Sigourney, huh?"

"Tell you what, we'll just stick with Sheena, anything else will just be too much for you."

"Right, Sheena, it is then." He sat back in his chair and took another sip of tea. "You know Sheena, I think I should call Pollock, with his connections someone is bound to turn up." Consuela aka Sheena, pondered for a moment and agreed.

"Yes, good idea, use your smartphone though, it will make it more interesting because he will have a secure line, you never know, we may hook in someone else."

"Sure, I'll give it a go, but he can be a real git to contact sometimes if he has something better to do. Mind you, it is a Saturday, no way would he expect me to call today, the shock of it might stop him from declining my call."

"He'll pick up Christian dear, your location will pop up somewhere, he will know where you are." Christian nodded, everyone seemed to know where he was anyway. The car and phone told them that, they just did not know why. He pushed away the totally inadequate remains of his brunch and stepped outside waiting for his smartphone to fire up. 'Sheena' just sat back with another cup of tea and watched as Christian paced up and down the road with a phone stuck to his ear.

After a couple of tries, Sir Jeffery eventually picked up, it was Saturday afternoon and he was on the sixteenth hole and losing badly.

"Simpkins! Where the hell are you?"

"Little Spudding sir, nice place I must say."

"What in heaven's name are you doing?"

"Well, sir, you mentioned that you had a summerhouse here, and you have a picture of it on your office wall."

"You notice far too much Simpkins, too much for your own good. You had better have a good reason for this?"

"Yes sir, just following up on things, George Willoughby is staying in your house here." The phone went quiet.

"You sure about this?"

"Pretty much, quite tall, black Labrador, left-hander and a little plump wife."

"My God, who have you told?"

"Just you, sir, I am parked up in the next village a couple of miles away, I think I should hang about for a bit, don't you?"

"Yes Simpkins, keep out of sight and do not approach George, he is an absolute whizz with a twelve bore, I'll work something out."

"Yes, sir."

"And Simpkins, shut down your ruddy phone, will you?"

"Sir," was all he could say before the call was terminated. The way Sir Jeffery reacted disturbed Christian's thought process a bit. If George Willoughby was a leading M.I.5 defector, he certainly did not plan anything helpful. He voiced his feelings to Consuela, and she suspected that his prognosis was probably right.

"You see, Christian, if Willoughby is in hiding, and it looks like it, the bad guys had to have a hold over him, it clearly dawned on him somewhere down the line that it would be in their best interest to eliminate him."

"My god, you mean kill him, don't you?"

"Of course, he probably has a good idea who is at the bottom of all this, Willoughby is a loose end that needs to be tidied up, but he left before they could do that. He left in some haste, that we have already worked out."

"And we can't call upon Rutherford and others in M.I.5 because the security breach is still ongoing. Maybe I should call Norman, you know…M.I.6"

"Unfortunately that is one number we don't have, very few people do, Sir Jeffery maybe?"

"Maybe Consuela er…Sheena, but I doubt it, wrong department. I guess we just have to wait and see what happens I suppose."

"Exactly, if the wrong people turn up, we cannot do much except put out a call. I have your little gun, but two clips of 32 calibre won't scare them off much. Presumably, if these people happened upon us, they would also be armed, let's hope for a nicely informed ending to this." Christian gulped and prayed that these 'people' whoever they were won't get wind of what may happen. "Anyway Christian, we are where we are and our ultimate goal is to try and track down Tsargrin, hopefully, alive and well." Christian nodded sagely, but the possibility of armed men descending on them barged through his subconscious to sit firmly in the forefront of his mind.

"We are going to have to drive down to Little Spudding if we are going to see anything," he said dryly.

"Yes, exactly that, see if we can hide the car away, somewhere out of sight if we can, look, we are going to be alright Christian, they have no idea that I am even here, they, like everybody else thinks that I am tucked away in the American Embassy. Try and relax Christian, we are here to observe er…hopefully."

"Yes, thanks for that Sheena, most calming."

"Yes, thought so. We will let them find the car, Rutherford will know exactly where it is, and that will I.D his people."

The corner of the pub car park appeared to be the only plan for even the slightest concealment of the Ford Focus, unfortunately, the incoming road could not be seen as the pub itself was in the line of sight. Christian just sat in it anyway whilst Consuela did whatever she did. She returned shortly with the helpful news that the road could be seen from the lounge bar but on the unhelpful side, he was forbidden to have any alcohol to calm his fraying nerves.

"We'll just bide our time a little, as a backup, I think I ought to book a room in one of the B-and-B's providing the view is right."

"Okay, sounds like a plan, just a thought, maybe you should remove your stuff from the car, if Rutherford turns up, we don't want him to work out that you are here."

"Good, precisely, you really are beginning to get a bit savvier. I still have the gun though, I think that it is for the best though, don't you?"

"Oh god, yes please."

After about an hour or so, Christian peered over the lip of his fourth cup of crap pub coffee.

"Aha Con…I mean Sheena, a very clean-looking saloon approaching quite slowly, it should pass us by in a few seconds." Consuela just nodded, she seemed to be switching over to spook mode, a look that Christian had witnessed several times over the years. The dark saloon cruised slowly past, Christian snorted into his coffee, slopping a heap of it down his trendy hiking trousers.

"That was Sir Jeffery, he had come by himself, didn't think that he would do that."

"What about the car?"

"That, standard pool car, Whitehall has dozens of them, oops…I think he has just told everyone where he is."

"That he has Christian, bloody idiot, keep your eyes peeled, if he has been followed, they shouldn't be too far behind. I'm going up to the guest house, somewhere to watch from with the binoculars, I'll also dump my stuff off there."

Christian wandered back outside and watched the road from the bus shelter. The publican had been paying them far too much attention, hogging a window table and barely spending any money never went down well. Consuela joined him after a couple of hours.

"I have a far better view from the second floor, or rather the attic. There is a motorbike approaching, if it acts suspiciously then we could be in trouble." Christian really didn't relish the 'we' part. Unfortunately, the motorbike did act a bit strange, quite slowly the rider brought the bike past the bus shelter. Consuela grabbed Christian's head and pulled it tight into her shoulder, as the bike passed, she studied it carefully and then let him go. The bike was equipped with two large panniers.

"Don't want him seeing you yet, go and see if you can get a line of sight on him, I am going back to the room, with the binoculars I can give you good notice. Make contact by text, use the dumb phone, okay?" Christian gave a thumbs-up sign and strolled up the road in the direction of the motorbike. The rider parked up the bike close to a telegraph pole, dismounted, fiddled with something low down, dusted himself down, remounted and then headed a little further up the hill. Christian was now trudging along in the mud behind an unkempt hedgerow. He managed to get a text off to Consuela describing what he had seen. He now paused again, the rider had stopped off in the shade of a leafy flowering shrub, he was literally a hundred paces from the little hamlet where the summerhouse was located. He opened one of the panniers and tinkered with some sort of device within. He then removed his helmet and carefully looked around, especially toward an east-facing farm track beyond the summer house, Again Christian relayed the event as he saw it but was cut short as his phone signal faded, but not before Consuela managed to instruct him to carefully return back to the car. Despite the amount of mud on his brand-new hiking boots, he plonked himself down in the driving seat of the Ford. Something was about to happen and he just knew it, his dodgy nervous system rarely got it wrong, Consuela appeared and sat next to him, she seemed extremely intense.

"Okay Christian, this is clearly not good, there is a black van up on the ridge maybe three miles at the most, it stopped, possibly to get some bearings, then disappeared down a farm track or a path of some sort. Check your phone signal please?" Christian obliged.

"Very weak, probably unworkable."

"Yes, mine too, and quite suddenly, the bike, you mentioned the rider tinkering with something in the pannier."

"Yes, the right hand one."

"Yep, the size is about right, that, if I am not mistaken Christian that is a phone bump, a signal disrupter, and I'll bet that when he stopped off at the telephone pole, he cut the landlines. The van must be the backup, they are coming on foot Christian, it's a hit, they will take everyone in that house down along with Willoughby."

"Bloody hell Consuela, what do we do? What's the plan?"

"No idea, we need to find a landline, try and call the police I think."

"Brilliant," said Christian enthusiastically, this was one plan that he wholeheartedly agreed upon. "There's a payphone by the door of the pub."

"Good, tell them that there's an armed robbery in progress, that will bring them." She watched him scoot across the carpark to the entrance only to reappear a few seconds later, looking somewhat dejected. She correctly reasoned that the lines to Little Spudding had also been cut. At that moment there were two boom-like retorts from a gun, Christian scuttled nervously back to the car.

"Right Christian, get this thing going now, up the hill as fast as you can, those were shotgun blasts."

"Surely, you mean down the hill," he said as they screeched out of the car park.

"No, up the hill to where the motorbike is, move it." Christian did as he was bid, it was only a quarter of a mile to the hamlet, and he'd be there in seconds. "As soon as we get there, get out, make for the hedgerow, find some cover, lie down and shut up!" she yelled above the screech of the wheels. He managed to slew the car around and then scrambled out and headed for cover, in the blur of things he noted that Consuela had already gone.

Another shotgun boom was followed by a succession of loud pops, by this time Christian was flying horizontally into a clump of thorny brambles, he felt as though he was in slow motion and the ground was coming up too slow to meet him. Another flurry of loud pops and metallic chinks told him that Rutherford's car had been wounded, immediately after, three loud cracks rent the air close to him, forcing him to squirm tighter into the ground, but these sounds he knew, small calibre, it was his gun, he twisted his head and thought he saw her spiriting herself across the road. She had put a few rounds into the bike's pannier, the phone bump, he now hoped was out of action. A familiar voice echoed out from the house.

"Is that you, Simpkins?"

"Yes, sir," retorted Christian loudly, before clamping his hand over his own mouth, as a few more pops and little tufts of earth flicked up by the roadside. It dawned on Christian that they didn't actually know where he was, the shots were generally directed to keep heads down, a tactic that worked very well on Christian. He heard his little gun speak again, someone cursed loudly, a couple more shotgun blasts and the sound of glass crashing.

"Simpkins," yelled Sir Jeffery, "there is one around the back."

Christian though, learns fast. He didn't reply or respond, he pulled out his phone, the smart one, and called the police in an overly loud whisper, apparently, they were already on their way. The villagers would have heard the gunfire, the shotguns would be a familiar sound but Christian's little automatic told a very different story. He lost count of the 'cracks' it made, he knew that she only had twenty bullets at most and she must have done over half a dozen already. There seemed to be a bit of a lull in the action, in the fading light, he could just make out a plume of white smoke, the coughing and cursing told him that it was some kind of gas, riot gas in all probability. The lull was broken by two very quick gunshots followed by a scream and a tirade of the foulest language. Christian flinched, Consuela was doing her stuff with his gun, then she will disappear and he will be left to blatantly lie about his escapades, provided he survives, that is.

Quite suddenly as if on a signal, two guns opened up at the front of the house, and rapid loud pops poured into the building punctuated by more shotgun blasts. Inside the house, George Willoughby, his wife and Sir Jeffery were corralled into the kitchen at the rear.

"Good man, that Simpkins, he must have got the chap out the back, we'd be stuffed otherwise, Jeffery."

"Yes, I suppose that he does have some qualities, I am down to my last two cartridges," he said snapping back his twelve bore.

"I am okay at the moment six left, Doris has my service revolver though." Doris, Willoughby's wife, nodded ashen-faced. They heard another crash, indicating more gas, it was only a matter of time before they were forced out.

"I think that there are only three of them, Jeffery, if Simpkins has taken the one out the back and one has just tossed another gas canister into the dining room, I think that he must be behind the flank wall." He then chose to crawl out and around the kitchen door, Sir Jeffery let loose another shot out of the window as some sort of distraction, it was clear that they were about to come in for the kill. Another shotgun blast, but this time from outside was rapidly followed by Willoughby darting back inside.

"Got the blighter, took part of his foot off I think." Christian's little gun again cracked several times in succession, much closer to the house now, then, like a cavalry bugle, police sirens could be discerned back down in the village.

One thick rough voice growled out above the noise, a heavy South African accent.

"Christian Simpkins, you are a fucking dead man, I will kill you, no matter how long it takes, you are dead, you hear me?"

"Ooops!" squealed Christian from his bed of brambles, a hand gripped his quivering shoulder.

"Shhh…it's me, dear, here is your gun, there is a guy up there behind the dry stone wall by the gate, he is wounded in the right shoulder and the right leg, he is out of action, I tossed his rifle into the copse nearby, M.I.5 will need him, see if you can get any info, I have to disappear pretty damn quick, erase my number from your dumb phone, oh yes, stay hidden until the police have made things safe, that South African guy might want to take a pot shot, okay?"

"Okay," replied Christian in the smallest of voices. He began to slowly extract himself from the brambles which snagged his clothes and tore at his flesh, in frustration he ripped himself from the last vestige of coiled up thorns, crawled over to a tree and put his back to it. He holstered his gun, it still felt warm to his hand, he would do exactly what he was told and wait until the police secured the area.

The first police car raced up the hill, out of nowhere a volley of loud pops sounded, the gunfire was directed toward the advancing police car, it screeched to a halt and reversed full tilt back down the hill almost as quick as it came up. Christian did not have time to act, he didn't have time to do anything, he just prayed that the officers in the car were unharmed. He was facing downhill toward the village, with the tree behind him sheltering him from any perils uphill. Over the next half hour, many more vehicles arrived, police cars, ambulances and the dreaded news vans complete with aerials and dishes. Christian now understood that the final volley of gunfire was but a simple but potentially lethal delaying tactic, a device that calls upon the worthy rules of health and safety to do its stuff. Presently a helicopter could be heard, and it immediately began its search, it was now dark but Christian knew quite well that the equipment it carried could identify anything on the ground whatever the conditions. Presumably, some sort of all-clear was given and black-clad armed policemen began to advance from every angle. Christian began to relax, for this particular nightmare was almost over, his nerves began to settle, he took a couple of deep breaths and wiped the sweat from his brow, his hands were wet with blood and for an instant, he believed that he was mortally wounded but found with the tips of his fingers a few jagged tears. He smiled to himself, it was just the brambles, and that, he could easily live with. Quite suddenly he was bathed in a fierce white light, the noise of a big powerful engine chopped the air above him. He could now hear angry urgent voices shouting at him, it was the police, this he knew, but they were all shouting urgently together and he couldn't make out a single word. He put his hands on his head and struggled to his feet. Two men covered him with complicated-looking machine guns, another roughly frisked him, ripped off his jacket and relieved him of his little gun. He was then brutally manhandled out of the bushes and into the road with the fierce white light still bearing down upon him. A little further downhill, he was made to kneel with a gun pointing at his head less than a metre away. With his hands still tight on his head, Christian understandably enough did not feel great, he was covered in wet mud, his skin was torn and now it had begun to rain. Somewhere in the back of his senses, he heard two more shots, not the pops of a muffled weapon or the blast of a shotgun, it was a different sound and Christian was perversely relieved that he couldn't get the blame for it. After about 15 minutes his knees began to hurt, every time he shifted to ease the discomfort the policeman growled at him to avoid any movement. Something was happening but he wasn't permitted to turn his head. The oncoming bout of drizzle just about did for him, he was going to get to his feet no matter what, as chance would have it, he was actually helped to his feet. He turned to face the tall figure of Sir Jeffery Pollock.

"My God Simpkins, you are in a dreadful state. You!" a man in a suit looked up. "Get this man some medical attention, he is one of ours, move!" He shouted in his natural-born authoritative tone, and the man did as he was bid. Christian could walk just fine, anything to get his knees working again. A policeman on one side and a concerned medic on the other walked him to a waiting ambulance lower down the hill. The fine drizzle had now turned his congealed scratches back to diluted blood. In the ambulance they wanted to give him all sorts of stuff, all Christian wanted though was a nice cup of tea, a request somewhat short of the professional medic résumé. Their response was to clean him up a bit and provide him with a blanket. From where he was, he could hear the voice of Bill Rutherford lambasting some poor soul, Sir Jeffery was listening intently to some important looking uniformed officer and George Willoughby had been handcuffed and led away under arrest.

When the time was right Bill Rutherford ushered Christian into the back of a dark saloon. There was a de-briefing to be had, there was always a de-briefing to be had whenever anything actually happens. It was getting late into the evening yet Christian still found himself to be hot and bothered. It took a while for all those vehicles to disperse. He lowered the dark tinted window and stared out at the scene beyond. He was almost adjacent to the pub, a woman was looking balefully back at him, she was sort of scruffy, lank-haired and a bit punkish, inside Christian was smiling, outwardly he was poker-faced. The car edged forward a few more car lengths, and another female face came into view, someone he had met several times, Anne Bottomley, she was a journalist, the driver overrode the window mechanism and locked it closed, but he was sure that she got a glimpse of him. This particular investigative journalist was clever, tenacious and bullish to the extreme. She really was the last thing he needed and his new trendy cropped beard would not fool her in the slightest.

The dreaded de-briefing took place at the regional police station, it involved a detective inspector from the police, Bill Rutherford and an M.I.5 interview specialist. Christian first of all had to explain what he was doing there in the first place. This was put down to a hunch that Sir Jeffery had let slip, it was an honest portrayal of the facts, minus the input from his secretary Mie. He told them how he followed the motorbike and how he discerned that the landline cables had been cut, he mentioned his hunch about the electronic gadgetry that disabled the mobile phone signals and that he guessed what was next to happen which caused him to return to the car and get his gun. After this point, his heroic actions became totally fictional. He claimed to have a bit of a headache and was consequently given some paracetamol, this he hoped would in some way derail anyone hoping to interpret his body language. Norman from M.I.6 was an ace at spotting a lie and Christian was thankful that he wasn't there. He proceeded to tell his three ardent listeners that he put a few shots into the motorbike pannier in the hope of disabling whatever was in it before he snuck across the road and verges to come up to the dry stoned wall next to an old gate, where he confronted a gunman with an unusual looking rifle, but he fired first hitting him in the shoulder and maybe the leg, which put him out of action. He then stated that because he had no idea how to use such a rifle, he just slung it into the bushes. After that, he approached the house from the blindside and loosed off a good few more shots in the direction of the attackers, after which, he retreated to the tree where the police found him, he forgot to count his shots and so was unsure about his remaining ammunition.

There was very little counter questioning and Christian displayed a little disbelief when he was told that the wounded man was dead. He knew Consuela too well and if she shot to wound the man then he should be alive but hospitalised. Bill Rutherford admitted that one of his people had to kill the man because he had retrieved his weapon, apparently, he had no choice but to shoot. Christian stated that this was hard to believe as he threw the gun a fair distance. Bill Rutherford countered this by stating that he was always amazed at what a wounded man could achieve in his experience. There were a few more questions concerning Sir Jeffery Pollock, and that if he were informed of George Willoughby's presence, then why was not the police or M.I.5, especially as he had all the correct contact numbers. This was a simple one for Christian as he truthfully had no idea what the man looked like in the first place, so it was but a calculated guess.

They returned his phones, and his wallet but not his gun as forensics wanted to do a rifling test on it, whatever that was. It was agreed that Christian's story tallied with both Sir Jeffery and the Willoughby's. The only other casualty was their black Labrador, murdered in cold blood as a distraught Doris Willoughby phrased it. Having been dismissed from the investigation for the time being at least Christian was permitted to go. He didn't know where to go, he didn't know what to do or where his car even was. It was 2.30 am Sunday morning. He was hungry, sore and felt like a complete idiot in his jazzy hiking wear in what was clearly an urban environment, plus it was still raining, that perpetual drizzle of fine rain that penetrated absolutely everything. Bill Rutherford came to his aid.

"You handled yourself pretty well in de-brief, Christian, a lot of people get totally flummoxed." Christian couldn't be bothered to tell him that he had been in a good few and that this was one of the easier ones.

"Yeah, thanks Bill, any idea where I am?"

"Not sure myself, but your, or rather my car will know, it is in the car park at the rear, got hit a few times, but it has been checked out and they brought it here. I think that I'll have to bill you for the holes," he said in a rather insincere way.

"Yeah, better the car than me I suppose."

"You did well today, stalking down that gunman at the rear was a huge feat, you must move like a ruddy panther or something to pull that off." Christian had to smile, he often thought that Consuela moved like a cat anyway. Bill took the smile as a recognition of the praise that he had just levied upon him. He pulled out a set of keys and rattled them in front of him before handing them over.

"Let's get this day over with, you must be shattered, during the week I shall make contact, we need to tie up a few loose ends." Christian nodded his agreement and headed for the car. Fortunately, he was in Oxfordshire and not in Cornwall or Wales. A couple of hours or so would see him back to his flat in Camden, North London, Christian did not quite make it, he slipped into the M25 services, had some much-needed food, got back into his car and latched onto the previous day's facts that tumbled around inside his head, in doing so, he promptly lapsed into a deep lifesaving sleep.

It was now a little before 4.30 early Sunday morning and outside the entrance to his tiny block of flats, an irate shadowy looking character got back into his car and waited, he made a couple of calls, waited some more and then paced up and down the road looking at his watch. He had somehow got the wrong information, for Simpkins had either got wind of his sinister intentions or headed off elsewhere instead of home. By 5.30 am the stallholders of Camden Market began setting up their stalls, forcing him to move on, then people, lots of people began venturing out of their homes and from that moment he was forced to abort his deadly mission. He was a professional in his trade and felt somewhat perturbed that he had been outmanoeuvred by Simpkins so easily. Christian knew nothing of these nefarious goings-on when he awoke a little cramped and cold at 6 am. He grabbed himself a fresh coffee and poodled through the suburbs of Barnet towards Camden and home. He well knew the hellish parking restraints around the area where he lived and parked as often before about a ten-minute walk away. The walk did him good, his tumbling mind freshened up and a worrying scenario began to take shape in his head. Although he was still convinced that Tsargrin Throtestabler was somewhere in hiding and in all probability, at his own accord, other things simply just didn't add up. By the time he got to his flat, quite unscathed he had made up a mental list of his worries.

Sir Jeffery's apparent eagerness to have his friend Willoughby arrested by the Oxfordshire police.
Why did it happen to be an M.I.5 operative that killed the wounded man when there were far more armed police around?

He had at first assumed that Sir Jeffery had led the killers to the summer house when he used the pool car, but why would they follow it? There was an underground garage full of similar cars in Whitehall. Sir Jeffery was completely unattached to the M.I.5 investigation.

It must therefore be assumed that they worked it out by the proximity of Christian's car, Rutherford's Ford Focus, yet the only way the connection could be made must have been from the phone call he made to Sir Jeffery. He could be certain that nothing now was safe or sure in Spyland.

Finally, was he, Christian, now a loose end that needed to be tidied up just like Willoughby.

In an act to dilute his fatigue, he took to his bed for another few hours, and then sometime around midday, he took a long hot soak in the bath. Come lunchtime he was sort of back on the ball. Tsargrin's welfare was as usual the driving force behind his rigour. He checked out his emails, dozens of them, but the only one that was a cause for concern was from Robyn, she needed to talk. He didn't even want to touch his smartphone for it had magically become a poisoned chalice capable of alerting all the evils on the planet. Out of necessity, he turned it on, glossed through the alerts and made some notes and then promptly shut it back down. Next, he reached for the dumb phone and recalled that it had been in other hands besides his, there wasn't much on it and he had already erased anything to do with Consuela. But now that the number was presumably now known it was also compromised. Christian sighed and also shut it down before popping out the Sim card, he would pick up another from the bustling street market below. He decided that he couldn't even trust his little flat, therefore he would call Consuela from one of the local pay-phones, Camden Market was by far the safest place ever, with crowds of countless people, wide-eyed tourists staring agog at the dodgy deals being haggled out by the hundred, bizarrely attired Goths, pseudo mechanoids and a host of people who thought that it was 1972 again, perfect. His call to Consuela was quick and to the point, when he told her that the wounded man had been shot dead because he had an assault rifle, her response confirmed his fears.

"He has been murdered then, Christian, those wounds of his were totally disabling, plus, when I hurled the gun into the copse, he was lying face down. No way could he find it in his condition, he wouldn't even know where to look. He has been silenced I'm afraid, so watch your back Christian dear, be so, so careful. Anything for me to work on?"

"I think I have a hunch as to where Tsargrin might be." Consuela's tone picked up somewhat.

"Go on?"

"I reckon that he has gone to the pub."

"Are you serious?"

"Completely, he is a local, isn't he? Everyone knows him, everyone likes him, I know I've touched on this before, but the more I read into it the likelier it becomes."

"Mmm, I've come to trust that intuitive streak of yours over the years, any idea what pub?"

"Not really but the Smugglers Arms is a good place to start, lots of little alcoves and a few rooms above that are sometimes let out."

"That sounds like dozens of pubs around there."

"True, but the Smugglers is Tsargrin's second choice local, just a guess though."

"Okay Christian, sounds feasible, but definitely not a watertight clue, I need more than that, but if you are right and he is safe then it is best to leave him there, anyway we can't stop looking, so back to Cornwall it is, shame, I like it here in the Cotswolds."

"I think I'll leave it with you for the time being, I have to check up on Robyn, I think she is frightened."

"And rightly so dear and she doesn't even know the half of it."

"Yeah, one other thing, my gun has been confiscated by the police."

"Yes, that figures," Consuela said little else, it was normally a sign of her analytical process cutting in, he gave her his latest new Sim card number and said his goodbyes.

Robyn Reilly was the next to phone and Christian had to wait a while before she picked up, she was still using her smartphone, she was scared and wanted to get back to the security of Tsargrin's facility, or even Wales, she considered that safe as well, anywhere but South London it seemed. She was sure that she was being watched, but not certain. Christian agreed that she would be far safer at the facility and that he would get her there. Tomorrow was Tuesday and a bit too soon for Christian but he promised her that it would be before the weekend. To this, she reluctantly agreed as the 'sooner the better' was her ideal. Christian decided that she needed a dumb phone as well.

Christian had already subconsciously decided that he now hated Bill Rutherford's Ford Focus, admittedly it was a dream to drive but he just did not want to be a red dot on somebody's screen. He didn't have an awful lot of money left, he knew that Consuela would need some funds and that would have to be in cash. He would have to put up with the Ford for another few days, get it to Cornwall and then hire something small but clean on his good 'ol credit card' and worry about the cost another day. Whilst in Cornwall he would make a concerted effort to track down any sign of Tsargrin, an oddly satisfying little pub crawl sprung to mind.

He slept well that night, he had the makings of a plan in his head, he liked plans, always had done, you could write it down like a recipe and follow it, everything in its own order, 'perfect' was his last opined word before he dropped off to sleep. He awoke quite early feeling fresh and able, he donned his last fresh grey suit, pushed his thick Devon adorned belt through his trouser loops, clipped on his holster and stuck his two phones in it. He didn't have the gun, but to be honest with himself he was a bit scared to use it properly anyway, he once wandered around the jungles of Central America with a stick in the holster and everyone just assumed that he was carrying, it worked a treat there eighteen months ago so why not now, but with phones.

Sitting down with a pint of strong tea, he turned on the TV and scrolled to the News, possibly not the best of choices. There was a high-profile piece on an armed robbery in the Cotswolds near the sleepy village of Little Spudding. Christian stared open-mouthed and cringed at the moment when he was dragged out of the hedgerow. Fortunately, the media were obliged to blur the faces of those that were directly involved, the smug face of Anne Bottomley seemed to speak to him directly. Christian thanked the lord for the right to anonymity, yet he knew that Bottomley knew that he knew that she knew. Every now and then he fired up his smartphone and at 7.45 am an alert came that he was half expecting, from Sir Jeffery. It simply read, 'Simpkins, my office 9 am sharp'.

Normally Christian abhorred any contact with his departmental head, but this time he felt that it was imperative for he needed to know about Willoughby and the result of his spurious actions. He still had a few thorn digs to his head and hands but most of these were minor and healing fast, one on the side of his neck needed a plaster as it sporadically bled and the other across the back of his right hand was inflamed and bright red. In the mirror and with a few deft adjustments, he was happy with his appearance, his mousey coloured hair had regained some of its lost bounce, enough to hide where his hair began to recede. His phones were in his holster, the weight of which still felt comforting, he felt good, confident even. October was reluctantly giving way to a cold autumn, which gave the need for an overcoat. Getting to Whitehall was a simple matter of getting the tube, the car, almost half a mile up the road could stay there, while he got on with his day.

Mie, Sir Jeffery's secretary greeted him with that wide bewildering smile, she seemed to be on the edge of her seat with excitement.

"Hi Christian, go in, go in, he is waiting for you." Christian did a double-take and headed for the office door, normally he was always made to wait, he knocked, got the usual laconic 'enter' and entered.

"Morning, sir, you wanted to see me?"

"Aah, Yes, Simpkins, quite an ordeal on Saturday, are you okay?" Christian was quite taken aback by the query about his health.

"Yes, I think so, how about you?"

"I'll do, thank you very much, but I will admit that I am not really cut out for this type of shenanigans. You proved yourself very able with that gun of yours and for once I can safely say that I was glad that you had it. However, Simpkins, this does cast a shadow over other similar events in your history. Up until now, here in Ancillaries, you have explained your gunmanship on other people present, in the Sahara, it was Petunia Cohen and the housekeeper Consuela, and in Central America, it was a Mexican woman named Maria, was it not?"

"Well…er…you see…" Christian was not prepared for this tack of questioning and unfortunately, Sir Jeffery continued.

"You were quite alone on Sunday and according to George Willoughby, you performed as a professional in the field. Do you have anything to say on this matter?"

"Not really, sir, I still maintain that everything I have said is as it was, I'm just exceedingly lucky I guess."

"Yes, I expected such an ambiguous answer, someone has clearly trained you and I expect that our security services will cast their nets out a bit further to find out when and who, if you get my drift." Christian did, but that problem would arise at a later date, it was the 'now' that he was most interested in.

"Can you tell me about George Willoughby, sir?" Sir Jeffery looked at the young man across the desk from him and nodded affirmatively.

"Yes, I suppose you should know the basics. Bit of a sad affair, really. Firstly, I made the big mistake of leading the insurgents to him at my summerhouse, which, incidentally, is seriously damaged…"

"I don't think you did, sir, I have a feeling that it was from my smartphone when I called you, plus I had Rutherford's car, he tells me that it is clean, but you can bet that it isn't."

"Yes, true enough and very astute of you to doubt it, but he is M.I.5 and they can't have all been turned. But I hear what you are saying and I will sleep better knowing that it was you or possibly your car that spilled the beans and not me. Now George Willoughby is actually a very decent sort, problem is, he likes to bet on things, horses mainly, but by his own account, he got himself into a pile of debt. Now bear that in mind for a bit. About three months back, he was approached by someone pertaining to be an investigative journalist for independent TV, this person, a man, said that they knew about the Cornish facility and wanted to get a peek behind the scenes. This first approach was immediately refused by George, however, they persisted over the next few weeks, found out about his debts, as they do, and offered to pay it, all he had to do was order a routine security check on the place, and this, perhaps in a moment of weakness, he agreed to. He was told that a TV van and presenter would appear during the check. Now, as far as George was concerned, his security people would deny them any chance of access anyway. It was the date he gave that proved to be his undoing, the M.I.5 infiltrators simply put their people in first and when the staff did their confirmation checks, it was all validated by George Willoughby the executive officer in charge. Someone knew what they were doing, two security men dead, heaps of classified information in their hands, Throtestabler missing, presumably taken and if that isn't bad enough, they also have the prototype of some sort of anti-gravity device and the intellectual property that goes with it. In short, a catastrophe of immense proportions Simpkins, absolutely devastating."

"You seem well informed, sir?"

"I bloody well am, 6 am this morning. I was having breakfast with a group of people, powerful people, Simpkins, not to mention a couple of cabinet ministers. This device of

Throtestabler's has to be found or destroyed if he has achieved what we think he has. The effects of this will be global, Simpkins, everything that ruddy flies would nigh on be obsolete, we invented this thing and we should damn well possess it. The Americans are even in on the act thanks to that blasted woman, no wonder she fled to their embassy, which I may add, they deny ever having seen her. So damn typical. But even they have cocked it up somewhere along the line, word has it that they cannot get their reworked version to work." Christian understood the importance of such a machine, tritely labelled as the 'Fridge Project', and the politics now involved, but at the top of his particular list was Tsargrin Throtestabler and his welfare.

"Have we any idea who we are dealing with, sir?"

"Not as yet, the man you shot on Sunday has been traced back to a mercenary agency as was the dead raider at the facility. They are exceptionally well informed and very well-funded, they knew what they wanted and were prepared to take huge risks. The fact that they sent a hit squad after George is a measure of their determination. Someone leaked the existence of this gravity device which surely leads to some nasty little tyke at Throtestabler's facility or possibly even the R.A.F. after they got wind of it."

"One particular thing does bother me though, sir."

"Go on."

"Well, if these insurgents, spies, raiders, whatever, have their prize, the prototype and possibly Mr Throtestabler, why bother to silence George Willoughby?"

"Yes, that was noted too in this morning's meeting, they are clearly trying to protect someone, someone in M.I.5 we presume, but who? George is currently reverse-engineering the whole operation regarding the breach, he is really good at this stuff and even from a police cell, he will do it, he is the only one that can but he has to move fast before they go to ground. Now young, Simpkins, you mentioned Throtestabler and the term 'possibly' are you suggesting that he may have somehow evaded capture or something?"

"I guess I am, very tentative evidence though, these people are looking for something or someone. Robyn Reilly's flat got broken into but nothing was really missing."

"And pray tell, who is this Robin Reilly chappie?"

"Erm…he is a she, sir, one of Mr Throtestabler's engineers, you know of her, she is in charge of the Welsh project, you know, the tidal generators?"

"Ahh, of course, carry on."

"Well, also my flat was broken into, nothing much gone except my hard drive, very little damage, they are after something big, they already have the Fridge thing so it has to be Tsargrin doesn't it?"

"Hmm…any ideas?"

"A few, but first I wish to divulge something, sir, just to get it on the record when the time comes."

"Of course, presumably you have not disclosed it to anybody else then."

"Not a soul, Mr Throtestabler tried to evade capture by trying to lock himself in his laboratory."

"That's hardly a disclosure, Simpkins, it's in this morning's minutes, common knowledge…"

"Sir, there is an emergency escape hatch built into the thing, it is not on any drawings or specifications."

"My God, are you sure?"

"I am, thanks to a cryptic clue, been through it. Comes out inside a bike shed. I aim to go back to Cornwall to see if I can work out how he got out of the grounds…"

"And you have told nobody, not even M.I.5?"

"Especially not M.I.5, I think that he is in hiding, he is a local, sir, everyone knows of him, this is the safest place for him I think?" Sir Jeffery, got to his feet and paced over to the window and back a few times.

"Okay Simpkins, thank you for that little gem. It is a bit of an offence to withhold information from our security forces, but if Throtestabler is alive and well somewhere, you should tread very carefully before reporting it, unfortunately, I should now tread very carefully as well, seeing as you have involved me. Thank you for that, not."

"I have promised to take Robyn Reilly with me to Cornwall, she is pretty spooked by all of this and swears blind that she is being followed."

"Mmm…probably is, by M.I.5. This is all top priority, unfortunately, just about anyone with anything to do with it, will be shadowed and that, Simpkins includes you, and now I suppose me. It's a bloody difficult affair, never sure who is who. It certainly didn't help with Throtestabler letting that thing off one Sunday morning. If we could see it zipping around the bloody sky at 40,000 feet, maybe others could too. Just too many variables, and talking of variables Simpkins what the hell do you think you are up to? Claiming to be seconded to G.C.H.Q., this is outrageous, everyone knows that they don't carry operatives, now they are not so sure."

"Sorry sir, it was the security bods here, had to tell them something to get them off my back."

"They are doing their job, and god knows, we bloody well need it."

"Sorry about that, sir, but it certainly worked though, the bad guys don't know what to think."

"Quite, but neither do the blasted good guys, Simpkins, try a bit harder will you? Now is there anything you need, be sensible though, eh?"

"Yes sir, just two things, I could do with a car that cannot be traced, you know, one without a tracker." Sir Jeffery just nodded slightly and made a small note on his blotter.

"And?"

"My gun, sir, do you think I could have it back?"

"That one, no, it has seen covert action, so it will go back to the issuer, M.I.6, I believe. In this case, though, I am somewhat further on with that particular request."

"Sir, is M.I.6 involved, that man Norman gave it to me."

"Not anymore, no. They are out of the picture and will stick to their remit overseas. We are quite able to extract ourselves from this mess in the very near future, er…hopefully." He reached for his desk phone and hit a blue key.

"Yes, Sir Jeffery, sir?" came Mie's enthusiastic voice, Sir Jeffery recoiled slightly, Christian risked a smirk.

"That package arrived yet?"

"Yes sir, about an hour ago, do you want me to bring it in?"

"No, Mr Simpkins is just leaving, make sure he signs for it and please keep it to yourself Ms er…Mie."

"Her surname is 'Ng', sir, pronounced as 'ung'."

"Shut up, Simpkins, for god's sake, can't a man even enjoy his own foibles sometimes?" Christian stood up.

"Right, sir, I'm off."

"Yes, I know."

"I'll keep in touch."

"Yes, you ruddy well will."

Christian closed the door behind him and turned around to face Mie at her desk.

"Sir Jeffery says that you have a package for me."

"Yes." She beamed, proffering him a shoebox-sized parcel. "You'd best open it up, it has to be signed for you know?" Christian reached across for it, she noticed the hefty plaster on the back of his right hand.

"Ooo, Christian, you have been wounded?"

"Just a scratch or two that's all."

"Ha, got you there, I saw you on the news Christian, all wet and muddy, I heard Sir Jeffery's voice so I knew it was you, despite the fuzzy face pictures they do."

"Okay Mie, what can I say, had a bit of a close shave, that's all."

"Much more than that I hear, anyway, shhh, I won't tell anyone, honest."

"Um…fine, er, can I have the package?"

"Oh, sure, I think it is your gun."

"Yep, pretty sure it is." He carefully removed the plastic covering and lifted the seal on the top of the box. It was indeed a gun, not his, this one was a bluish-grey colour, his previous one was black but of the same .32 calibre, Walther, German, with it was a spare magazine and a box of maybe 50 shiny bullets. This gun seemed brand new, although the model was over forty years old. He took out the accompanying paperwork and studied it carefully. It was actually a refurbished gun and the issuer was, unbelievably so,

Ancillaries and Procurement. He checked the serial number to make sure it tallied and signed for it there and then in front of an excitable Mie Ng.

"Well, aren't you going to take it out and stuff?"

"And stuff?" he repeated.

"Yes, you know, check if it works, click on the magazine thing, that stuff. Anyway, you may as well wear it, otherwise, you would have to carry it. You wouldn't want to leave that thing on a tube train would you?" Christian couldn't really argue with that sentiment.

"Look, is there somewhere else I could do this? I mean, Sir Jeffery would not be too happy and anyone could just walk in, couldn't they?"

"Oh, we're all fine here, everyone knows, but that's okay, the photocopy room should do."

"Everyone?"

"Well, not everyone, come with me…" she said happily, skipping from around her desk and escorting him through to the photocopy room. Here he found a flat surface, took out the gun, cocked it and released the trigger with a satisfying 'snick'. He then ejected the empty magazine, took ten bullets from the box and eased them gently back into it; he could feel Mie's breath on the back of his neck as she peered over his shoulder. Snapping it back into the gun, he made it safe and placed it into his hip holster, the rest of the paraphernalia plus his two phones went into a handy plastic carrier bag. He felt pleasantly thrilled to have the gun back where it should be, although, it must be said that Mie was twice as thrilled as he. Her face was less than two inches from his, instinctively he leant slightly forward and planted a kiss on her forehead and said 'thank you', she just nodded happily and watched him go.

Robyn

Later that week, he went to collect Robyn to ferry her safely over to the Cornish facility, five hours or so away, he probably had better things to do with his time but a moving car happened to be the best interviewing venue of all time. She wouldn't be forced to make eye contact, she couldn't disappear on some imagined errand or pretend that she hadn't heard. He had a few things to ask and this would easily be the best way, plus, he quite liked her company, she was clever, very able and comfortably confident. It dawned on him that he didn't actually know where she was, he knew the area and would give her a call when he got there. However, her timing was pretty perfect for as he climbed into the Ford Focus, an alert popped up on his phone with a number, street name and a postcode. She was ahead of the game and that was good. Camden to Streatham in London was a torturous route at the best of times, just over an hour at least. Eventually, he found the house, a nice big period semi. Fate smiled at him briefly as he pulled up by her house, another car pulled away. He had made good time, the sun had decided to shine and he was in quite a buoyant mood when he rang the bell, this mood dampened somewhat when a man, a young man opened the door, he was taller than the doorway and almost as wide, big, dark and oozing with raw power. Christian smiled weakly and fought for the right words.

"Er…hi I'm um Chr—"

"Yeah, Christian right?" He nodded and dutifully followed him to the rear of the house, another man, smaller in stature with tightly braided hair passed Christian without a glimpse, he was heading back toward the front door. Christian found himself being ushered through a doorway which closed immediately behind him. Robyn was there, he looked at her questionably.

"Oh right, that was Billy, my kid brother, he is only twenty you know, he is a good boy, plays American football, clever too."

"Ahh…I see, that's good having people around you. Well, Robyn, you are not wrong, you, I and anybody else embroiled in this thing is under some sort of scrutiny. It is M.I.5 and believe it or not they are there for your benefit, mine too I guess."

"Coffee?"

"Please, kind of black, just a touch of milk."

"Right, Americano man huh, I can do that, the other guy you saw was our Malcolm, into I.T, complete whizz, bit of a petrol head as well. I described your car to him, he went out to have a look, do you mind?"

"No, not at all," and if he did, he surmised, it would make no difference whatsoever. Malcolm soon returned from his keen-eyed observation of the car. He stared intensely at Christian before turning to Robyn, his sister.

"Yeah, great car, well kitted out but could do with a paint job, needs a bit of care. However the fucking thing has bullet holes in it, three at least, new too, no rust. What the fuck are we getting into, Sis?" Robyn thought for a bit as she looked over to a rather sheepish Christian.

"Not only that, as soon as he pulled in, the other car, the saloon pulled away and left. I guess this bloke here is your protection, don't look much."

"Oh c'mon, Malcolm, let's be nice." Christian remained mute despite the barely veiled criticism.

"Bullet holes, really! There are scratches on your neck and your hand looks like it has had a knock or something."

"Forget it, just a bit of a to-do that's all." Robyn stepped back and appraised him.

"Bullet holes huh, new ones huh, hey Malcolm be a darling, there was a news item of a shoot-out in the Cotswolds several days back, something rings a bell." Malcolm was certainly adept with a computer, in a matter of seconds he had called up the news item on his screen in the corner of the room. She briefly watched it through, she asked him to freeze it at a certain point. Christian, still silent, tried to look casually bored. It was an image of Christian walking with the policeman and the medic. All three faces were effectively digitally blurred, but Robyn was not looking at their faces, she had seen something else.

"This is you, Christian, come on now, be honest."

"Nope, not me," he said shaking his head.

"No, really, look at the belt, little pictures all over it, magnify it please." Malcolm did his stuff, she reached out and pulled back the front of his jacket to reveal the offending evidence. "Still want to say 'nope' huh." Christian raised his hands.

"Okay, okay, sorry, classified stuff and all that." By this time Malcolm had gone into overdrive and onto 'You-Tube' where he had conjured up the scene without the blurring. He replayed it from where Christian was on his knees with his hands on his head and a police marksman pointing a gun at him less than a yard away. Christian hadn't seen this footage himself and inched closer for a better view, he seemed to be covered in mud and blood, but his grey eyes were clear and he eyed the policeman with some disdain, he recalled that it was the pain in his knees that made him so fractious. On film, as it were, his look was misinterpreted as pure defiance. A deep voice behind him said…

"Cool, so cool." Christian glanced around to big Billy. He didn't think he was cool at all, but being on the skinny side a camera was normally quite kind to him. The footage soon wound around to the point when he was escorted to the ambulance, he looked like someone in a 'Die Hard' action movie. He blinked a couple of times and backed away from the screen. Robyn and her two brothers just stared at him, she reached up and snapped Billy's gaping mouth shut, she then flicked up the right-side flap of Christian's jacket to expose his gun, both brothers instinctively stepped back a pace. Christian just shrugged.

"Erm…sorry, you weren't supposed to see any of that, bit embarrassing, sorry."

"Stop saying sorry, Christian, you were just doing what you do, well, whatever that is anyway."

"I, er, think that we ought to get going, Robyn."

"Whatever you say hot-shot." On their way out, Billy just had to ask.

"Um Christian, I mean Mr Christian, no, Mr Simpkins Sir, do you shoot people, I mean for real, like the films?" Christian found the emotion to smile.

"Only the bad guys, Billy, films aren't real, are they?" he gave Billy a friendly wink, a tiny detail that Robyn noted with some satisfaction.

Christian left South London and headed for the M4 motorway heading west. He didn't say a word to Robyn for a good while, he could feel her studying him, this he ignored and continued onward in moral discomfort. He had gotten himself into yet another huge lie that he couldn't extract himself from. Billy, her brother was left in awe of him and she, Robyn, felt safe and secure with him beside her in the car. He now felt like one almighty phoney, all he wanted to do was to try and track down Tsargrin, that was all, but now he found himself in the dangerous middle of just about everything and he didn't like to do dangerous, it was something that he normally avoided like the plague. Before his mind lapsed into some strange form of depression a ping from the dumb phone on the central console clicked him back into the reality of the situation.

"Oh, that's a text, could you read it for me, Robyn, not great on phones at 70 mph." She picked up the old phone and looked at it with some doubt, it took her a moment or two to familiarise herself with actual physical buttons.

"Well, there is no message, just a smiley face followed by a pound sign, it's from someone called Sheena?" Christian smiled, it was Consuela, she was on the move and would need some cash just as he assumed.

"Okay, that's fine."

"Oh, it makes some sense then?"

"To me yes, you okay, Robyn? Sorry that I haven't spoken much, it is just that I have …."

"Don't be silly, you have a lot on your plate and god knows what else, you are a cool customer, Chris, nothing seems to get to you, oh sorry, can I call you 'Chris'?"

"Of course, Chris is fine, but listen, I am a bag of nerves under this suit."

"Yeah, right," she responded flippantly, "what is with the shitty phone anyway?"

"It's called a dumb phone, no internet connection, no 4G, really hard to track, nigh on impossible to hack."

"Really, shit, hang on." She rummaged around in her bag, pulled out her smartphone and shut it down. "Oh my god, they know where we are now, don't they?"

"They do indeed, even if it is turned off sometimes, they can track the car too, this one belongs to Bill Rutherford. As for that phone, I have another in the boot for you, sometimes you will need a bit of privacy, well I guess so anyway."

"Oh yes, how very true, thank you," she responded after some thought.

The first leg of the trip went just fine, at the halfway point they put in for petrol and some welcome coffee. Christian noted that she rarely strayed from his side, she was nervous and edgy, but he couldn't blame her considering the traumas of their last trip. Back safely on the road Christian tactfully suggested that she should voice any of her concerns. She mentioned all the small stuff at first and then got around to the 'Fridge Project'.

"You see, Chris, sooner or later, maybe next week, they will have replicated the prototype at the facility and they will find that it doesn't really work. I feel that I am the key to all this because of what Mr Throtestabler asked me to do in Salisbury Plain with the gravimeter configuration."

"Yes Robyn, you very possibly are, you see, the Americans have also re-made the device and they cannot get the thing to work either, so presumably the raiders who stole the original prototype have the same problem."

"So, when it comes to it, do I tell them or just suggest it to them. The thing is, I don't have the exact settings Mr Throtestabler has, but I have a pretty good idea of where I took the readings from. It is all about fine-tuning the compensator. You need a benchmark you see, something stable. It would be like trying to calibrate a thermometer without knowing where zero is. Think about it Chris, a datum of sorts is vital, that fridge thing accelerated up to 40,000 feet, the height itself we are talking about relies on a datum, in this case, mean sea level. He knew he needed this so he picked on Salisbury Plain as the point of stability, heaven only knows how he knew where, but he was bloody right, really stable readings, bit spooky if you ask me. I proved it for him though, I set the readings into the compensator and brought it back. Now it transpires that any record of my doing that work had been erased from the work records, by presumably Mr Throtestabler himself long before the raid. I'm guessing that he recognised something long before anybody else, huh?"

"Yeah, nothing unusual about that, Robyn, when the time comes, we will discuss it. Now I want you to think back to when Mr Throtestabler first approached you, he picks his people very carefully, so you have to be more than just good at what you do as an engineer. The money you get paid will be way over the average, am I right?"

"Well, yes, I suppose so, quite a bit actually."

"That's because he expects a lot from you, I'm sure he would have mentioned going that extra mile even if things get really tough." She took her mind back to that moment and nodded her agreement.

"Well, unfortunately, this is it, but hey, I believe that he knew that you had some grit and I think so too, otherwise you wouldn't be here now, would you?" Robyn said nothing for a short while and gazed out of the passenger window.

"Thank you, Christian Simpkins," was all she said, more to the window than to him.

The atmosphere at the facility had now lightened somewhat, the hard-nosed security men had left as had most of the technical observers, the latter, Christian could easily understand as they were now dealing with new science and consequently would be totally lost. He went for a stroll to stretch his legs. The two security men in the car outside were fully alert. They recognised Christian and gave him an encouraging nod as they entered his name into the log. Walking at that speed it would take him around twenty minutes to go full circle to arrive back to his present position. It was a bit damp but not too cold considering it was now the onset of October, so he decided to do his little tour. He still had the conundrum regarding the manner of Tsargrin's escape from the grounds if, of course, he escaped at all, he hoped that the walk may furnish him with some inspiration, anything. Although the perimeter wall was old, it was wide and quite sturdy, strong enough to bear the many steel uprights that angled slightly outward to support the alarmed wires and the newly installed camera arrays. At the eastern stretch of the wall, the little lane narrowed substantially and Christian had to step onto the tiny verge to let the local bus creep past. It wasn't even a big bus, no upper deck, just a tad wide for the little lane, Christian thought. As it passed the driver gave him a little wave, he did not know him but nevertheless, he returned the wave anyway, *one of the locals,* he correctly surmised. Maintaining his pace, he came upon the entrance to the rear gate where a neatly dressed security man addressed him.

"Coming through, Mr Simpkins?" It perturbed Christian a little that everybody knew of him. The gate was there, the man was there, so he curtailed his walk and entered. It was hard to believe that slightly less than three weeks ago, this place was under armed siege. He walked uphill along the winding path and stopped at the old tennis court. It looked grubby and unkempt but somehow it became the launchpad of possibly one of the greatest technical achievements in history. Christian looked up into the endless sky wondering how on earth his friend Tsargrin managed to propel a fridge shaped object from this grubby setting to such a height that it spooked the air force. He walked its length and looked beyond at the two big barn-like structures and the rambling old farmhouse which was Tsargrin's home. Much closer to him was the bike shed that housed the hidden escape from the laboratory. Turning 180 degrees he looked back down the path and then back up the hill to the gardener's hut that abutted the perimeter wall. A picture was taking shape in his mind, it was the wall itself, the security stanchions and wires were angled down toward the road. The old wall was eighteen inches wide, 'that wall' was possibly Tsargrin's path out of the facility, he thought. Christian strode briskly toward the gardener's hut, without any hesitation he stepped upon an old rusty roller, then a water butt and then onto the roof. The security wires looked dangerous and foreboding as he stepped onto the wall, he then walked calmly down its length peering down at the lane which he had just walked. Presently he came to the first of five big oak trees, this one like the others had a large bough but it had been cut short, although this bough hindered his progress he examined it more closely, at one time this particular bough had caused some type of problem before it was cut away, this left a gap that had been wired across as an afterthought. To Christian, this makeshift wiring didn't seem to be connected. Tentatively he touched one and then the other, he even gave it a good shake, no alarms and thankfully no shocks. It was quite simple to unhook if one wanted but the drop-down to the lane was still well beyond Tsargrin's physical capabilities even though it was a little over ten feet from the overhanging branches to the ground. He stood on the edge of the wall, re-hooked the wires behind him and jumped down onto the grass verge of the narrow lane, looking back up, the security failure was all but invisible. Deep in thought he headed back to the rear gate, as an afterthought he returned to the place where he dropped and examined the scene, there wasn't much to find except a couple of shards of glass that glinted in the pale sun and a bit of litter which he dutifully picked up. The security man at the rear gate did a double-take when Christian approached, he tried to say something but Christian told him not to bother and to just let him in. It would have been a nice thought if he could have, perhaps proved that Tsargrin just might have escaped. He made a mental note to report a possible security breach in the perimeter wires.

He didn't have that much to do now and he was sure that some people would be wondering what he was doing at the facility in the first place, something he couldn't answer as he didn't really know himself.

Robyn managed to secure one of the upper rooms in the farmhouse and although late in the day, she checked in with the chief engineer so that she could get a good start in the morning. Christian had no alternative but to check into one of the small hotels in the locality, it was now into the second week of October and the season was over so he knew that some good deals could be had. He, without putting too much thought into it, booked himself into the same hotel as before, in a small town maybe ten miles from Tsargrin's facility. It was near where he met Consuela early one morning in a pub lock-in. It was at this pub where he would park his car, a good ten minutes away from the hotel.

Whilst close to the pub, he decided to savour a pint of the local brew, it went down exceptionally well and shortly another followed, and then another for the road, as it were. Although not inebriated, he felt more carefree than he should have; he looked forward to a nice dinner and an early night. Tomorrow, of course, was another day, but he had no clue as to what it may bring. On his way to the overly quaint hotel, he turned to look at the source of some angry motorist tooting. It was just some impatient fool of a driver trying to overtake a bus, the driver of which appeared to be totally unphased, *another local,* he mused as he watched the petty event unfold. Something about that bus stirred his relaxed mind, by the time he had reached the hotel that stirring turned into a click. He had sussed it; he knew how Tsargrin escaped the facility grounds; he was sure as he could be.

Very soon he was ensconced in his hotel room, it was a good room, big and airy. His door was locked, there were no bugs or eavesdroppers and for once he felt snug and safe. He kicked off his shoes, stuck his gun under the pillow and then laid on the bed to reassess his thoughts, several times over he reran his thought process and then, when happy with his prognosis, he punched the air whilst hissing the word 'yessss'. There was only one person he could call and that was with the dumb phone, Consuela, or rather her alter-ego, Sheena. He calmed himself down, for this was one call that he had to get right. There was every chance that his dumb phone was secure, but from experience, he was overly cautious as he had no real idea what could be achieved these days in the dark art of spookery. The text had to be short and to the point, it came to him in a flash.

'Hi Sheena, Charlie is at the pub, hopefully, I will be at the lock-in,' the response was immediate.

'Good boy, wait for me, X?'

He looked forward to seeing Consuela, he had no idea when they would meet, but undoubtedly they would and very soon. He had a nice hot shower, spruced himself up and headed down a couple of floors to the restaurant and a decent wholesome dinner, he was still feeling quite buoyant, the hotel bar beckoned but he resisted its allure and took a tour of the rather splendid gardens that the hotel boasted about in its brochure. Come 9 pm he headed back up the stairs to his room for a nice bit of TV and *a welcome early night that should finish this particular Wednesday quite nicely,* he thought. He closed the door, stripped off, did his bathroom stuff and climbed gratefully into bed and started scrolling through the channels. Then one of the most bizarre moments happened, the en-suite door opened and a woman, very much like Consuela, glided out with a towel around her, she smiled at Christian and slid into bed.

"Touch me if you dare Christian dear, and I will kill you," she said sweetly.

"But wot! I mean how? I've been in the bathroom?"

"I know, I saw you, I was in the bath, had to have one, I was getting a little stinky, you weren't very observant I'm afraid, not to worry though."

"But Consuela—"

"Shhh, Sheena?"

"Oh bollocks, okay Sheena then, you are in my bed?"

"Got to sleep somewhere, up until now I have been camping out, not to be recommended though, everything is so darn wet. I wasn't that far anyway and I get around by bike, nice to see you, dear, even nicer to hear about your news. Are you sure?" Christian was still flummoxed, he fumbled for the off button on the remote.

"Erm…well yes, pretty sure I know how he got out of the facility, but I was in the bathroom, I had no clothes on, why didn't you say something?"

"I had no clothes on either, now relax and tell me all about it."

"God I could do with a drink, I've got a mini-bar here, want something?"

"Good idea, bit of white wine would go down a treat."

"Oops I'm not wearing anything, so um…don't look."

"What's the point, you have been wandering about in the bathroom buck naked, God, you British amaze me sometimes, tell you what, I'll stick my head under the covers huh?"

"Oh, bloody hell, don't bother, wine you say?"

"Yes please, white." Christian obliged and when they both felt comfortable, he began.

Firstly, he described the thickness of the wall and how it could be easily walked upon like a narrow path, then the bigger trees and the makeshift security wirework.

"Okay Christian, fine so far, but how did he get down to the lane itself, no way could Tsargrin undertake a ten-foot drop and then get up and run, he wouldn't even be able to lower himself down."

"Well, um…Sheena, he didn't, he just got on the bus."

"Excuse me, am I missing something?"

"He knew the bus times, he took his bike with him as he walked on top of the wall, lots of foliage for cover, when he got to some makeshift wiring he unhooked it, tossed the bike into the lane, re-hooked up the wire behind him and stood on the outer edge. Because of the bike, the bus would have to stop and when it did Tsargrin simply stepped onto its roof. The lane is really narrow at this point, the drivers are all local folk, they all know him and have all had a chuckle at his various pub antics etcetera. He and the driver would have had a quick chat, his bike would have been stuck inside the bus and Tsargrin would have remained on the roof until the driver found him a safe place to get him down, any other passengers would just find it all a bit of a hoot."

"Proof?"

"Not much, but parts of a broken mirror, he had one on his bike, which, if you remember, is missing from the bike shed. The timing is right too. The raiders made their escape maybe ten minutes after the police arrived, blue lights and sirens and all. No time for any road closures to be in place at that juncture. It all works for me?"

"Mmm…good reasoning Christian, not exactly watertight though is it?"

"Possibly not, but it ticks a lot of boxes, if the bad guys had all they wanted, then they wouldn't still be around would they?"

"True enough I guess, but it is certainly worth pursuing though, have you told anyone else?"

"No, to be honest, I do not know who to tell or even who I should tell if proven right."

"Yes, I can understand that, find that man Norman. He is M.I.6 and pretty high up, he knows you and even if you don't much like him, we know that he is straight." Christian had to agree, but he had no idea how to find him, Norman normally found you. He turned and looked at her, she had short clipped black hair now and didn't look at all punkish. She noted his object of scrutiny and ran her fingers through her hair.

"It kind of works, you know, really easy to maintain and perfect under a decent wig. I have two of them now, what should I be tomorrow, a blonde or a redhead, what do you think?"

"Blonde is good."

"Okay, I'll be a redhead then." Christian laughed.

"Dammit, I knew I should have said redhead, then I would have got the blonde, ho-hum."

"Goodnight, Christian dear."

"Yeah, okay Sheena." Consuela snorted a laugh, turned onto her side and clicked the light off.

Fortunately, Christian found himself alive and well in the morning, and surprisingly enough he slept very well. Consuela was no longer in the bed with him and a red-haired woman was at the dresser making herself up. She needed money, cash and Christian gave her his last £200, he had no more and was already attacking his credit card in earnest.

They needed breakfast and a plan, Consuela grimaced when she tasted the coffee.

"That's the way the Cornish have it, Sheena, you really must try harder," he said quietly, smirking over the lip of a steaming mug of tea. She tilted her head and stuck her tongue out at him. Red hair suited her he thought and marvelled at the way she had somehow magically applied freckles to her cheeks and around the bridge of her nose. It was decided that at lunchtime when they knew that Sir Jeffery would be out, he would call Mie, the secretary; he needed her to see if she could find a contact for the mysterious Norman. Sir Jeffery abhorred M.I.6 for some reason, however, he was the best-connected person that either of them knew, so Mie, as before, could maybe help him again as she had some access. Tsargrin, was as usual at the top of their list, Christian was convinced that he would be holed up locally, possibly with friends or at a hotel similar to the one they were in now and of course a pub, possibly, maybe. Consuela pointed out that Tsargrin was unlikely to be in plain sight, being as recognisable as he was. After a bit of deliberation, they homed in on Tsargrin's lifestyle. Near or actually in a pub would suit his needs best. He also had a habit of getting up at 5.30 every morning, whatever the day, so it was judged that they should check out the more local pubs really early to see if any lights were on or other signs of people being up at that time. After a short bout of research, Christian located fourteen pubs or inns in a ten-mile radius and about the same number of small hotels and guesthouses. He discounted the smaller ones, the franchised set-ups and anything without a decent bar which left nine to be investigated, he then got these down to five as the other four were on main tourist routes. It was clear that he couldn't really use Rutherford's Ford Focus for this, although he trusted him, he never knew who else had access to the tracking software. Later on that morning, he booked a hire car, he had to use his own credit card and so rented the smallest cheapest thing he could find, he also knew that by using his card he was increasing his risk but he did know that the little car could not be tracked as yet. Obviously, his chancy plan could not be implemented until the following morning. Consuela decided that it would be best if he took the Ford back to the facility to check on Robyn. Consuela 'aka Sheena' or an unnamed redhead would take the hire car to undertake a bit of a recce of the said pubs they would need to check in the morning.

For once, Robyn was genuinely glad to see him and almost demanded that he should take her out for lunch. This time she played her part well and held his hand as they walked to the car followed by the knowing glances of the security bods. They avoided going to the pub this time and so went to a place where the fare was much better, Robyn swore that she would never eat another Cornish pasty again. The Rosemount Hotel, a few miles further out, had a good rating although it turned out to be just another pub or 'old inn' suitably extended. They had a nice window table, Robyn had some greenish Italian thing whilst he had a sort of posher version of a pasty with a pint of Cornish ale to wash it down. They had barely placed their order when Christian noted that she seemed a little fazed.

"Is something up?" he queried.

"Yes, I think so, there is a woman paying me a bit too much attention, I noticed her when I came in." Christian made to turn, but Robyn hissed at him to stop.

"Now you can look, quick, she is reading something, it is the woman with the red hair." Christian turned, gave the redhead a quick glance and inwardly smiled, Robyn read him correctly.

"You know her, don't you, Christian?"

"Oh yes, that is Sheena, she is one of the security bods, it's okay, she is on our side."

"Then why is she watching us then, she must be a bit stupid, I'm with you, and you have that thingy as well don't you?" Christian subconsciously tapped his holster with his elbow and nodded.

"Tell you what, I'll have a quick word with her and suggest that she take a hike, um…nicely though, of course."

"Please Christian, I find all this a bit suffocating." He ambled over to Consuela as casually as he could and then leant over the table to speak to her, he was aware that Robyn would be watching his every move.

"Hi, um, we need you to disappear if you could, Robyn's a bit on edge."

"No problem, I just wanted to make contact, small world isn't it, I am just doing my rounds, speak to you later, bye." She then stood, turned her back and walked away. Christian returned to his table, Robyn looked more than satisfied.

"Wow, one word from you is all it takes huh?"

"No not really, if she needed to, she could just watch us from afar, it is just circumstance, that's all."

"Oh right." She eyed him dubiously as if suspecting something else.

The lunch did its job and she began to relax, Christian took a slug of his pint and sat back a bit' she looked at it and then at him.

"Is that a pint of that Proper Job, like in the other place?"

"Yes, it is, a bit heavy but quite excellent if you like that kind of thing."

"Mmm…could I have one please?" Christian couldn't think of anything to say and to avoid an awkward pause he summoned the waitress who soon obliged with another pint.

"Cheers," she said happily taking a huge slurp, Christian touched glasses as a way of returning the salute.

"Right, Robyn, a bit of business I'm afraid, how is the prototype going?"

"Oh, pretty well I suppose, I still haven't told them how to balance the compensator and to be honest, I don't actually know, the readings in my head just don't stack up, or maybe they do, I just don't know. There is no paperwork to back things up you see? Anyway, they are not onto the settings yet, they are still messing with the disc motors. There is not much I can really do, so I am back on the Welsh Project, which I may add is progressing splendidly, unlike their efforts to achieve the Norton Effect."

"Norton? What's that?"

"It is not a what, but a he, he's an American bloke called James Norton who identified it first. Counter rotary helicopters suffered from it. You know, they built these things, two rotors, one above the other but rotating different ways so you wouldn't need a tail rotor. But somehow, sometimes these helicopters would lose power, conflicting centrifuges if I remember rightly. That unexplained power loss is why they do not make them anymore, the Norton Effect, he published heaps of work about it."

"Right, of course, possibly, actually I haven't got a clue about any of this, but I will take your word for it."

"And so you should." Christian nodded dumbly, his mind was turning to other things, he glanced at his watch.

"I think I ought to get you back now?" Robyn reluctantly agreed and polished off her Cornish ale with noticeable satisfaction.

"By the way," she added, "Bill Rutherford is expected to arrive in the morning, thought I'd let you know. His people are always snooping around these days, drives me insane. I mean, what on earth are they expecting to find? There is nothing to find until they build the damn thing, so why huh?"

Christian nodded his agreement and stood up, Robyn did have a point, why were they actually inside the facility's buildings in the first place.

It was still a little before 2 pm. He needed to contact Mie, Sir Jeffery's secretary, to get her to find Norman's contact number. It was a big favour to ask of her yet he felt that he had to, for something was still amiss in the ranks of M.I.5 as far as he was concerned and it was more than just poor old George Willoughby. Again, as Christian pulled up into the facility's drive, Robyn played her part and hung casually on his arm as they approached security. For some reason, Christian was no longer permitted to go beyond the curtilage of the farmhouse, when he queried this, he was just told that it was a new directive that non-essential personnel were not permitted to enter either of the 'barns'. To Christian it seemed perfectly logical despite everyone there being on first-name terms with him, he didn't push it. He parked up Rutherford's car and headed out for a walk down the lane. He needed the space to make his call to Mie. It was nearing 2.30 pm, and Sir Jeffery wouldn't even leave his lunch club for another half hour or so.

When he called her, using his dumb phone, her bright response forced him to smile, Christian adored buoyant people and often tried hard to emulate that particular character trait, but alas, with very little success.

"Hi Mie, it's me Christian!"

"Yes, I know."

"But how? I am on a different number."

"No idea, that is what it says on my screen, you are in Cornwall, no?"

"Yes but? No matter, listen, Mie, I need a little favour from you."

"Ooo, well you will have to be extra nice to me then." He laughed and made her a promise.

"I think it's best if I ask you now before Sir Jeffery gets back?"

"He hasn't been out yet, something important I think."

"Mmm…must be something desperately important if he has had to miss his lunch club, can I talk to him please, Mie?"

"Not sure, I'll ask." There were a couple of clicks, a little buzz and then Sir Jeffery.

"Ah, Simpkins, good of you to call."

"Yes, hello, sir, just checking in. Is it okay to speak?"

"Well, you are not on a smartphone and my encrypted line is very secure, so go ahead."

"Right, we, or rather I, have a very good reason to believe that Mr Throtestabler was not taken by the raiders, he managed to escape from the facility via a rather special route…"

"Simpkins, you said 'we' in the first instance, who is 'we'?" Christian cursed himself briefly and then countered with a swift ad-hoc response.

"Yes, right, it is Robyn Reilly, the engineer, I am not allowed into the facility itself, apparently I am not essential."

"Yes, I was thinking the same thing myself," he added laconically. Christian was well used to his demeaning banter.

"Of course you were, sir, well she, Robyn, has become my access, hence 'we'. Now 'we' are pretty convinced that he has not been taken, by the insurgents, for want of a better word, they are still looking for him and getting far more desperate."

"Now, this is news, something positive for a change, where is he then?"

"Here in Cornwall, somewhere local, I haven't located him yet or tried to make contact, I feel he is safest where he is."

"And you haven't mentioned any of this to anyone else, well I sincerely hope not anyway."

"Of course not, sir, you are my first point of contact, just as you requested."

"Good, nice to see that you are on the ball, Now George Willoughby has been cooperating fully, he tells us that there are still two active rogue members still at large, plus another somewhere in the wings. These people have very good inside information, in fact, too good, and this is what put George onto them. In George's eyes, there could only be one logical outcome and that is why he fled, alerting his family to do the same. These people are using a mercenary team to do their dirty work. A very organised bunch of miscreants originating from somewhere in Kyiv in Ukraine and now operating out of South Africa, they are very well funded and utterly ruthless. Both the C.I.A and M.I.6 amongst others are on their tail but unfortunately with little success at the moment. Now, Simpkins, if they do have Throtestabler's worrying little toy and are able to make it work, it will be off to the highest bidder for a couple of billion quid or whatever or whoever their client is. Some Chinese mega-consortium or suchlike springs to mind, doesn't it?"

"Yes, the usual suspects, I suppose. Sir, it seems to me that they were trying to silence Willoughby, presumably because they think that he is a danger. Something he knows or something he can find out, maybe?"

"Yes, and we are aware of that, he, his wife and family are quite safe I can assure you. George is an exceptionally clever man and although they have covered their tracks quite thoroughly, he will pick his way through it all until he finds them, and Simpkins, he will do this, I know him well."

"Okay then, sir. So who is running the show now in his place?"

"That I cannot tell you, it is confidential despite your dodgy clearance category. Stay close to Throtestabler, any trouble, get Bill Rutherford on the case, he knows the score."

"Sorry sir, I do not quite know who to really trust at the moment, I am sure Rutherford is fine but if you don't mind, I would rather liaise with you in the first instance. I know that we don't really see eye to eye, but at least I know where I am."

"Okay, Simpkins, I will take that as a compliment, now remember, try not to kill anybody else please, it is so damn annoying."

"Yes, of course, sir," he added before hanging up. He studied his dumb phone for a moment and wondered how on earth Mie could identify him on her screen, even more spookery he just didn't get.

The Rosemount Hotel

As luck would have it the local bus swung into view and he waved it down. It didn't go quite to where he wanted and for the last half mile or so, he had to walk. In a way, he was glad to have rid himself of Bill Rutherford's Ford Focus. Strangely, he recalled his own words to Sir Jeffery regarding Rutherford and possibly others, he didn't trust them but he didn't know 'why' as yet. Back in his hotel, he went straight to his room, Tsargrin was at the forefront of his mind yet again thankfully.

He checked out his room more thoroughly this time, the maid had clearly been the last one in, even so, he crept into the bathroom and peered behind the shower door and checked the bath. Wherever she was she *wasn't here*, he thought. He waited a while, left the room and meandered around the bar area, the lounge and the gardens, a little bit flummoxed he returned to his room and found her sitting on his bed.

"Blimey, I've been looking all over the place for you?"

"Yes, me too, Christian dear, you took your time?"

"I know, I got caught up in a conversation with Sir Jeffery, then I had to get the bus plus a half-mile walk. Anyway, what do we have, any idea?"

"Not absolutely certain, but I am sure that we are closing in. It was once just a pub, very old too, it is called the Sycamore Inn, comes up a lot in the local history archives, bit of a smugglers retreat in the past, it backs onto a bit of a rocky outcrop. Apparently, there are tunnels and what-not around."

"Yeah, sounds very possible, but there are a good few places like that around the Lizard, difficult to check out as well," he replied in a somewhat dejected tone.

"Have some faith, dear, there is something else. On the new part, the restaurant extension, someone has turned the satellite dish around, it should point due South, this one points East and if you look at one of the chimneys in the old bit there is something sticking out, looks like the tip of a high-frequency aerial. Are you getting this?" Christian dumbly nodded, but he needed something more, something that said 'Tsargrin' on it.

"You are looking for closure on this aren't you, well here it is. This place wasn't even on our list as it didn't appear to rent out rooms, but apparently, it does, but only a few. It is pretty old and a bit of a sprawl, I just stopped to check it out by chance when I saw the satellite dish. You see, Christian, it was the bins, the big wheelie type, they had been put out in the front for collection so I took a little peek and 'bingo' there it was."

"What was, Consuela, what?" she smiled at his frustration.

"A beer mug, right on top, it was broken, whatever was in it wasn't beer, it wasn't sticky, remember Tsargrin making his brew, he always left the spoon in as it conducted the heat, if you didn't do that the glass, a beer glass would break every time, somebody didn't know the trick, it broke, it got binned."

"God, it's Tsargrin, it just has to be, I think."

"Yep, exactly, you know what we do now?"

"Oh yes, leave him be, he is safest where he is."

"Good boy, you are really beginning to get the hang of all this."

A little while later as Consuela was getting her stuff together, Christian voiced his unease about finding out that his new dumb phone number was already on file, it was so new that he had trouble remembering it himself, he had only used it four times. For once Consuela was stumped, but he had obviously set some wheels in motion, for she lapsed into one of her very sincere thoughtful moods. Out of the blue, she demanded to see Christian's gun, her face was severe and her tone almost menacing. He did not hesitate or even question her as he handed it over without either a please or a thank you. Christian looked somewhat aghast as she stripped it down to its many components. She paid great attention to the firing pin, then the auto-mechanism and then finally to the ten-shot magazine.

"Aha, there you are," she said to herself.

"Er…I think it is quite new," he said helpfully.

"No, it isn't dear, they haven't made these things in years, it is almost a museum piece, it has just been refurbished that is all. You got this thing from Sir Jeffery's department, didn't you? Well, the only place he could have got it was M.I.5, legally of course. This gun Christian has been tampered with and quite cleverly too, normally if one wanted to make a gun covertly safe you would shorten the firing pin, saw or file a bit off it so that it doesn't reach the cartridge. However, the way that they have done this is to mess with the magazine lock, here I will show you." She reassembled the little Walther too expertly for comfort, she then handed it to him without the magazine. "Well, go on then, cock it, then fire it." This, Christian did, a satisfying 'snick' and it was cocked and with a squeeze of the trigger it clicked perfectly. He shrugged his shoulders and looked at her stupidly as she handed him the empty magazine, he took it, gave it a quick check-over and slid it into the butt of the gun, he then cocked it as before, the slider pulled back okay but would not return, the trigger was solid, the thing had jammed up.

"You see, no good to anyone like that." Christian looked dumbfounded and went to peer down the end of the barrel as Consuela quickly relieved him of it. "Tut-tut, never do that dear, bad move." She stripped it down again and looked carefully at the loading mechanism.

"My God, it's been sabotaged, what if I needed to use it?"

"That is the whole point, they don't want you to use it, whoever 'they' are, now, find me a tiny screwdriver or something, I should be able to fix it."

"Ah yes, 'they' apparently are from a mercenary outfit from the Ukraine, Kyiv, they operate out of South Africa," he said in a slightly triumphant tone, as he rummaged through his holdall to find a tiny pouch with a thin Swiss army knife inside it. After fifteen minutes of delicate tinkering the gun was reassembled with a smooth jamb-free action.

"The British security services have one almighty headache, Christian, despite them being hunted down, they are still brazen enough to be active enough to access whatever goes on even in Ancillaries and Procurement."

"We need Norman," opined Christian loudly, Consuela nodded her agreement.

"Now I have to get out of here, they will have worked out that you are here, but not I, I'm still hiding away in the American Embassy I think."

"Maybe you could stay in one of those rooms in the Sycamore Inn where Tsargrin is."

"Shhhh, yes, my very thought. Problem is, we are going to need money, cash that is, we cannot risk using a card."

"Well, I can use my cards here as they probably know where I am anyway, see if you can book into the Sycamore, it is out of season, after all, use the room phone."

"Yes, I will, the ironic thing is that my house is only a fifteen-minute drive from here. John, my husband, is in the States as we speak and will stay there until all this blows over. I have a lot of cash in the house and there are a few other things I could do with."

"Yeah, but you can bet that your place is under observation."

"Of course, but it will be remote, the slightest incursion would show on somebody's screen somewhere. Plus, you can bet that it has already been turned over. It is all getting exceedingly dangerous now, I think they are getting desperate. Their window of opportunity is shrinking fast as Willoughby will obviously be on the case, it is his department and he will know it inside out, once he identifies just one, the others will soon follow. It was incredibly fortunate that we managed to frustrate that hit team."

"Consuela?" Christian said pensively. "What if I go around to your house, I'll use Rutherford's Ford and just openly go, if I get questioned then I'll just say I was snooping for clues."

"What clues, Christian? We can't mention Robyn's field trip or even give anyone an inkling that we might have found Tsargrin, M.I.5 are probably wondering what you are doing in Cornwall anyway."

"Well, I have made it appear that Robyn and I are an item."

"Are you?"

"No, but we put on a good performance, I could also say that my flat is unsafe because of death threats, remember that South African bloke, Pollock would verify that, I'm sure."

"No, not good enough, think of something else."

"Right, what about you then, I've gone around to your house to see you because the American Embassy tells us that you are not with them, how's that?"

"Actually, that is really clever as the embassy would deny I was there even if I was. You would look a bit green, you know, painfully naïve."

"Yep, I should be able to act that out without a problem. Now just tell me where and what you need and I'll fetch it." Consuela, as one would expect, was thorough. She explained that the remote cameras would be covering the entrances and the front and rear elevations and that the house alarm would take thirty seconds to activate. He was to be quite brazen and not the slightest bit covert. He should, as was agreed, take the Ford Focus and drive right up to the front of the house, ring the doorbell then go around to the side entrance and as it would be undoubtedly locked, he should break the small window next to the door, reach around and unlock it. Once in, he should turn on the lights briefly and then off before leaving, he should get in and out of the house in three or four minutes, grab the hidden cash and a certain overnight rucksack, put one in the other and then drop it out of the upstairs toilet side window to a gap between the wheelie bins and the garage wall so that she could collect it later. It was most important that he leaves the house empty-handed and drives casually away as there was a good probability that he may be stopped on the way back or by waiting for him at the hotel. Christian got her ruse quite quickly, he would just be the gormless amateur trying to find the odd lead. This scenario ran uncomfortably close to the truth in his eyes.

Looking ahead Christian could see that his hire car might cause some contradictions but he had an idea how to defuse it if questions were asked in the morning when Bill Rutherford arrived at the facility. Despite M.I.5s problems, he trusted Rutherford but not necessarily the people behind him, and in this, he was pretty certain for if Consuela shoots to wound, they stay wounded and would not have a gun to hand. Someone from M.I.5 killed or rather murdered that man and this was a thought that permanently lurked in the back of his mind. Just to make things even more complicated, Christian received a message from Robyn that one of the technicians remembered her field trip to Salisbury Plain and her return with the compensator. She had to explain that at the time she didn't think that it was important but she guessed that they knew it was a lie, especially with the last remaining M.I.5 eavesdropper still wandering around the place annoying everyone. With the aforementioned in mind, Robyn needed to be taken out for dinner that very night. She was frightened and rightly assumed that she was being corralled into a corner.

It was nearing 5 pm now and it was suggested by a newly transformed blonde woman that he should go to the facility and collect the Ford Focus, do the deed at Consuela's house and then do the dinner thing with Robyn.

Consuela's house turned out to be a doddle, he was in and out in minutes, the side door had already been broken into and the make-shift repairs were easy to overcome, he found the hidden cash and the travel bag, although previously opened by others the contents were intact, these, as discussed were dropped from the first-floor side window to a gap behind the wheelie bins. Empty-handed, he strolled out of the house with the alarm screaming, he got back into the car and headed off to the facility to collect an overly upset Robyn Reilly. It was just after 6 pm, darkish, damp and October.

"Jesus Christ! You took your time, I mean, how clear could I be, they know about ruddy Salisbury don't they?"

"Okay Robyn, it is okay, the car is just outside on the street, c'mon." He put his arm around her shoulder and escorted her past security and the main gate.

"God…" she said as she slid into the car, "get me out of here for Christ's sake."

"Okay, we are safe, where do you want to go?"

"Africa sounds nice, Ghana even better."

"Ghana huh, you got roots there?"

"Not really. Mum is from Brixton and Dad comes from Tunbridge Wells; anyway, mind your own damn business."

"Oops, sorry, we are off to the hotel where I am staying, the restaurant is really good."

"Wherever, anywhere is better than the facility, I thought it would be fine, I thought I would be safe. I can't go back there, Chris, I just can't, I feel like I don't have a fucking friend in the world."

"Don't be silly Robyn, of course you have."

She looked around at Christian's irritating smirk and tried a high-pitched laugh, "You?"

"Yep, the best friend you ever had."

"Oh, really!"

"Definitely, now have a little faith. How goes the tidal project in Wales?"

"What, what! Yeah, well, actually it is going very well, the contractor's engineers seem to have it all sussed, I just have to sign a few dockets, approve some calculations and throw some 'fucks' at the odd underperformer, bit of okay really…" Christian let her talk, he knew nerves when he saw it, and Robyn was going down that track as they spoke. His own dodgy nervous system would do exactly the same in her predicament.

Although the dinner was quite decent, she didn't really eat, she just pushed the food around her plate a little. He wasn't quite sure what to say. Quite conveniently, his dumb phone rang.

"Sorry," he mouthed across the table as he accepted the call.

"Hi Christian," came the cheery voice of Mie, loud enough for Robyn to gather that it was a girl.

"Hi Mie, thanks for getting back to me, I'm sorry, but I need a little help?"

"Which is?"

"I need a restricted number, I only have one name but I'm not sure if it is a surname, could even be made up I guess. The name I have is simply 'Norman', it is really important to me."

"This is not going to be easy, restricted numbers are, well you know; restricted."

"An e-mail address would do?"

"Yes, that would be easier I think, you are asking a lot from me Christian. The last time I helped you, it ended up as a shoot-out."

"Mmm, it did, and I guess I am asking a lot, but will you have a go, please?"

"Alright, I'll see what I can do, no promises mind and I can assure you that this will cost you a lot more than a dinner, okay?"

"Yes Mie, I understand, thanks, I'll see you when I can."

"Don't leave it too long sweetie." Christian flinched as he terminated the call, Robyn looked at him incredulously.
"Did she just call you 'sweetie'?"
"Mmm...I suppose she did, erm, she gets a bit hyper sometimes if you know what I mean?"
"No."
After dinner, Robyn made it known that she needed to make some private calls, the best place would be from his room phone. He led her up to his room to find that it hadn't

been made up, which was understandable because Consuela had been there for most of the day up until a couple of hours ago. There were two used coffee cups, a barely noticeable whiff of female deodorant and some lipstick-stained tissues in the waste bin, which he tried to manoeuvre out of view with his foot. Robyn was as sharp as she was clever and picked up a long red hair from the dresser and looked at Christian curiously.

"Um…it is not what you think, Robyn."

"You have no idea what I think and probably never will," she said sitting on the edge of the bed and reaching for the phone, she paused, pulled a couple of long blonde hairs from the headboard and gestured to him with an open palm.

"Ah, the maid is not very good," he countered.

"One must wonder what she is good at then?" Christian wilted and then left the room as she began to make her calls, he wandered down the stairs to reception to see if any other rooms were vacant for Robyn, fortunately, they had one, a single on the upper floor. When he returned, he handed over the keys to her room on the above floor, he kicked off his shoes, removed his jacket and stuck his gun and holster inside the bedside cabinet, he then plonked himself down heavily next to where she was sitting.

"Feeling any better?" he muttered.

"Yes thanks, had a good chat, and now I have a room, thank you for that." She looked across at him and frowned. "You look like shit though, you know, knackered?"

"Yep, busy day."

"Yes, I should imagine so, that security woman in the restaurant had long red hair, didn't she?" Christian took a deep, long-drawn breath.

"Does it matter?"

"No, not at all, just curious that's all, I am going up to my room now."

"Fine, I am going to clean myself up and have an early night." She turned at the doorway and sarcastically retorted.

"Okay sweetie, good night." Christian sighed and headed for the shower.

The following morning Christian was up, breakfasted and out by 7.30 am. He left Robyn on her own but slipped the keys to the hire car under her door before he left for the facility. He had barely got out of the car when a rather irate Bill Rutherford came striding up to him.

"Christian Simpkins, a word in your ear if you please?" Christian was not sure what to expect but he felt that he had most things covered.

"Oh, hi Bill, of course, something up?"

"Oh yes Christian, you are the 'something up', what on earth are you doing here now?"

"Me, oh, just returning your car actually, fantastic vehicle but I am afraid that it still has a few bullet holes in it, getting some unwanted attention I'm afraid." Rutherford examined the car overly carefully, checking both rear seats and the boot, to Christian he seemed to be gearing himself up to say something.

"Okay, see what you mean, fair enough, I can get those fixed easily, you did well out there in the Cotswolds, cool head, nothing stupid, but god only knows how you managed to stalk down an ex-special forces man and strategically shooting to wound."

"Not so hard really." Christian was thinking fast. "I just moved every time those big shotguns opened up, I sort of stumbled across him, he was side-on, those wounds were pure luck. I didn't know how to use the assault rifle, so I chucked it in the copse, worked rather well, I thought."

"Yes, on that I have to agree, you should have finished him though, when my man found him, he had recovered the rifle, he had to kill him, no choice. Now, while I have your undivided attention what the hell were you doing at that American's ruddy house, it is strictly off-limits. Got you on camera, you even set the alarm off."

"Well, actually I was looking for Consuela, I heard from Sir Jeffery Pollock that the US embassy has stated that she was not there and never had been. So I thought, why I was down here, I would check it out. There is no one there I can assure you."

"This is really amateur shit, Christian, no embassy, especially the American embassy would ever admit to harbouring someone. She has probably been spirited off to the USA by now, back with her CIA buddies, you really have a lot to learn. Now what else, yes, Robyn Reilly the research engineer, you have something going with her, don't you? Is that why you are still hanging around this place?"

"Sort of, yes, but I also had a death threat from one of those men and people are watching my flat, so, taking that in mind I have checked into a local hotel and I have also hired a car so I could return yours." Rutherford carefully assimilated Christian's responses and nodded in agreement.

"Okay, Chris, I hear what you are saying and it sort of fits. The guys watching your flat are my men keeping an eye out, should have informed you, anyway, you know now. Right, where is Robyn Reilly, back at your hotel I assume?"

"No gone now, early start." Christian was in full lie mode now and had to pace around a little to hide his deceit.

"Gone, gone where?" There was a slight grate to his voice now, something that Christian instantly picked up on.

"Wales, of course, the project there is augmented by the facility's engineers, she is needed, part of her job really."

"Tell you what, Christian, while I am here I may as well drive you out to your hotel, busses are such a headache." To this, Christian found that he couldn't refuse, he had no business to be where he was anyway, he voiced his agreement and climbed into the passenger seat. Bill Rutherford drove quickly and expertly safe, within ten minutes they passed the village pub, where Christian noted that his hire car was still there, it had become a useful habit to park away from one's personal presence. He halted the car outside the main entrance of his hotel, it dawned on Christian that he hadn't actually told him which hotel he was in. He cut the engine and looked around.

"Your car here?" he said gruffly.

"No," said Christian honestly, "my car, the hired car, is not here."

"Right, now don't take this personally, but I am going to check your room, okay?" It wasn't okay but there was nothing to do but nod, it was still early, a bit after 8 am. Briefly, he checked out the restaurant area and then followed Christian up to his room. Rutherford was a professional, he too, noticed the two coffee cups, the lipstick on the tissue and probably more. "Well, we've clearly missed her." Christian sensed that he was getting a little anxious now.

"I've got the details though, it's South Wales, takes about three hours if the going is good." He just looked at him, and demanded that he text his car hire details, he then turned on his heel, headed out toward his car and left. To Christian, Bill Rutherford seemed distinctly suspect, his demeanour today, his line of conversation and his overly sincere pursuit of Robyn Reilly's whereabouts. Being quite early Christian assumed that she was still upstairs in her room. He went down to the restaurant to grab a coffee, it was here that he met Robyn tucking into a croissant. It had been a close call, as he and Rutherford were going up the stairs she must have been coming down in the little lift.

"Hi Robyn, and good morning," he said as brightly as possible.

"Oh hello, Christian, I got the car keys thanks, I don't really know where I should go though."

"Me neither, look, do me a favour, don't pick up any calls on your mobile phone please."

"No chance of that, it is permanently off, had a nice chat with my brothers though, I told them that everything is fine and well, and I suppose it is, now you have got me out of the facility."

"Ah well, sorry to break it to you but Rutherford is on your tail, he was here, had a quick look around down here and then checked my room out, stroke of luck you being in the lift and him on the stairs."

"I didn't take the lift."

"Well, in that case, he missed you by seconds, how is the room?"

"Just fine thanks, I am feeling a lot better, well I was until you told me that they are after me."

"You should be just fine, they are on our side, remember, they can't all be infiltrators, they probably just want to keep you safe in their own particular way."

"Huh, and whatever that is, they can keep it."

"Right, point taken, now I have a few things to tell you."

"Okay, try and make it nice, you know, something bloody positive for once."

"Right, but keep it to yourself, I mean it. I think I have found Mr Throtestabler, he is alive and hopefully well at an undisclosed location."

"My God, that's wonderful, so the raiders didn't take him after all."

"No, they didn't, but they are hunting for him. Like the Americans and your copy of the prototype, neither can make the thing work."

"Just Mr Throtestabler and me huh, how nice."

"Yes, sorry it has turned out like this but it bloody well has. I am really not sure about Bill Rutherford, but there are still some infiltrators active at M.I.5 and that, I am sure of."

"So where do I stand, Christian, what are you going to do with me?"

"Not a lot at the moment, as far as the hotel is concerned, you are a middle-aged woman named Bernice Bates…"

"Bernice Bates, is that the best you could come up with, 'Bernice'?"

"'Fraid so, it's all I could think of in the time given, erm…sorry."

"You will be, so what now?"

"You will have to stay here for a few days, try and look inconspicuous."

"Inconspicuous! Really, I am the only black person for miles around, how the hell am I supposed to look fucking inconspicuous?"

"Ow…c'mon, you are only a bit black, you'll get by."

"Jesus, are you for fucking real?"

"Er…yup, suppose so."

"Then God help me! Find something better, Christian, a lot better."

"I'm trying to, I need a man, Norman but it's a bit tricky, sorry."

"For god's sake stop saying sorry you are driving me insane."

"Sorry."

"Idiot."

Later on that morning, Christian got a call from Mie in Whitehall, she had what he wanted and insisted that he meet her tomorrow night. This would mean another six-hour drive but this time in a pokey little hire car. Christian's stamina was not quite up to the trip. There was not much happening in Cornwall anyway, Robyn had taken to wearing a headscarf and answered to the name 'Bernice', she used room service instead of the restaurant. Consuela, in some disguise or whatever, kept a wary eye over the Sycamore Tavern where Tsargrin had presumably taken up residence. Christian, after some thought, decided to take the train back to London from nearby Falmouth.

This time, when he met up with Mie it was in a nice Italian restaurant in Camden, a short walk from where he lived, Mie apparently, was more than happy to make the tube trip in from Barnet on London's outskirts. She had been very busy, she had an email address, which was good, albeit a little unusual and a phone number that was dug out from some restricted archive, this too was a little obscure as the international code tallied with somewhere in Morocco. Christian was elated, it was only a one-off chance and she had come up trumps, he now had something tangible to work with. Mie was by now ploughing into a plate of fresh pasta, it was clearly her favourite dish, he had a plate of fine risotto complimented with a really nice bottle of red wine.

"It was hard work and more than a little dodgy getting that stuff together, Christian," she said as she finished her pasta.

"Yes, I imagine so, I can't thank you enough, Mie."

"Yes, you can."

"Oh yes, you said it would cost me, fair enough, what do you want?" Mie pushed her empty plate aside and took a long slow sip of the wine.

"Take me home, Christian."

"Oh well, right, yes, of course, I can order a taxi from here at the restaurant I suppose."

"Not my home, you Muppet! Yours." Christian tilted his head slightly toward her, her big smile was beaming and her eyes were gleaming, she was brimming with confidence. He struggled slightly to find the right words and emitted a soft, throaty cough.

"Yes, right, wonderful idea, um, no need for a taxi then, my place?"

"Ah-ha Christian, it is Thursday, I'm free on Thursdays, Mum takes the twins, who's a lucky boy then?" By now his cheeks were filling with blood and he was blushing uncontrollably, his throat was dry and all he could do was produce an awkward smile. Mie found all of his squirmy embarrassing traits more than just funny.

On entering his small block of flats, it was she that led him up the stairs to his flat at the top. Christian knew that he should be the one skipping up those stairs to relish the promise that awaited him but his mind was still reeling. Mie's unquenchable wanton confidence appeared to have no boundaries. Once inside, he didn't even have the chance to brew the customary cup of coffee, a traditional happening when one brought a young lady home. However, as fate, or rather Mie would have it, the evening turned out to be forever memorable. Once Christian had got his head around her mindset, he found that total control and girls-on-top appeared to suit her best. He was good at unconditional surrender and eased into the role perfectly. After a torrid and unquantifiable period, he lay back wet with sweat and gasping happily for breath. He noted though that she, although happily sated, didn't perhaps reach the moment she yearned for. Christian, with his forever shifting lifestyle and a rather grey exterior did not normally score that well with the fairer sex. Something went really well for him, maybe it was his new aftershave or perhaps just some good old-fashioned sex appeal just beginning to surface.

They chatted for a while and Mie settled into a peaceful sleep. Christian's metabolism hadn't quite settled down yet and he was left staring up at the ceiling, he swung his gaze across to her laying by his side. She was certainly pretty with absolutely beautiful skin, physically she was quite a sturdy girl, short and relatively compact, she clearly made a point of keeping herself trim. It was a nice observation and one that eventually took him to sleep.

In the morning when he awoke, Mie had gone, although it was Friday he knew that she had family duties awaiting. The kettle was still warm which was a good sign that she didn't have to leave in too much haste. He checked his phone as he always did first thing, she had left him a sweet little message and a smiling emoji blowing him a kiss. He had a slow morning, he was feeling good, he knew that the people watching his flat on occasion were on his side and he had no specific agenda as such for once. He also now had, thanks to Mie, what he needed. It did strike him that maybe he should dream up some more nefarious tasks for her as he thought the payment terms she demanded were fabulous.

Clean and fresh and hopefully with his wits back in order, he decided to make the call to Norman on the dumb phone. The number he called rang a few times before being tentatively answered.

"Who is this?" a voice demanded, the line wasn't so good but it sounded like Norman.

"Hello Norman, this is Christian Simpkins."

"What! How did you get this number?"

"Well, I—"

"Never mind, what do you want, I am overseas so this had better be good, make it quick Simpkins?" Already Christian could feel the pressure rising.

"Okay, right, I think I have located Charlie, I have also had to put Robyn Reilly into hiding, she is not safe. In short, I'm beginning to have my doubts on Rutherford."

"Explain?"

"Too much circumstance going on, I can list them if you can give me time, basically I am stuck. I'm not sure where to turn."

"Okay Christian, M.I.5 has some really good people in their ranks." Christian greatly appreciated his change of tone, *"I can't do much from here, but I know some who can, where are they?"*

"Sorry Norman, the line is pretty bad."

"Where are they Christian, Robyn Reilly and Mr Throtestabler?" he repeated.

"Cornwall…we are in Cornwall, Robyn is with me at my hotel and Tsargrin—"
"Right, I hear you; stay where you are," he interrupted, *"I will get an email link to you, do not call this number again, we will talk another time about this and by the way…"* again the call faded, he tried to speak more and lapsed into garbled expletives, and the call was ended.

Christian peered into the handset and scratched his head, he was happy that he didn't divulge any exact addresses, he was sure about Norman but not really confident about his phone or about the technical security of his flat despite it being checked after the break-in. The only thing he did reveal was that Tsargrin was alive and in hiding somewhere in Cornwall. He cursed himself for not going down the road to the call-box, but then again, they could bug that number too as it was such an obvious alternative. Thinking about the conversation, he noted how quick Norman was to interrupt him before he gave out the finer details. *Possibly for the best,* he thought.

For once, it all felt comfortably quiet on the Cornish front. Consuela confirmed that she has got a visual on Tsargrin at last and although very brief, from one door through to the next, he seemed well and in fair health. No news from Robyn probably meant that she was well and a polite email from Sir Jeffery reminded him to keep in touch. He also received a message from Bill Rutherford informing him that George Willoughby had eventually worked out who the inside man at the facility was. Unlikely as it seemed it was the old guy who ran the communication's (comms.) desk, he had been at that job for many years and many were aghast that he ended up being the informer, they paid him by cracking his skull, he was said to be still too poorly to be interviewed. The only good thing from that piece of news was that it helpfully allayed some of Christian's suspicions regarding Rutherford. Saturday morning arrived with no incident and Christian took full advantage of a free day to update Sir Jeffery, catch up with all the neglected matters, and put in writing a summary of what had happened in the last few weeks. By doing this he had, by dint of recollection, put things in some sort of order inside his head, something tangible he could deliberate on, maybe a light at the end of a long tunnel. Monday morning should, he thought, have some promise regarding the help and advice Norman's contact should bring. He had barely arisen from his bed when someone could be heard banging loudly on his front door, he took a peek through the spy hole but all he could see was someone's chest. That, someone, was quite huge and in an effort to save his front door he fetched his little gun. Gingerly he inched open the door and looked up, he knew the face and slipped the gun into his dressing gown pocket, it was Billy, Robyn's enormous kid brother, Christian stepped aside and ushered him in.

"My sister is in trouble," was all he said while producing the tiniest mobile phone ever.

"Go on, Billy."

"Well, before she left with you, my brother Malcolm gave her one of these, it is really small isn't it." Christian nodded to him to proceed, it struck him that any phone would look small in those huge hands. "You see," he continued. "Malcolm knows all the right people in all the wrong places, these are the kind of things that get smuggled into prisons, any sim card you like and it runs on three xxx batteries, no charger, not much money, but they work. Robyn says that she got arrested by the police at the hotel, a terrorist charge of all things, then the police handed her over to some security people, M.I.5 she thinks." Christian's mind was already whirring.

"Where is she, Billy?" From another pocket, he pulled out a smartphone and consulted it briefly.

"Here it is, Falmouth, she is in Falmouth, she is on a boat she says, oh yeah and it smells of fish a lot. I guess that they weren't real police then?"

"Billy they would have been real police but bogus M.I.5 people who just get the police to do their dirty work, how did you know where to find me?"

"Robyn left your details just in case, I thought that you would be with her, you know, protecting her but you are here, why Christian, I mean Mr Simpkins?"

"I was there until Thursday morning, but unfortunately duty called and I had to come back. Now I am going to call someone in Cornwall to get on the case, then I'll be on my way, we will find her, Billy, every time she calls you, you call me understand?"

He quickly scribbled out his dumb phone number on a scrap of paper and handed it to him. "Be careful with that, and don't put my name on it." Billy just looked at it blankly before nodding okay. Christian paused briefly for thought, trying to formulate some kind of plan.

"Billy," he said, "did you drive here?"

"Yeah, what's wrong with that, I've probably got a ticket anyway."

"Well, I haven't got a car, can I borrow yours?" Billy looked a bit sad, but reluctantly nodded his huge head, his car was apparently very special to him. Christian rapidly got dressed and stuck a few things into a holdall, he knew that he should call Rutherford but something wasn't right, in fact worryingly wrong. Downstairs in the minuscule lobby, Christian wanted to peer out to see if he could spot any big clean saloons, he noted that the front door catch had twisted off.

"Oh yeah, I'm sorry about that, I didn't know that the door had a lock on it when I gave it a shove, wasn't thinking right I guess." Christian had to suppress a little laugh due to the severity of the situation, he couldn't easily spot a security services car, so made his move following Billy to one of the side streets. He slipped into the driver's seat of a low-slung BMW coupe, it was quite old but well looked after and spotlessly clean.

"Find Robyn," was all he said as Christian pulled away, "and mind the paintwork," he added, out of earshot.

By the time Christian reached the motorway, he had just about fathomed the ins and outs of the car, it had so many extras and unmarked switches that needed to be sampled, the sound system was definitely off-limits, a hugely complicated set-up with volume control that just did, loud, louder and stupidly loud, another switch turned out to be a horn that played tunes. *Oh, to be a 20-year-old*, he mused as he roared up the fast lane.

He had already left Consuela a voicemail regarding Robyn and her being locked up in a boat but thinking onward, it was quite logical and probably the only viable way to get a bunch of hardened mercenaries into the country along with all their hardware, assault rifles and other deadly kit, a boat would be the obvious choice. The helicopter they dumped was near the sea as was the lizard peninsular which was actually in it, also they would need to have somewhere to put Tsargrin, if they had him, plus his flying fridge of course. A boat or boats, a ship even, it was now painfully obvious. Robyn told Billy that it smelled of fish and to Christian a fishing boat would be the perfect choice for these people, something local, something the coast guard would be familiar with. He didn't really anticipate the enormity of the problem until he got to the dockside of Falmouth. There were boats of every description everywhere on both sides of the river Fal, yachts, pleasure craft, fishing boats and others much, much larger. He continued to liaise with Consuela, she on the west side and he on the east and both with next to no idea as to what they were looking for. A lot of boats were moored away from the shoreline of the river which consequently made them impossible to survey. With no clear plan in mind, Christian began at the head of the estuary, working his way slowly upriver examining everything that floats for some kind of biblical revelation. Presently he came across a line of little souvenir shops and cafes despite it being an October Monday afternoon the sun was out and it was quite busy, he reached Falmouth in pretty good time, slightly under five hours and possibly a speeding fine or two, Billy's car easily rose to the challenge. Christian grabbed a take-away coffee and engaged his mind to confront the improbable task of finding one boat among so many. At that moment, he got a call from Billy, he had heard from Robyn, the signal from such a device within the confines of possibly a steel hull would be nominal, all that Billy could interpret was that she could hear many people around and that the boat had the sharp end pointing downriver, the shore was on her left, still no name or location but to Christian the few clues were invaluable, this meant that she was on the east side of the river, as was he, the boat wasn't moored mid-river and that it was pointing south. He passed the message on to Consuela on the other side of the river and briskly walked upriver to where he thought most people were, this was more like an angling convention, tackle shops and bait stalls with people walking around with rods, nets and weird fishermen's attire. A group of six boats moored a little way off seemed to attract a fair bit of attention. He didn't have to guess the signs were clear and concise, they were fishing boats okay, but not commercial, these were the boats that everyone knew, you paid your money and the boat takes you somewhere special where you catch your own. Christian remembered going out on such things with his parents many years ago, every resort had them. His thought process was now taking a different tack.

Such a boat, like the ones now in front of him, would be ideal for the task, perfect almost. The coast guard or customs would rarely challenge them, they were big and robust enough to handle the Atlantic's inshore cross tides and nobody would bat an eyelid on the comings and goings of such a vessel and its cargo of amateur fishermen and their buckets of freshly caught mackerel. Christian approached the nearest for a summary investigation although up close it looked a bit on the small side. The signboard welcomed all and sundry to the delights of sea fishing on the cutely named, *Happy Suzy*. An oldish man in green waxed overalls, probably the skipper, eyed his suit a little curiously.

"Yer ain't really dressed for fishing if ye don't mind me saying so, sir?" Christian took his cue.

"No, no, not now, just checking things out, how many fishing people can you take?"

"Ahargh! You'd be wanting a fishing party then?"

"Erm…yes. How many?"

"Well, young sir, the Happy Suzi here will take seven, maybe eight, we'll supply the rods and the lures, there won't be a finer fisher boat than this around these parts I'll have you know."

"Well, thanks anyway, we are eleven people, need a bigger boat I guess."

"Eleven you say, nay too many boats here could do an eleven, the old 'Emily Jane' at the end there could I suppose, bit of a rust bucket if you know what I mean."

"Okay thanks, maybe I ought to check that out then."

"Ahh…! Rather you than me matey, the skipper is a surly old fool, but manages to get a few parties, all the same, remember though Suzi here could do nine, maybe even ten if you have some kids."

"Okay thanks, I will."

"Mind you do, young sir, mind you do, keep yer jib up…" Christian nodded his thanks and made his way up to where the Emily Jane was birthed, he was trying to work out if the old fisherman's banter was for real or just a tourist attraction.

"Ahargh," he muttered to himself as he neared the last boat, somewhat bigger than the other, but far scruffier. The little gangway was roped off and despite his efforts to glean some attention, the boat seemed empty. Whatever the uncomfortable risk, he needed to make an effort and have a quick check, it was just a chance, not even a gut feeling, but it was pointing the right way and it most definitely smelled of fish. He took a quick look around, literally, to check if the coast was clear, he unhooked the rope, the boat was, as the man had said, a rust bucket. Plastic bottles and bits of blue rope littered the deck along with buckets, stale bait and sea grime. He took a peek inside the wheelhouse and then through the open door that led below. There were two tiny sparse doorless cabins, something resembling a broken toilet and an engine compartment to the rear, to the front, a galley of sorts and some sort of storage place, there was nothing of any interest, going back up the steps he noted something while looking down upon the galley, something that rang a sinister bell, it was a foil wrapper, gingerly he back-tracked, picked it up and scanned the label before giving it a good sniff, it was biltong, a type of dried beef not dissimilar to the jerky found in America but biltong was South African and a very acquired taste. This scrap of evidence was hardly conclusive, but to Christian, it was enough to need to take some sort of action, right or wrong. He knew very little about boats and thought hard about trying to disable it. Without much of a clue he grabbed a half-full mop bucket, entered the engine compartment identified what he thought was possibly a fuel cap and tipped the contents in, he now needed to get off the boat and contact Consuela. In one of fate's ironic twists, he could hear the sound of several footprints on the steel deck above, repeating the word 'shit' several times under his breath, he left the engine compartment and hid in the store upfront which was really just a void stuffed with old rotting nets and small plastic buoys. He squirmed into the foetid mess, it stank, he stank but it was an excellent place to hide. From where he was concealed, he could see the galley area quite clearly. He had no idea who had just boarded, if it were just a bunch of amateur fishermen, he would extract himself, make loads of apologies, accept the humiliation and move on to the next boat that fitted the bill. He dreaded to think what he should do if it were the mercenaries or whatever, for if he just surrendered, normally his default plan, he would become fish food anyway. He tried to text Consuela but like Robyn's attempts, his signal just bounced off the metal walls around him. Before he could even conceive a next move a man herded an extremely frightened Robyn Reilly down and into the left-hand cabin, thankfully she seemed unharmed, physically anyway, she also had the spirit to glower at the man with cold fury. To Christian, this was a good sign for it meant that she still had heart. The man shied back slightly in the face of Robyn's wrath.

"Now, now, Missy, calm down, there is nothing you can do, we ain't gonna hurt ya. You've had your coffee, you've been to the loo, now we are back in the boat so settle down, in about three hours you are gonna be somewhere much nicer." The man then stepped across to the galley pulled out a laptop and proceeded to occupy himself. To Christian the situation was getting trickier every minute, without warning, ropes were unhooked, the gangplank raised and the engine then sprung into life, and they were in motion, *impossibly trickier now,* he thought.

Christian lay hidden in that pile of festering nets for the best part of an hour, his famous depth of ideas and cunning plans had dried up. Aboard, as far as he could work out, there were two men and someone, a gruff speaking local, presumably the skipper, they were up on deck, plus the man in the galley and, of course, himself and Robyn. He was armed, which was a huge bonus, although he was hopeless with the thing, he had a reasonable talent for bluffing for as long as his nerves held out, the downside was that they too would be armed and exceedingly able. He decided that his best chance would be to remain hidden until the boat met its rendezvous, hope that they all disembarked and then make the call, police, coast guard, M.I.5 or 6, whoever.

The Boat

In due course the engine began to splutter, the man on the computer blurted out some obscenity and pulled open the metal door to the engine compartment, he tweaked something or other and the engine regained its rhythm. Again the engine spluttered and again the man began to tinker with it, but now the splutter turned into a mechanical cough for a number of seconds and then dwindled into silence. There was a loud curse from the skipper at the wheel up top, and another man came clambering down the steep ladder-like steps. The man in the engine compartment was yelling out for some tools, with a loud clattering these were provided, the skipper was now hollering some sort of nautical blasphemy to the boat in general. The two men appeared to be making little progress with the engine, a third man now descended with some sort of manual, he was big, heavy and mean and packed an automatic in a shoulder holster. Christian identified him as the South African, his attitude gave him away. He stood in the doorway of the engine compartment, he was fumbling his way through the manual between accented curses. It wasn't so big in there and with the engine, it would be pretty cramped, the door itself was relatively small as it was designed to be sealed if there was a flood, this forced the big man to dip his head up inside to gain entry, everyone in there seemed to have a different idea as to what the problem was. At this moment, Christian saw his chance, the only chance that just had to be taken, he knew that if he hesitated his nerves would never let him do it, in a frenzied dash he exited the store and headed for the compartment, he collided with the broad back of the South African sending him reeling into the engine and in that one fluid movement he slammed the door and pulled across the dog locks, A dog lock is a sturdy metal lever one near each corner, an iron device used to water-seal the closed door if ever the sea breached it.

"Ahargh!" he sang to himself in triumph as Robyn emerged from the cabin.

"Oh my god, Christian! Oh my god but how?" Christian hushed her and quickly tried to explain the situation as she leapt into his arms. Suddenly there were two huge booms and a couple of holes appeared in the metal door, Christian involuntary ducked and twisted with Robyn latched onto him, and they both crashed to the floor to one side of the door, somewhere in that split second of madness he found his little gun in his hand, another boom and another hole appeared quite low down, correctly they had guessed that they would be on the floor.

"Stop shooting," screamed Christian, "stop shooting now, I am armed and you are trapped." There was a stunned muted silence from within until a familiar gruff voice roared.

"Fuck me, is that you, Simpkins? I don't fucking believe it?"

"Well believe it now, stop shooting, you have nowhere to go, think about it." There was another bout of silence followed by a few muffled sentences.

"Fuck you, Simpkins," said the South African, again his gun boomed and a hole appeared adjacent to the top dog lock. Christian then fired his gun at the door, but it was of a far smaller calibre and its velocity somewhat lighter, his shot zinged off the metal door, whanged off the ceiling beam, skidded off the bulkhead and zipped past Christian's head. Again there was a bout of silence, Christian still on the floor cushioned by a pained Robyn beneath him, she was staring intently back up the steps, Christian followed her gaze to see the skipper making his way down with a big old-fashioned revolver in his hand. He never made the final step as the gun boomed again through the door clipping the other upper dog lock and straight into the man's chest. He now realised the mercenary's tactic, he was trying to shoot away the dog-locks and from his point of view, he soon would. His little gun could not puncture the door, it was only a couple of feet away up to his right in front of him, he had to do something, he forgot about the struggling Robyn beneath him, he crawled forward a bit and stuck the barrel of his gun tight up against the lowest exit hole from the larger calibre weapon. It was only a thought, an off-chance that could go horribly wrong. His first shot seemed to go through, but to where, he had no idea but lacking any alternative he loosed off another five, maybe six shots. There was the sound of pained pandemonium from inside the engine compartment, screams and curses underlined the mayhem he was causing and this prompted him to fire another series of shots through one of the other holes. He was now out of ammunition but could hear the sound of anguished groans. For some reason, Christian's nerves had for once held out, but he knew that shortly they would strike him with a vengeance. On all fours, he scrambled across to the stricken man laying on the steps and relieved him of the big old revolver. Robyn looked dazed and horrified as she watched Christian struggling with the body of the man as he tried to clear the step access, there was a mass of bloody gore oozing out everywhere.

"Listen up," he said to the bullet-ridden door, "stay where you are, I have another gun now, a big one too, the man at the wheel is dead, keep away from that door or I shall shoot through it from this side, understand?"

There were a couple of groans and the odd grunt. "Understand?" repeated Christian louder.

"Fuck you, Simpkins," came a faint reply.

Christian by now was doing his best to get Robyn up all ten treads of the steps to the safety of the upper deck, she was baulking at the sight of the dead man and heaved and gagged as she inched her gory way up with Christian behind her, revolver in hand.

Up on deck, sitting in the hatchway, he could just see the bottom of the steel door and on this he kept the big revolver levelled. He handed his smartphone over to her shaking hands.

"Robyn, you have to do this, go to settings and activate our location, then call the police, 999 they'll notify the coast guard, tell them it is an armed kidnapping, anything, just get them here, terrorists even." Having something to focus on alleviated Robyn's acute anxiety a little, she was recovering fast and thankfully her well-functioning sense of priority took over. Christian smiled weakly at her, his legs dangling through the hatchway were beginning to shake and his voice had all but dried up, but he was not letting the revolver drift from its mark. It took almost twenty minutes before the first sign of rescue appeared in the form of an enormous helicopter. Christian took his eye off the steel door and looked up at it hovering overhead, the feeling in his legs began to ease back. They were perhaps two miles off the coast, a couple of black-clad commando types descended down onto the deck by rope. Robyn was by now in full efficiency mode as she described the scene to them, another two men appeared from the sky, one of them gently relieved Christian of the revolver and told him to get out of the way, Robyn took his arm and they both went up front and sat on a bench.

"How are you feeling?" he croaked, trying to get his voice to carry over the sound of the helicopter.

"I think I'm okay," she shouted, "it's all a bit of a shock, these guys will take care of everything now, they said that a coast guard cutter will be alongside soon. Wow, you look awful, all that blood, are you hurt?"

"No, don't think so, it's not mine, hah, you don't look so cool yourself. Fantastic weather, though."

"Yeah well…thanks for that, Chris." The clear sea air began to chill them as their metabolism struggled to right itself. Robyn slid closer to him, her voice sounded desperately tired. "We're going to be all right now, aren't we? This must be the end of all this shit, surely."

"Generally yes, guess so, these things though, tend to leave loose ends, but hey, we are the good guys, right?" Robyn tried an encouraging smile and looked up as the helicopter pulled away. Without that monster hovering over them, they could now converse. The men in black were doing their stuff and had started to investigate the chaotic scene below.

"To the rear, one dead, two injured, one is critical," one reported through his radio set, "plus one other in the galley is also dead, all firearm injuries."

"Guess I shot someone then," said Christian without a tinge of emotion in his voice.

"Yes, you did, and we are okay, Christian, you saved me, god knows how you found me, it must have been nigh on impossible with all the boats around."

"Mmm…lucky I guess."

"Bullshit, I'll find out."

Presently, a huge coast guard cutter pulled up alongside and roped itself to the far smaller fishing vessel. Christian stood up and tried to brush himself down only to fail miserably. One of the coast guard men, younger than the others, approached him smiling.

"Hey, you're Chris Simpkins aren't you?" Christian nodded.

"Erm…do I know you?"

"No, never met, just seen you on the news that's all, you have quite a following these days."

"Oh, God."

"Anyway, glad to meet you, don't worry, us coast guard boys will look after you and your girl here. Wow, one man, four casualties, that is some going." Christian hated the thought of being some weird celebrity, he turned back to Robyn and helped her to her feet.

"Apparently, I am your girl?"

"That's what the man said."

"Oh well, whatever!"

"Well, that is an improvement of sorts, the last time that was suggested, you just said 'eew'."

"Yes, I suppose I did, seemed right at the time."

The medical team on board the coast guard cutter was far too busy to deal with either Robyn or Christian, but they managed to grab a welcome shower and a pair of pale blue overalls.

Conveniently, the cutter returned them to a secure place onshore where they were met by the police, more medics and the inevitable men in suits. Christian had been in this situation a good few times and knew what to expect: statements, debriefings, evidential events and a thorough medical. Poor Robyn, he knew, would be put through a psychological assessment. He had been through a couple himself but after so many near-death experiences over the last five years, the authorities had given up on him, as he often knew more about the probing than the assessors did.

By 9 pm that night, Robyn was given leave to, well…leave, given her choices she chose to stay over at the facility that night, just twenty-five minutes away in a polished dark saloon. By 1 am the authorities had done with Christian, it was an awkward time of morning but they had some holding cells in the custom and excise building next to the Coast guard's complex; it wasn't perfect but he managed to avail himself of one of the cleaner ones for the night with the door being politely left ajar.

In the morning, he was awoken by a smiling customs and excise man with a large mug of tea.

"Nice to see that you are okay, I must say that I am quite impressed at the way you cut your jib." The mariner's phraseology was quite lost on Christian, but he smiled back and took the tea. "Yeah, great day for me, young sir, my wife was quite thrilled when I told her that I've got that Christian

Simpkins in my cells, anyway, you have a visitor, a bloke, he wants to have a talk." His visitor was the operations manager from M.I.5, Sean Holmes, they had met several times before.

"Well, Christian, what can I say, well done, you have certainly turned a few things upside down, one of those wounded guys is more than happy to talk, which we shall take full advantage of once the doctors let us at him. That boat you were on, the Emily Jane, was to liaise with another vessel at sea, we need to find that quite quickly, any ideas?"

"Not at all, I'm afraid, Mr Holmes, I was kind of busy."

"Yes, of course, had to ask though. Now listen to this, as soon as all this got out, Bill Rutherford went missing along with another operative from M.I.5, a man named Kaye. Willoughby has put some rather damning evidence to the test which proved that they were the principal insiders, there is a warrant out for them as we speak. George Willoughby has been temporarily re-instated to see this case to the end. I must admit, I didn't think a man like Rutherford could be bought, having known him for years but there you go. Right, we are going to get you back to London today."

"Fair enough, how is Robyn? She isn't used to any of this, in fact, I doubt that anyone is."

"She is fine, one of our councillors is with her, she is a very able young lady I am told, she learns quick and adapts fast, I'm sure that she'll be okay. She is back at the facility."

"Can I see her before I go?"

"Sure, no problem, I'll arrange a car."

"Well, actually I still have a hire car at the station, oh yeah, I have another at the quayside, just get me there if you will, the station is best. Can I have my phone back?"

"Afraid not, Christian, it's evidence, it is your phone that made the alert, you can have the dumb phone though, we can't do anything with that."

"Yeah, thanks, and my gun?"

"Not a chance, ballistics have it and they never work fast, you know the form."

"Did you know that my gun had been tampered with before I got it, it was made to jam up once cocked."

"Now that, I did not know but guess what, it was an M.I.5 issue and the boys there are shit hot with their firearms log, anyone who gets to handle it is on it. You will need to file a readiness report, um…It's a C26 form I believe."

"Yeah, wonderful, do I have to wear these overalls for the rest of the day, I think that they are made out of paper or something?"

"Yes, we don't normally do clothes, I'll see what I can do."

Christian, once again in his tiny hire car, did not go directly to the facility to see Robyn, he was bug-free, as was his car so he went to see Consuela at the inn where Tsargrin was hiding out. She found him first, she had reverted to the freckled red-head. She looked at him dubiously and drew a sharp intake of breath. Mr Holmes had indeed dug out some clothes for him from somewhere in or around the eighties, in this particular case a rather baggy, shiny shell suit with a hood and if that wasn't bad enough, it was worn with his black business shoes. Quite briskly she ushered him up to her room, to Christian this was the first time he had ever seen her panic, she closed the door behind them and gave a sigh of relief.

"What is wrong with you, Christian, you stick out like a sore thumb, you look like that Jimmy Saville guy."

"I know, my clothes got wrecked, it was either this or some light blue paper overalls with 'Customs Official' written on the back." He went on to brief her on the past events, from locating the boat to being rescued by the rapid response squad and ferried by the coast guard. Consuela was adequately impressed.

"God, you were lucky with that little gun of yours, if you didn't line that barrel upon the hole exactly you would have clipped the door, and the bullet, and in all probability your gun would have come flying back at you, a really cool head at just the right moment, well done." All this was news to him as that scenario didn't even cross his mind. "Perfect response, though in a metallic environment, those little bullets of yours would have been wanging around the place until they found something softer, brilliant."

"I don't know about 'brilliant'; 'traumatic' sounds more apt."

"I've seen Tsargrin, he knows that I'm here, but we haven't spoken yet."

"Good, keep it that way though, now we know that Rutherford is the man alongside an agent named Kaye we have to keep everything so tight, nobody knows about you, Consuela, which gives us a huge advantage but until those two and the rest of the mercenaries have been found, nothing is safe. Hopefully, they have all headed for the hills or simply quit, which I very much doubt. They will be still active and still well-armed, unlike me at this moment."

"Rutherford…who would have thought, but it figures, he was senior enough to access almost anything. He is a danger to the British security forces and they shall be all out to find him. Thing is, to me, Rutherford seems to be extraordinarily well informed. If the price is right and I have no doubt that it is and they cannot make the fridge thing work then their only option would be to deprive us, or rather you, the UK of it. If they can't take Tsargrin, then they must eliminate him and possibly Robyn too, no doubt about it."

"Shit, you are probably right, any Ideas?"

"No, not really, my cover here is good, to them I'm someone who writes up travel guides so they are pleased that I am here. Christian, I need a gun, if these guys come calling, there is little I can do. The people looking after him at the moment are his friends, they are not professionals, and they are not even properly armed. They won't stand a chance if Rutherford and whoever shows up."

"Well, maybe George Willoughby can think of something?"

"Possibly yes, but it's unlikely to work as Rutherford knows the men, bit of a disadvantage if he sees them hanging around somewhere. Get me a gun, c'mon, you are the one with the creative bent, you can do it. You're in contact with Norman, he can help you with a gun, he has before."

"Okay, Norman is a good bet, I have to go back to London this morning, no alternative I'm afraid, but as soon as I get done. I'll come back here."

"Make sure you do, I have a feeling that it's all going to get a bit tricky, keep your hood up as you go, you look like an idiot but better that than giving yourself away."

"Erm...okay, no change there then."

Christian wasn't overly enthused by his shell suit but in reality, it was far more comfortable than the grey suit he was about to change into at his hotel. From there he headed directly for the facility and Robyn Reilly. Robyn was pleased to see him but she seemed withdrawn and quiet. She preferred to stay in the farmhouse than go home, there were people here, people she knew and trusted. A softly spoken woman next to her suggested that her current mood was to be expected. A natural process apparently, for only yesterday did she watch a man die, something difficult to witness that would undoubtedly take some emotional toll. He stayed with her for a little while, quietly chatting over some coffee. She thanked him for caring enough to visit her, he gave her a little peck on the cheek before saying his goodbye, a tiny tear glistened in his eye.

His next job was to return his hired car and wait for the big saloon to arrive and take him to London. He still had Billy's BMW at the quayside, but he was in no condition for a prolonged drive, Mr Holmes was to deal with that also. Hanging around Falmouth high street, he popped into a sports shop and selected a decent tracksuit, grey of course, and a pair of recommended trainers. He liked the comfort and changed into it there and then. It was a five-hour journey and he hoped for a decent nap in the back. He was no longer surprised at the popularity of the shell suit all those years ago and could quite understand how it evolved into the garment of today, this was his very first item of sportswear, such was his life. The car duly arrived and the driver eyed him cautiously as he slid into the back seat, by the time they hit the motorway he was out for the count until he awoke in London as they approached Whitehall and not his little flat in Camden. The electrifying smile of Mie greeted him as he entered.

"Ah there you are," she trilled, "we've been waiting for you. Look." She swivelled her screen around and brought up a picture of a distant helicopter hovering over a stricken boat. "This was on the news, it's you isn't it?"

"No, it isn't," he lied.

"Really! Then look at this then." Another series of zoomed images came up, one of them clearly showed a bloodied Christian talking to an armed soldier at the front of the boat, his heart sank, there was another of him boarding the cutter with Robyn clinging to his arm.

"Christian Simpkins, what are you like! See it's you." Before he could respond an impatient cough alerted him to the presence of Sir Jeffery Pollock. Mie emitted a tiny 'oops' spun her screen back around and sat down.

"Sorry, ah, afternoon, sir."

"You see, Simpkins, if you insist on larking around near the coast you have to expect that every Tom, Dick or ruddy Harry living near the shore will possess a half-decent lens, binoculars, telescopes and occasionally a massive zoom lens connected to a camera, two miles out or not, you were clearly visible. I would strongly suggest that you keep away from all sorts of social media for the time being, now into my office if you will." Christian closed the door behind him, he prepared himself for yet another barrage of asinine remarks.

"Now, Simpkins, this should be an interesting conversation, first off though, what do you think this is, some kind of sports club?" Christian glanced down at his tracksuit, held out his palms and lamely replied.

"Sorry, sir, my clothes have sort of been impounded I guess."

"Don't tell me, that girl lost her clothes too I suppose?"

"Well yes, but…"

"Thought so, well at least it's not my secretary again, that would be so tiresome." Christian held his tongue on that particular comment.

"Well sir, quite a lot to report, I haven't had time to write it all up yet."

"Yes. I suppose that is understandable. However; I do think that I am in possession of most of the facts. A rather efficient man going by the name of Holmes of all things, he furnished me with the information this morning. Two men dead, two wounded, one of which is critical, armed as well it seems. You had a bit of a field day on that boat, Simpkins."

"Sorry sir, but believe me, it was necessary, they would have killed me and Robyn if they could."

"Yes, so I understand, it wouldn't do to have that innocent girl killed, now would it?" Christian smiled inwardly at the connotations of Sir Jeffery's last sentence.

"Listen, Simpkins, I don't much care for all this gun stuff, this is Ancillaries and Procurement, this is England and you are not, I repeat, 'not' James Bond."

"I don't like it either, sir, I just find myself in certain situations. However, I have to confess that these recent events were not of your department's making, er…sir."

"Are you trying to lecture me, Simpkins? I would well advise against that."

"No sir, wouldn't dare. Saw you in action up in the Cotswolds though, you didn't seem to mind then and I must admit that you and George were more than able."

"Was that a compliment, Simpkins?"

"Of course not, sir, I wouldn't dare." It was now Sir Jeffery's turn to conceal a wry smile.

Sir Jeffery was, as he said, extremely well informed, he appeared to know a lot more than Christian, and he was there. With George Willoughby temporarily back in charge, things were moving fast.

"Now pay attention, Simpkins, that boat you were on was to meet up with a certain trawler, and that trawler was to enter international waters for a rendezvous with a ship named the Caravel, we are currently searching for this ship although it has been suggested that it might bear a false name. This whole affair seems to be sponsored by a bunch of executives from a conglomerate in Macao, China. This, as yet we cannot prove, but when we do, we shall air a diplomatic complaint to the Chinese government."

"Yes sir, I am sure that it will have them worried."

"You may mock, Simpkins, but hear this, if we, that is the UK, found out the origins of a fridge like object at forty thousand feet, we too would launch an effort to borrow it or steal it, and if not, we too would seek to destroy it. Anti-gravity is the grail in the world of physics, no one can even describe it as yet and whoever possesses it has an insurmountable advantage over everyone else."

"Hence the Americans going all out to get it?"

"Exactly, now I hope that you appreciate the enormity of this unfolding epic. The security forces are still erm…not secure yet. We know for a fact that there is still one informer and he is very active, oh and by the way, I should actually thank you properly for rescuing Robyn Reilly. You have to understand that if that was M.I.5 or 6 undertaking the rescue, and the rescue failed, they would be duty-bound to shoot her." The blood drained from Christian's face as his jaw dropped slightly. "Good," continued Sir Jeffery, "you now understand.

It is not all rosy trying to pretend that we are the good guys, we have to do what we have to, no matter what the cost. Now I think that we have covered most of what is relevant, do you have anything to add?"

"Yes, sir."

"Well, spit it out then?"

"Okay, I can now confirm that I have Tsargrin tucked away somewhere in Cornwall." Sir Jeffery looked gobsmacked, he stood up, paced around a bit and pushed his glasses up to the top of his head.

"Hell, are you serious?"

"Of course, sir, although I'd rather not say where, just yet. He is being looked after by some of his friends, he is a local down there sir, everyone knows of him."

"Is he safe?"

"For the time being, yes but the people with him are poorly armed sir, maybe a shotgun or two, just local folk, that's all."

"Who else knows about this?"

"Rutherford knows that he escaped and that he is alive, but I lied to him about the exact whereabouts."

"Good lord, so you suspected him then?"

"Not really, I suspected everyone, still do I guess."

"Right then, what do we do?"

"Nothing for the time being sir, he is safest where he is. I hate to be a pain but I need another gun, mine has been confiscated by the police in Falmouth, but I am sure the police in the Cotswolds will be finished with my old one sir, could you make a few calls?"

"Of course, I shall explain your needs to George, he has the bit between the teeth now."

"A car would be nice as well, I did mention it before, but events sort of took over, something clean, I mean bug-free as opposed to polished."

"Fair enough, George again, it shouldn't be a problem. Listen, Simpkins, try and make this bloody debacle work, aside from your curious antics very little is happening elsewhere. Anyway, it will be a splendid achievement for the department as well, of course."

"Yes sir, of course."

Overt to Covert

Deep in thought, he left Sir Jeffery's office, he hardly noticed Mie's cheery goodbye. Exiting the lift he came across a throng of busy people, inadvertently, distracted by his thoughts, he had forgotten to take the smaller side exit. The main entrance hall to that part of Whitehall was always busy whatever the time, he was the only one wearing a tracksuit. Almost immediately he was hi-fived by someone he barely knew.

"Good work Chris", "Well done, Chris", "Brilliant", "Yo Christian" and so forth followed his route through the main lobby. Someone began to applaud, others joined in, and phones were flashing everywhere. Eventually, with his face the colour of beetroot, he slid his hood up and exited the building, and slunk away to obscurity. His mind was reeling, too many people, far too much attention. He couldn't be doing with the tube or a bus, nor a taxi even or anything. It was a good hour's walk home but he knew of a little obscure pub just north of Oxford Street, and to this place, he headed to murder a couple of pints of fine ale, without having to talk to anyone. Here he felt safe, tucked away in a little alcove. The staff were nice, the beer good and a warming open fire completed the moment, for a moment was all he had. A voice broke his short reverie, he knew the voice, female, slightly well to do, and with an educated clip at the end of a sentence.

"Hello Anne Bottomley," he said without looking up, "I guess I should have been expecting you after all this attention."

"And so you should, Christian, I'm a journalist, it's what I do. You first brushed me off in the Sahara, four years back, then you ran away from me in Belize, but this is London, ha, my turf. You just have to talk to me for once."

"Aww…c'mon, Anne, I really can't be doing with this, anyway, what can I say, I've signed the Official Secrets Act."

"That is tosh and you know it, I know that act better than anyone, shift over I've got something to show you." Reluctantly Christian slid over to give her room to sit down, she then produced a tablet screen.

"Look I am really not in the mood."

"Shhhh, just watch." Christian's attention was taken up by a range of news stills from Western Sahara, Belize and now the Cotswolds followed by the most recent off the coast of Cornwall. Because he was slight of build, dull-looking in real life, the cameras loved him although unfortunately, he didn't. "You see, Christian, these pics along with their own storylines would make interesting reading to an awful lot of people. Not only have you weathered die-hard type skirmishes you have also brought water to the desert and peace and prosperity to a little chunk of Central America. I and probably many others have been following your progress most carefully. I just need to know what is really going on here. A gunfight in the Cotswolds, for God's sake, and now, all nicely videoed, a daring sea rescue of a young kidnapped girl. These, Christian, are not the actions of a low-ranking Foreign Office official.

Now talk to me, if you don't, I shall simply guess what is in the gaps and release it all as a grand expose. 'Our man in Procurements' as it were. Christian, there is easily a book here, and if you don't do it, someone like me will."

"What! Jesus Anne don't do that, I promise that I'll give you some time when this is all over, I'm still hurting."

"Oh hell, are you wounded or something? I didn't know."

"No, no not that kind of hurt, you know anguish, trauma, loss even."

"Okay, point taken. I've heard from certain sources that you are working for GCHQ, is that right?" Christian glanced sideways at her, catching her bi-spectacled eye, she nodded knowingly.

"Aha, I got that one right then!" Christian wilted, he only mentioned that as an aside to get a security guard off his back. Clearly, Anne Bottomley knew her trade.

"Okay Anne, I don't, but say I do, but it means that I still can't talk to you. A lot of those pictures of me are genuine, but very few have my name on them. Anyway I was featured in a Sunday supplement after the Sahara and I was on TV for a bit with the Skyship, this is not new news surely."

"Put it all together and it is, but okay, I get what you are saying and I don't want to compromise anything, but after…You've made me a promise okay?"

"Yes, okay, I will, listen Anne you are pretty good at what you do, huh, this investigative stuff."

"To me, I am the best at what I do, you want something? What is it?"

"A ship is what I want, it is called the Caravel we think, but it might have changed its name. It was last seen in international waters off the southwest coast on Sunday. I'm not sure how big it is but it is ocean going"

"Well, that's not much to go on, but it is not so easy to change the name on a big ship, it'll be written in big letters on either side of the bow. It would have to have its real name when it hit port, any port. The name Caravel is the Spanish form of the French Caravelle. A ship bearing that type of name wouldn't really be so big but quite fast. It doesn't lend itself to being a cargo vessel, any idea what flag it is flying under?"

"No, afraid not."

"Mmm…There are probably a few ships that share that name, some kind of super yacht maybe, but the Spanish name makes it interesting, the same spelling is used in Portuguese as well. Okay, we're cutting it down a bit already, I'll speak to a few people."

"Thank you, Anne, you have done better than us already." She looked at him thoughtfully.

"You going to be alright, Christian?"

"You won't believe this, Anne, but I hate guns and the damage they do, it really is horrific if you are up close." She just nodded almost knowingly.

"You on the same number?" she said quietly.

"No, anyway my phone has been confiscated again." He pulled out his dumb phone to prove the point, she looked at it dubiously and made a note of the number, she seemed to sense his melancholic mood and quietly left without a further word. With Anne Bottomley now gone, Christian sat back to regain his uninterrupted calming of thought. Another hour passed and eventually, slightly wobbly he made his way home, a lot less cautious than usual he forgot to take his normal precautions, he stumbled up the stairs, wrote off any thoughts of dinner and put himself to bed. Outside in the street, an M.I.5 man in an overly clean dark saloon logged the moment and continued to monitor his charge. George Willoughby had put a lot of markers in place and refused to compromise his ace in hand, Christian Simpkins. Christian awoke relatively early the following morning, dry in the mouth and very hungry, he slipped into his comfy new tracksuit and made his way down the stairs. A full English breakfast was now on his agenda, he checked his phone as he went, there was nothing much to interest him except a couple of missed calls. He ambled past the ever-present saloon car and its driver, hiding clumsily behind his newspaper, without even a glance, either way, the local café beckoned him with the promise of a fully loaded plate, a mug of hot tea and a free read of the morning's tabloid. On his return, full and feeling much more human, he tapped lightly on the saloon's window. The driver let him in.

"Hello, been here all night, huh? Here, have some coffee, black, no sugar." This, the driver gratefully accepted. Abject prolonged boredom was a pain that Christian was well aware of.

"Am I so bloody obvious?" said the man.

"Afraid so, but sometimes that is the whole point, you are like a big red flag saying keep away from Simpkins or else. If you get my drift."

"Yeah, I guess that is a way of looking at it, can't say that it really fits in with my training though, but there you go."

"Mmm…suppose so, car's a bit too clean though, look at the others?" This he did and nodded his head in agreement.

"Shit, I make myself a bit of a target don't I?"

"Just a bit, but hey, it takes the attention away from me doesn't it. Now can I borrow your phone, no, not your personal one, I mean the agency one, I need to make a call but my phone is absolute crap."

"Well, I'm not sure, to be honest, I don't think anybody has really asked this."

"It is okay, you can listen in if you like, key up George Willoughby please." The man did a double-take at the name, unlocked his phone, hit a key or two, handed it over to Christian and went for a walk.

"Ah, there you are Christian," said George Willoughby, *"I've been trying to get hold of you."*

"Yes, I know, but my phone is pretty crappy, you know, unsafe."

"This is my operator's phone is it not?"

"Yep, he keyed you up for me, he has just gone for a short walk, nice bloke."

"Perhaps yes, possibly a bit green though. Now, you must make your way to Millbank tomorrow, M.I.5 headquarters 9 am sharp, Sean Holmes will meet you in the lobby, you know him, he will tell you the rest. Need to get you a firearm and a bit of kit and whatnot."

"Oh, okay, I could definitely do with one, I think that I can smell a bit of action on the way." He was thinking of Consuela and the reason for her request. George though read it in a different way.

"Look Christian, I am aware that you prefer to operate on your own?" This was news to Christian as he usually spent an inordinate amount of time begging for assistance in any form from Sir Jeffry's department.

"You will not be permitted to act by yourself, this is an important operation. You will have all the help you need and more, two trusted men will accompany you, and you will not be asked to disclose the whereabouts of, um…Charlie, until you get there. So tomorrow morning then, try and be on time and please, no tracksuit." Christian laughed to himself, *for what the hell difference would it make?*

It occurred to him that he had the rest of the day, Wednesday, free. In one way it was good as he had a bunch of less important things to sort out but Cornwall beckoned and he needed to get back there. He sent Consuela a rather cryptic update of what was happening, he then had a long conversation with Robyn, she was still at the facility but felt quite safe. She seemed to have thrown her 'all' into the Welsh project and its tidal generators and apparently it was now all going very much to plan. She explained very carefully that she needed to keep very busy, busy enough to distract her mind from the traumas of recent events. Sadly, Christian agreed, for he too also had horrific memories of the past that came back and haunted him, they would always be there, and this he knew only too well.

Bright and early, Christian emerged from the underground station and headed up Millbank towards the secret services offices of both, M.I.5 and 6. He had never been there before and the huge riverside building that now confronted him looked more like a grand classical hotel than anything else. Still awed by its grandeur, he confirmed the address by checking the sign. *This*, he thought, *was possibly the most unsecret, secret service building in the world.* Inside the huge galleried lobby, he met up with Sean Holmes as planned, he was then politely escorted through various security checks after which he went up a few floors to a large open planned office and then to a glass-walled meeting room affair.

"This is George Willoughby's department," confirmed Mr Holmes, "as you can imagine, it is quite safe and secure. It is continually checked for any unwanted devices or remote applications, this glass is soundproofed and with a click, it can turn opaque if needed."

"Hmm, very nice, what's the coffee like?" Sean Holmes smiled widely and offered him a seat.

"Our coffee! Well, it really is the finest, we check that as well."

"Glad to hear it. So Mr Holmes erm, Sean, what am I doing here exactly? I should really be back in Cornwall."

"Just a bit of a briefing, that's all, followed by a bit of prep."

"De-briefing! Not again, I don't think I have anything else to add."

"No, no, just a little talk about what we are proposing to do. If it all goes horribly wrong and you are taken out of the picture, so to speak, we will be almost back to square one." Christian baulked at the thought, he had no intention of putting his life on the line and never really had, and if he was really honest with himself, everything he had done regarding risk was purely unintentional. He nodded his assent meekly.

"Good," said Mr Holmes rubbing his hands. "Right, this is where we are, or rather you are, you know that Mr Throtestabler is alive and apparently well and has not as we had feared, been abducted and sent to somewhere unknown. Our Mr Throtestabler is crucial to many projects and especially the gravity device which everyone is so currently keen on. We need to get Mr Throtestabler to a secure place, his facility was okay but not watertight, you have proved this yourself. Plymouth for example has a very secure naval base, as does Portsmouth of course." Christian nodded his head in bland agreement as he knew that Tsargrin would resist any change. "So we shall effect a coordinated rescue operation to secure his safety, we intend to deploy a rapid response team with helicopters, plus some men on the ground to ensure that the operation will happen."

"Yes, that sounds all perfectly logical although knowing Mr Throtestabler as I do, he will not relish the thought of any type of confinement if that is what you intend."

"That is crap, Christian, and you know it, I mean look where he is now, he has incarcerated himself in some pokey building somewhere for weeks."

"Possibly, yes, but that was his choice, and the correct one if you consider his choices at the time."

"Granted, but supposing he does have a few issues, we secure his safety first and sort those out at a later date." To this, Christian had to agree, get him somewhere safe and secure. Slightly reluctantly he divulged Tsargrin's true whereabouts and together they formulated a plan of action. In its most basic form, he, Christian was to make contact with him and then persuade him that everything is secure and then escort him to a waiting car and into the custody of specially trained men. He would be taken back to his facility from where a waiting helicopter would take him to somewhere unknown, presumably secure. Cautious as always Christian neglected to inform Mr Holmes about the presence of Consuela. Quite cheerfully Sean Holmes stood up and again rubbed his hands together. Clearly, like Christian, he was someone who loved a good plan.

"Good, good, this should run like clockwork, Christian."

"I hope so, but you still haven't neutralised the raiders yet, I mean how many are they, and you still have an active informer here don't you?"

"Unfortunately, yes, a bit of a thorn admittedly, however, only the two of us, me and you know the exact location and it won't be logged or communicated or even scribbled out until afterwards. As for the raiders, thanks to you they are somewhat less in number, but they will probably have some in reserve and presumably all the weaponry they need. We know the location, we have the advantage, we have the men and the kit and believe me Christian you would be hard pushed to find better men than we have. The response team will only be minutes away if we need to call them in. In this operation, the raiders' only practical choice will be a sniper but the squad will get around that easily."

Christian understood, he hadn't even dreamt of there being a sniper, Sir Jeffery had already implied that they will try to kill Tsargrin simply to deprive the UK of him. Dutifully, he followed Sean Holmes out of the glass office and to the lifts. Down they went, to maybe half a dozen floors below street level, the very bowels of that magnificent building.

"Right-ho, Christian, here we are, this is where we keep our hardware." It was a cavernous but busy place full of subdivisions and side rooms. There was a slightly oily scent in the air. Sean Holmes was speaking quietly to someone at a desk next to the entrance, where they waited for a short while until a youngish-looking man approached, he was the first person Christian had seen not wearing a suit, instead, he wore a pocketless type of blue overall.

"Ah, hello, John. I have Christian Simpkins here for you, you have the operation brief I assume?"

"Of course, sir, we've even got the 'Triggs' in hand."

"Good man, they can really make you wait at times. Okay Christian, stick with John here, he knows the form, tell them to give me a bleep when they are done okay?"

"Right, erm, well yes I suppose, but?"

"What?"

"Oh, nothing…I'm fine."

"Good, on your way then, see you later." John was an affable young man, almost too carefree if one considered the nature of his trade.

"Hello, Mr Simpkins, so nice to meet you, at last, we have all been following your progress, actually it must be said that outside our military affairs you are our most active operator, currently anyway. What you managed to achieve with that tiny Walther automatic is a lesson to us all, I mean stalking down that ex-special forces guy in the Cotswolds was classic, showed a lot of bottle."

"Er…I didn't know he was in the Special Forces, if I had I wouldn't have gone near him." John took Christian's remark as a bit of light banter and grinned accordingly.

"We are off to the armoury first, try not to touch anything please, because if you do, we will have to check it again, house rules I'm afraid."

To Christian, the armoury looked more like an American gun shop. There were weapons of death and destruction everywhere, each one spotlessly clean and labelled accordingly. He stared around him, dumbly trying to take in the scene. He found himself being ushered over to a big steel topped counter.

"Unfortunately," said the man behind the counter, "you've had our last little 32. Walther. They are very old and frankly, quite obsolete. We do try to cater for our operator's individual various wants and needs. We have far better guns here, more powerful, accurate and most of all reliable. I bet that old Walther fired low didn't it?"

"It did," mumbled Christian. The man then ran off a list of suitable replacements backed up by gun talk and meaningless stats. Despairingly, Christian realised that everyone here assumed that he was a field operative of sorts, highly trained and educated in the dark arts of war. He began to feel a bit silly, he took John by the elbow and guided him to one side.

"Look John, I am not a field operative and hopefully will never be, I haven't received that type of training, I just need a gun that will do the job. You don't have the Walther, which is my particular preference so I need something else, without the sales pitch if you get my meaning."

"Okay, Mr Simpkins, we are aware of this anomaly, but you do have the clearance, and trained up-operative or not, you certainly are at this present time. Just pick a gun, old Charlie here tends to pour out a little too much information sometimes, he just loves his job that is all. Now personally I would recommend the Glock." Christian knew of this particular gun as it was the weapon of choice for Commander

Teddington Back in Central America, he remembered having to look down the business end of it, the Commander knew his guns, so in his eyes, the Glock was okay for him.

"Yes, I'll take the Glock." Old Charlie readily agreed with his choice and scuttled off to a certain shelf to retrieve one.

"'Ere you go, young Mr Simpkins, Glock 17 gen 4." He removed it from its box and handed it to Christian, it was a big powerful looking weapon but in his hand, it wasn't so heavy. "Lots of plastic parts, very reliable and so quite popular, it carries a 17-round double stack magazine, 9mm parabellum ammunition. You can fire one if you like, we have a test range on this very floor."

"Er, no thanks." He couldn't think of anything worse to do, but now he was thinking of Consuela's needs and this particular gun would fit the bill nicely. Charlie was still rambling on about the gun's fine attributes and he got to the holster requirements just before his eyes glazed over. He didn't know what holster, this gun was certainly far too big to sit on his hip, the shoulder holster was gender fitted so he opted for the normal sidearm holster that hung off his belt against his thigh, although in reality, it would be in Consuela's handbag. Eventually, old Charlie boxed the whole set up and placed it carefully on a different shelf as he began the necessary paperwork, this struck a chord with Christian. He now had a question, something that would cause some unease to old Charlie and John.

"Are you familiar with the Walther P37?" he asked.

"Of course," said Charlie, "I remember it well, good little gun in its time, why do you ask?"

"Well, what would happen if you removed the magazine and tweaked that little linear clasp in the gun's butt to make it tighter?"

"What, the feeder return, well if you did that it would be stupid because it would just jamb up if you tried to cock it with the magazine in place. You would have to strip the thing down to free it."

"Right, thanks for that, now tell me what happens to a firearm once it gets allocated. Presumably, you check it out first?"

"Of course," he said a little warily, looking at his colleague, John.

"So what happens after that, what's the procedure?"

"Well, I am not sure that you really should be asking—" John then cut in, there was a story unfolding and he didn't like the sound of it.

"Okay, Mr Simpkins, once the gun is checked, it is sealed in a cardboard box similar to the one that you have just seen, it is sealed closed with a numbered sticker and barcode. It is then collected right here or it is sent to the relevant department."

"And these relevant departments are normally in this building, right?"

"That's right, but sometimes they are couriered out, can I ask you where you are going with this, if one of our weapons has been compromised, we need to know?"

"Okay John, I'll be straight with you, my little Walther, the one you delivered to Ancillaries had been tampered with prior to me receiving it. I received it, I checked the seal and opened it, the mechanism seemed fine at the time when it wasn't loaded. Could have been a bit tricky for me to say the least." Old Charlie behind the counter was shaking his head and the normally laid-back John looked racked with injustice.

"My God, that could have been fatal, have you filed a report?"

"No, not yet, but I'll get around to it, been a bit busy." Christian's verbal revelations had soured the mood a bit for their professionalism had been directly challenged. John led Christian over to another desk at the far end of the room.

"Sorry, John, I did not mean to infer that Charlie was culpable in any way, I guess I could have handled it better."

"Yes, point taken, but there are procedures in place for this sort of thing, rare as they are. Please do not say any more about this until the report has been filed." Christian nodded and looked curiously at a row of strange looking sleeveless jackets.

"Those, Mr Simpkins, are flak jackets, good for bullets too but no good for you, we have something much better." John unhooked something from a certain rack and pressed a buzzer, a woman appeared with a tape measure draping from her neck. John held up a pale grey waistcoat seemingly made from plastic.

"See this, Mr Simpkins, it is the latest development in body armour, although mostly still Kevlar, it is interwoven with a Graphene-based material. It is thinner and lighter but still with a good capacity to stop a bullet from normal velocity small arms. Penny here will measure you up for one, it can be worn under a loose-fitting jacket." Christian was more than content with a bullet-proof vest and with his history of constant near-death experiences, he hoped that they would let him keep it. Eventually, he was done with the hardware section and John ushered him off elsewhere.

"Right, Mr Simpkins, time for 'Triggs' now this you will like."

"What is 'Triggs' John?"

"Aha, come with me." The next room off the wide corridor looked and smelled more like a salon. John handed a sheet of paper to a young woman with spruced up hair, she turned and smiled at Christian while politely closing the door on John.

"Hello Christian Simpkins," she said, "we have heard so much about you much like everybody else, which is why you are here of course."

"Erm…Excuse me for asking, but what is 'Triggs'?"

"Oh, that! Well, it's a type of nickname I suppose, it stands for 'trigger point' which is the term used for something that stands out on a person, and sticks in their memory, big red hair, bushy beards, Elton John style glasses, that sort of thing. Our little team is going to work on you, a disguise is no good for any prolonged duplicity, not real enough. Our methods are much longer-lasting. Far too many people can put a name to your face, which can't be good can it?" Christian smiled, they could do whatever they wanted to him, anything to avoid unwanted attention.

The Triggs team were very good and although he had never had this type of treatment before, he correctly guessed that their techniques could not be found on the average high street. First off, they stripped him down to his boxer shorts and applied some sort of fake tan with an impressive-looking spray gun. It was just a light tan but Christian, looking at his transformation in the mirror, was pleased to lose the pasty white hue of his skin. Next, they did his hair and changed it from thin and mousey to a rich dark brown, his effort of a beard also got some attention and was coloured darker and remodelled into a fashionable goatee. His eyebrows were clipped and now he had cheekbones or the appearance of some simply by not tanning the area beneath his eyes, the white shining through emphasised the little he had. He was thrilled thus far, a pair of snazzy specs with plain glass and a small mole on the side of his cheek completed the transformation. They then furnished him with some designer clothes of the type he would never ever have thought to buy himself. He could not believe it, the Triggs team was as proud as he was. Plus, everything they had done would last for weeks. Before they let him go, they gave him a few tips; he had to lengthen his stride a little bit to change his gait and had to practice speaking in a loud whisper instead of his normal conversation voice and most importantly he was to lay off wearing his grey suits. Presently, John returned and escorted him back to the department entrance with a few brief instructions to find Sean Holmes' office. Christian loved his new look, he had never even considered that he could look cool. He practiced his new walk along the lengthy corridors and although some people smiled at him, none displayed that air of recognition. Sean Holmes was also impressed and had to do a double-take as he walked in.

"Bloody hell, Christian, you have come out well, the guys at Triggs have really pulled out all the stops, I like the beard, you should keep that."

"Thank you, to be honest, I'd like to keep the lot. Now what happens next, I really must be getting back to Cornwall, I've spent most of the day here."

"Yes, you have and we are almost done, we are hoping that you can get Mr Throtestabler to come with you on his own accord, he trusts you Christian so it shouldn't be much of an ordeal. However, in the light of what has happened before, we intend to take no chances. Only you and I know his whereabouts, and that whereabouts has, as I have said, not been entered anywhere, no software, no paper trail, just us. Tomorrow morning you will be collected by two men, not M.I.5 but extremely professional, they will bring your weapon, your body armour and another set of Triggs' clothes etc. You will also receive some credible I.D under the name of Gordon James Knox, aged 33 and you are a surveyor for English Heritage, there is a room already booked under his name, same hotel. You will find all the information you need in the envelope that they'll give you. You will also receive a rather smart watch and phone, I haven't a clue what the watch does but I am sure that you will work it out in the car. I think that's all for now." Christian was beginning to get a bit bewildered, he also knew that if Tsargrin was a target, then he was too.

"What about money, I have almost exhausted my rather meagre savings and I daren't use my credit card."

"Ah yes, good point, in the envelope there is a card issued under Gordon Knox, lots of credit on it, um…try and keep a few receipts if you can and don't lose the body armour, it is the latest generation, and costs a ruddy fortune."

Back down in the grand main entrance lobby, he thanked Sean Holmes for his efforts and in return he was wished good luck, 'hopefully' Christian thought, luck would not be needed. He caught a good look at himself in the glass doors as he exited the building, he still felt cool, a brand-new sensation he now had to deal with. It had just turned 5 pm and the streets were beginning to fill, somewhere along the line he had missed lunch and his stomach began to growl with the pangs of hunger. For some reason he thought of a decent plate of pasta and from there he thought of Mie, she should be just finishing work now, on the off chance he gave her a call, she seemed delighted that he rang.

"Christian!" she squealed. "I thought you had forgotten about me, where are you?"

"Not far, just the other side of Millbank, I have to go to Cornwall tomorrow, but I thought, maybe we could meet up, I fancy some pasta."

"Christian Simpkins, what are you like! I need to call Mum, call you back, bye." He stared at his handset and blinked at her instant response as she cut him off. But now he couldn't get the tube, otherwise, he might miss her call. He decided to get a bus, after all, he was now plain old Gordon Knox. Up on the top deck, he received her call on his dumb phone, the only phone he currently possessed.

"Can't believe it, Mum says yes, brilliant huh, I can't go out tomorrow though, but I don't mind, pasta sounds good, I love pasta."

"Me too, how about the place we went to before, that was pretty good. I'm pretty hungry, 6.30 maybe?"

"Good, anything is good, wow, so unexpected. 7.30 is better, need to go home first, I'll see you at the restaurant at 7.30 then, yes?"

"Excellent, looking forward to it..." he said his gooey goodbyes, sat back and looked out of the window as London life passed on by. He was feeling good, he felt cool and untroubled for once and now had a date with Mie in a Camden restaurant, a short walk from his flat, by chance.

Christian liked Mie, she was so buoyant and positive about everything and he hoped to see a lot more of her.

Back in his flat he used his time well, he was a bit wary of the men that were to take him to Cornwall, Sean Holmes had told him that they weren't M.1.5, then who, he pondered. He adored his new look and carefully hung up his new clothes on a door in the hall. He looked different now, few would recognise him and only a select few, just three, Consuela, Holmes and himself knew where Tsargrin was, the odds for once, he felt, were in his favour and if not, he literally had an army behind him. He felt that he didn't need a gun and was sure that Consuela would be pleased with the new Glock automatic when he presented her with it.

Despite all the Bondish hype he was receiving via the media, friends and foe alike. He was quite aware of his misgivings, he didn't really know much about guns, he was not physically equipped for any form of combat and he had an extremely shaky nervous system. Hardly a man of action in any form, his latest effort on the boat had been his best and that was spent squashing Robyn, the abductee, into the steel deck whilst firing his little gun blind through a little hole in a steel door, *nothing fantastic about that* he thought.

He was pleased to see Mie and she him, they had a good chat, a good bottle of Chianti, and a huge plate of pasta apiece. She too liked his new look, he explained to her that he needed to be less recognisable and found the right people to do the job, this, she could quite understand.

"You do look very different, but in a nice way, you know, kind of stylish," she said as she hooked her arm into his as they left the restaurant.

"Thanks, I appreciate that, I was getting far too obvious in those grey suits."

"And the hair, darker, richer, the beard too, what else is new?"

"Ah, well, I've yet to find out."

"You mean, I have to find that out?" They both laughed together, Christian gave his M.I.5 man in the saloon car a short nod of recognition, Mie didn't seem to notice or even care. Up the stairs and safely in his flat, again they didn't even bother with the niceties of coffee. Within five minutes, she was the girl on top doing what she did, when her hip thrusts abated, she leant down on him and whispered that he should hang on a minute. Slightly puzzled but not perturbed Christian maintained his position and put his hands behind his head as she hopped off and delved into her handbag, she produced two lengths of soft thick rope. Christian widened his eyes.

"Can we use these please?" she giggled. This sounded quite okay to Christian, he wasn't really good at knots but he would of course give it his best shot. As usual, he had got the wrong end of the proverbial stick, Mie wanted to tie him up. He thought back to their last rampant tryst and recalled that she didn't quite reach her own particular special moment so maybe the bondage thing was that missing catalyst.

"Er…sure, bit of a first for me, though."

"Oh, it's okay silly, people do it all the time." Christian felt a bit out of touch, apparently, he was plainly missing something. She was a bit too practiced with the knots but the binding was secure yet not tight, they went from his wrists to the legs of the bed. He felt that he didn't really mind too much because being bound as such ensured that very little was expected of him. Within minutes, she was again doing what she did and reached the peak of her passion fairly quickly and kept it there until he too got there. Eventually, she dismounted, gave him a big wet kiss and skipped off to the bathroom, leaving him to stare up to the ceiling, again feeling a bit like a spent racehorse. However, the moment, ropes or not, certainly worked for the both of them, Mie returned and gently freed him, she pulled the duvet back over them. He clicked off the bedside lamp, held her close and fell asleep grinning like a Cheshire cat in the dark. It was an early morning start for the pair of them although they did manage a quick rummage under the sheets to prepare them for the day ahead, she to the desk at Sir Jeffery's department and he into the unknown care of a pair of heavies who would ferry him to Cornwall and to the perceived threats thereafter.

It was the best start of a day, he embraced his goodbyes to Mie and looked around for his transport, an SUV of sorts he was told. There was only one that fitted the bill and as he approached a powerful-looking man stepped out of the driver's door, he smiled broadly as did Christian.

"My god! Dave? Whoa, this is brilliant, I can't believe it, I don't suppose you have the other Dave with you?"

"Yep, in the car, good to see you again, Christian, you've been causing a bit of a stir everywhere, thought we'd turn up to give you a hand." Christian almost bounced into the rear of the big SUV where he met the other Dave and shook him warmly by the hand.

"Wow I haven't seen you guys since Western Sahara, what…three or four years ago?"

"Almost four, yeah," said Big Dave as he pulled away into the westbound traffic, "but actually we were also with you in Belize, in the Royal Marine detachment. I smiled at you, gave a little thumbs-up sign if you remember."

"Ahh so that was you, all that camouflage grease, sorry, couldn't make you out. I am really glad you two are on board, I've had a hellish time trying to figure out who the bad guys are, driving me insane."

"Yeah, bound to I suppose," said the other Dave, "anyway, we've brought your kit with us plus some nasty stuff of our own. I'll tell you what though if you want to lose that bit of body armour in the back then I'd appreciate it if it comes my way, wouldn't fit Dave here though, too fat."

"Who the fuck are you calling fat?" The other Dave just laughed, as did Christian.

"Oh, just drive," he said.

"'Ere," commented big Dave, "that girl, isn't she Pollock's secretary? It is ain't it?"

"Erm…suppose so, I guess, you know how it is."

"Ha-ha, it's not the first time you've up-ended his secretary huh, you old dog."

"It's not like that, she is a very nice person you know…" The two Daves roared with laughter, and thus their journey continued until the halfway fuel stop.

The second leg of the journey to Cornwall was dedicated to the business at hand, Christian trusted these two men with his life and left very little out as he explained the events as he saw them, they were very pleased when he told them that Consuela was also in on the act and had located Tsargrin.

They also thought that she was holed up in the American embassy or possibly the U.S by now. They knew of Christian's limitations and marvelled that he was, in fact still alive and kicking. Big Dave who was now in the passenger seat passed a thick brown envelope back to Christian.

"Not quite sure what is in it but I have a fair idea."

"Me too, I believe I'm supposed to be a surveyor, I am now Gordon James Knox apparently, could be worse though, another Dave would be even more confusing." He opened the package and spread the contents on the seat next to him. Driver's licence, debit and credit card, business cards and a bunch of small value notes. Apparently, it was all he needed to be someone else. He studied his fictitious date of birth, address and pin numbers and tried to commit them to his memory. The last piece of paper appeared to be a shortlist of particular codes, puzzled he muttered some mild expletives which prompted big Dave to hand over a clear plastic bag containing a phone and a small box. The phone was something special, it was a multi-band smartphone with a satellite enabler built-in, and the small box contained a blank-faced watch. It took Christian the best part of an hour to work out what the phone does and which code went where and with which number. Before he even got to the workings of the watch, car sickness took him and he had to take a break until the nausea passed. It appeared that the two Daves had already been allocated a house reasonably close to the facility. He hoped that he too could stay overnight there, but the Dave's were having none of it and insisted that he stay at the same hotel as before. At the time he didn't really understand why, but when the Daves say something, it is normally for your own good. They were on target to reach the peninsular by 2 pm and Christian planned to do lunch with Robyn if he could, he aired his minuscule agenda with them and they had no problem with it except that he should ensure that Consuela got the gun before anything else.

The Dave's accommodation was a good choice, vacant and secluded with very little natural cover surrounding it. As soon as they pulled up the other Dave, not the big Dave, scampered out of the car and did a quick survey of the area and cautiously entered the building, in a few minutes, he re-emerged and emitted a quick sharp whistle which prompted Dave to cut the engine. They began to stretch, to ease off the cramps of a five-hour journey, Christian did the same, for if they felt safe, then so did he. The amount of kit that they had crammed into the back of the car took him by surprise, cases, boxes, bags and a couple of steel-framed rucksacks. Christian followed them inside with a couple of bags, immediately they selected a large holdall, unzipped it and spread the contents out on the kitchen table, taking a cloth bag out from the bottom, big Dave weighed it in his hand, nodded his approval and handed it to Christian, it was his body armour, Gen 4, the latest, well, apparently. It was something like a body warmer and still felt a little bulky to him. He had seen flak jackets and Kevlar waistcoats and such like on the news and the one he now held up seemed positively tailored in comparison. He tried it on, it had two thick zips on either side, it was sleeveless but high in the neck and low at the groin, and it moved well in all the right places, unfortunately, his trendy new jacket would not go over it but he had an overcoat that easily would.

"Nice try, Christian, except it is back to front, you'll find some tensioning in the inner lining, might be a good idea to give them a tug as well." Christian nodded his assent and wondered why none of this spooky stuff ever came with instructions. Once happy with the fit, he removed it and checked out the Glock, it was brand new, its weight quite comforting in his hand but he was learning so he asked Dave to check it out for him. It took him less than a minute before he slid a magazine in and cocked and ejected a few rounds.

"Perfect," he said, "what are you doing for a holster, you can't strap that thing to your side."

"Putting it in my man-bag, of course, it's the thing these days, wouldn't be without one you know." They looked at one another, laughed a little and shook their heads in despair.

"You sorted your watch out, Christian?"

"Afraid not, I got car sick, I'll do it when I get back to the hotel."

"Make sure you do, it will be the quickest way to reach us, like the phone it won't be too affected by a phone bump or any disruptor, voice won't be much but text will always work. There's an app on the watch, a bug finder, keep using it, it will find anything that has the ability to transmit. Now listen up, Dave and I here have a job to do, and that is to get Mr Throtestabler somewhere safe, we are relying on you to do your bit. It should be plain sailing, we will only be minutes away from you, that watch will tell us and only us, get it." Christian gave a rather lame thumbs up. He had never seen the Dave's so sincere. "Whatever it is, whatever you think, let us know and remember there will be a Lynx helicopter full of action hungry buddies, when we move him those rotors will be turning just waiting for a sign, okay, remember, plain sailing, that is what we are looking for. Check it out with Consuela and the old boy, we want to do it tomorrow, get it?" Christian again just nodded, they were beginning to scare him a little, he just thanked the stars that they were on his side. He was issued with more dire warnings, more precise do's and don'ts and then out of the blue a cheery 'good luck'. Big Dave hung a paw on his shoulder and steered him back to the front door.

"Relax Gordon, it will be okay," said the other Dave from the kitchen. Christian flinched, for, of course, he was Gordon Knox now, a desperately important thing he had already forgotten. Big Dave drove him a few miles back to the picturesque village where his hotel was.

Playing his part, goatee beard, darkened hair, tinted glasses and perfectly stylish attire he approached the desk, he recognised the receptionist, his heart did a tiny summersault, he remembered to talk in his loud whisper, like someone with a sore throat.

"Ahem…Gordon Knox, you have a room for me?" The girl looked up and smiled, *this was it,* he thought, *I am scuppered.*

"Of course, Mr Knox, we've been expecting you, nice trip?"

"Oh, er, yep, just fine, thanks." He breathed a sigh of relief.

His room was fine, much like the other he had on the floor below. Although he wanted to check on Robyn, he did as he was bid and put Consuela at the top of his mental list. He ordered a taxi, popped the Glock back inside his man bag and arrived at the Sycamore hotel as the casually suave Mr Knox. He ordered a coffee at the bar and sent a smiley face to her. Her response was almost instant and in less than a minute, she was with him, still a redhead and still called Sheena. Christian couldn't work out how she recognised him so easily.

"Hello, Sheena," he said as she sat down opposite him.

"And you are?" she said smiling.

"Gordon Knox at your service," he responded with his familiar smirk, "I've brought you a present." So saying he passed his man bag over the table to her. She felt its weight and took a little peek inside.

"Whoee, you darling young man, just what I've always wanted, marvellous taste."

"Thank you, it comes with a couple of nice magazines as well." She flashed him a dark look warning him not to get above himself. "You have done well, who is with you?"

"Couple of guys called Dave, you've met them before." Her eyes widened.

"The Dave's, now we are cooking and about time too, are they kitted?"

"Totally."

"Fantastic."

"Is Charlie about, I'd love to see him?"

"Yes, lots of people would, I'm afraid, shouldn't be too hard as it's you. By the way, who dressed you? I like the get-up."

"Ha, just upping my game a bit, grey suits are out this year."

"And all the other years I hope," she said under her breath. "Tell me, Gordon, do we have a date for the removal?"

"Yes, we are hoping for tomorrow if it suits."

"Excellent, I just hope Charlie is up for it." To this, Christian readily agreed, it was always difficult to get Tsargrin to do something if he didn't want to. Another reason to see him before the event.

Out of professional courtesy or rather, helpful interest, Consuela took Christian for a little tour of the old Sycamore Tavern. The newer part with the hotel rooms was pretty self-evident, rectangular, three stories, twenty rooms, restaurant and bar, all built and decorated with the tourist season in mind. The original tavern, a little under three hundred years old, had little nooks and alcoves, a main bar and of course the snug, a listed building with the interior decoration consisting of raw brickwork and heavy black timbers. Being a tavern in the traditional sense it also had its own selection of rooms, small and dark with minute windows, nice to see from a historical aspect but appalling to stay in for an extended period. It was in one of these that Tsargrin slept. The exterior was much more enamouring, with meandering paths of stone branching off to rose gardens, old walls of ancient crumbling brickwork, a well house and even a secret herb garden with no visible access, flower beds abounded. Christian gazed upward following the trail of a mighty wisteria that snaked up the side of the old building. An alternative route up or down, he surmised. Consuela interrupted their tour at the far end of the gardens adjacent to a banked mound.

"See this, Christian," she said tapping lightly on an overgrown rusted iron door, "this is what is called a smugglers' run, there are a couple of earthen tunnels inside, once they had timber shoring but now it is metal, still pretty old though, pre-war maybe, but that is not the point, this leads into the old cellar, this is Tsargrin's escape route should he need it. Despite the state of the door, it has been made to open from the inside. The sea is only about half a mile from here going south, hopefully, though it shan't be needed." Christian nodded, he could feel the sea breeze from where he stood, fresh and salty, he buttoned up his stylish new jacket and wished that he had worn his overcoat instead. They went back to the hotel via a different route and so encircling the place with Consuela pointing out various facts and follies as they went. Back inside the tiny Sycamore lobby she checked her watch and looked at Christian.

"It's almost four, shall we see him now?"

"Who?"

"Charlie! You twonk, come on." She led him to a small reception office in the old part and had a word with the woman there. She looked hard at Christian and was satisfied that it was him. She called out to a person called Tiny in another room and he or rather it came lolloping into the office, the man was a giant in all proportions, far heavier than Robyn's brother Billy, he had to turn sideways to manoeuvre himself through the doorway. Christian stared at Consuela for a few seconds before following her who was following Tiny. It wasn't really ideal for such a man, with low oaken beams, narrow hallways and random steps either up or down. Presently he stooped down to knock upon an arched door. A voice within signalled that they should enter, Tiny did his best to stand to one side as they passed him before heading back to whence he came. The room they subsequently entered appeared to be empty, Tsargrin could not be seen. Christian looked around, piles of paper everywhere, an old blackboard full of unintelligible calculations, books, lots of books and a battered old computer with far too many cables leading to, or possibly coming from it. He shuffled slightly to allow his gaze to continue around, he stopped at the old iron fireplace, he was smiling now, it was a half-full pint mug of tea, probably cold. A loud and familiar voice from seemingly nowhere echoed around the old room.

"Ah, so there you are my boy, I knew you wouldn't let me down, what gave me away?" Christian still couldn't see him, the voice, Tsargrin's voice seemed to be emanating up through the floor, Christian answered anyway.

"Sheena Ventura did it, empty and vacuous, you once described her, that picture in your lab was the first clue, clever stuff."

"Yes, wasn't it, that idiot couldn't even work out the airlock, gave me all the time in the world." Christian just nodded and tried to hone in on the sound of his voice. Tsargrin was standing on a very steep stairway up from the cellar, just his head bobbing up and down in an opening next to an old leather sofa.

"Ah, so there you are, should I come down or are you coming up?"

"No, no, I mean yes, help me up will you, not much to hold on to I'm afraid." Christian obliged and Tsargrin clambered out, using the arm of the sofa for some added leverage. Looking down through the opening he identified another room, windowless and musty. Tsargrin seemed to be very much himself, rotund, red-faced, mad hair and a powerful glint in his eyes, he was very pleased to see Christian, he rarely shook hands and much preferred a decent hug from those closest.

"So Christian, you sussed out the escape hatch, what then? Those M.I.5 bods couldn't work it out, but you did, didn't you?"

"Mmm…suppose so, you just followed the wall around, using the top of it like a path, you found the opening by the big oak and simply caught the bus when it came, or rather the roof of the bus."

"Exactly, yes, you know, I told them that you would work it out, and this place, the Sycamore, how did you find us, come on, I thought I had that angle covered."

"Well, Consuela and I narrowed it down to about a dozen pubs and hotels, you being local and all that, then Consuela here found some evidence and sure enough you were here."

"Evidence pah! What evidence, not me I can assure you."

"It was your tea, you drink it by the pint amongst other things."

"And?"

"Well, Tsargrin, you forgot to tell your people here that you have to leave the spoon in it to conduct away the heat, stop it cracking, and that is what she found, a tea-stained broken pint mug in the top of the bin."

"Bah, luck, it was just luck, you guessed that's all."

"Didn't."

"Did—" At that juncture, Consuela cut in.

"C'mon boys, now, now." At that, they both conceded simultaneously. The three of them then squashed into the sofa and talked just about everything that had recently happened. After all that should be aired, was aired, they came across the present, here and now as it were. When Christian informed him that they were to move him back into the now highly securitised facility complete with armed men and helicopters he was distinctly unhappy.

"Listen, my boy, I'm not entirely sure what you have been through recently but I will assure you that I am going nowhere in a hurry, it is peaceful here and I can do all sorts of scientific theorising with Tiny prowling around the place I feel pretty secure and remember that M.I.5 have not got their act entirely back together yet, so who do you trust eh? Answer me that then Mr Christian Simpkins with the funny beard."

"I'll have you know that it is not a funny beard, it happens to be the er…happening thing in London. Anyway, I do understand your concerns, but George Willoughby is back in charge for the time being."

"Mmm…Willoughby, well he is okay, certainly clever enough to deal with most things that come his way, but maybe the er…whatever you call them 'interlopers'? Will also know that and re-plan or whatever they do. Rutherford is still out there and he definitely is nobody's fool."

"Granted, but Tsargrin, it is better for you and to be honest, the rest of us if you were back in the facility. If I can find you, then maybe they can, anyway, we have a helping hand, I think that Norman is on the case to give us an advantage. So we have a couple of very good independent operators. You have met these guys, Tsargrin, they think on their feet, you won't find any better."

"I hope you are talking about the Daves, you must be?"

"I am and they are very close. Plus, we have Consuela, and she is better kitted out than normal." Consuela nodded sagely and patted the man-bag on her shoulder.

"And you, Christian, what have you got, that little pop-gun I presume?"

"No, not at all, I am unarmed."

"Probably for the best, I think." Consuela stifled a laugh and Christian looked at the ceiling and shook his head.

"Come on, Tsargrin, please say you will come, you are a national treasure remember?"

"Excuse me, when you say that I feel like a piece of valuable furniture."

"Possibly yes, I suppose, but we need you, not because you are the only person on the planet to understand gravity, but because you are Tsargrin Throtestabler, friend and mentor."

"The Daves, are they fully kitted?"

"Oh yes, very much so, they are seconded from the Royal Marine Commandos. Norman has pulled a few strings."

"Norman, it's not like him to entangle himself in domestic matters."

"This affair stretches overseas Tsargrin, he is on the case, he issued me a gun from M.I.6."

"Who else knows I'm here?"

"Just us and a man named Holmes from M.I.5, I trust him."

"Okay Christian, right, you've got the Daves, Consuela, your unarmed self and Mr Holmes and a rapid response team with a helicopter I believe. Well okay, I will come, but if I get killed in the process, I'll never talk to you again, might haunt you though."

"No, haunting is not okay, everybody knows that there are limits you know. Anyway, we'll come tomorrow afternoon, it will give you some time to get all this gubbins together."

"Gubbins boy, gubbins! Every bit of paper here is crucial to something or other, national importance even, well maybe."

"Yes, maybe."

"Tomorrow afternoon you say?"

"Yep, so don't go anywhere."

"Anywhere Christian! Anywhere, I've been incarcerated here for weeks, and when I get to the facility, I'm going to be incarcerated there as well."

"Sorry, just my little joke."

"Hmph" – he then turned to Consuela – "have you mentioned anything about young Robyn?"

"No, not yet, one of our better-kept secrets."

"What do you mean, secrets," said Christian a little too indignantly, "Robyn, have you seen her?"

"No Christian my boy, I haven't seen her but I certainly needed to speak to her, so Consuela, under her guise as Sheena, set things up so that we could communicate. Payphones brilliant ruse, at lunchtime she goes out to the pub, closely watched, of course, the payphone is just inside the front door, small space, difficult to eavesdrop, our conversations are somewhat cryptic but it works. Bit strange though, she has taken to eating Cornish pasties for lunch, washed down with a pint of Proper of all things, even when we don't need to talk. By the way, she is in Wales as we speak, got there yesterday. She is quite safe, your tidal generator concept is really ploughing ahead."

"Hardly mine. Tsargrin, I just borrowed the tide driven water pump system you put together in Western Sahara, that old semi-submersible rig is still working by the way. You were really busy at the time, so I just reasoned that, if that set-up could piston pump water, then it should be able to produce power. That's all, those enormous pistons gave me the clue and the tide in that part of Wales is astonishingly high. I sketched it out and Robyn did the rest, I borrowed your calculations for the power output on ten thousand tons lift per hour. We only needed five thousand tons so I just halved everything, Robyn agreed that it was an awful lot of joules to work with, whatever that meant."

"Yes Christian, an awful lot, but halving calcs like that just do not work, but the concept was yours, and as for the calculations, any half-decent maths man would have worked it out, no problem, so let's not be shy about it, it is going to turn out to be a real winner. To be honest, Robyn really needs it to be, she is happy with it too. The current situation had really got to her, quite understandably I would add, she doesn't want to go home and she is really on edge at the facility I'm told. In Wales, she is using a different name in a different hotel and travels back and forth by bus. She told security that she was going home to stay with one of her brothers. All neatly devised by our resident red-head." Christian realised that he had been paying Robyn far more attention than needed, it even pained him a little that he wasn't in on the secret. Consuela noted his pause for thought, she read his body language in an instant and cracked a knowing smile while arching her eyebrows, Christian cringed slightly, Robyn was on his mind and he really didn't need diversions like this. Back outside and into the damp misery of an autumn drizzle that seemed to permeate everything, he waited for a taxi back to his hotel. He had planned to see Robyn to check on how she was holding out but it was a little too late now for lunch. He laughed softly to himself when he recalled her eating a pasty washed down with a pint of Proper, a really strong ale. He decided to use his time well before an early night, he hung up his damp jacket in the bathroom, kicked off his damp shoes and then got down to business. After much faffing about he managed to pair his smart watch with his special super smartphone. He decided that he trusted the

Daves enough to tell them the location of Tsargrin's Hotel, despite all his gizmos, he used the public phone in the bar, quick and concisely he relayed every pertinent point as soon as Dave confirmed that the line was clean. From now on all he had to do was ping an icon on his watch and they would home in on him if needed, everywhere his left arm went they would follow. Another feature of the watch was that he could enable it to scan and source any device capable of transmitting, a very useful tool amongst other things to detect location devices, phones and trackers. He tried it out on his dumb phone, it gave a buzz and a noticeable vibration, its range was only a metre or so, but was all he needed, perfect for checking out a car and of course a hotel room, his room was clean, he ascertained. Satisfied that everything should go smoothly tomorrow especially as Tsargrin had agreed to comply, he treated himself to a steak dinner complimented with a nice glass of Chianti, he deliberated on the coming day, a Saturday and all the things that had been put in place, Consuela, the Daves, the rapid response unit, plus the helicopter, the disguise and every other little bit that made up this particular plan of action. Tomorrow afternoon, if it went without a hitch, the operation from the Sycamore Hotel to the Facility should take only about fifteen minutes for Tsargrin to be safe and sound and the rest of the UK's security forces could then breathe a sigh of relief.

Daves

Before bed, Christian headed to the bathroom for his customary ablutions, his new smart watch was supposed to do everything, but he wasn't sure if it was waterproof, out of idle curiosity when removing it he enabled the searcher app and it began bleeping immediately with a slight tut, he made his way out of the bathroom to check his phone, the bleeping stopped, he went back in and it started bleeping again. His mind flew into an instant panic, he homed in with his app and it settled over his jacket drying from the shower rail. Frantically he searched every pocket yet the bleeping continued, he felt through the lining material and came across something resembling a small credit card. Fashion clothes are not renowned for their robustness and so he ripped the lining apart, what he now held in his hand was something similar to a large sim card, he recognised it for the something it was, a tracker. His mind was filling with drastic scenarios, he tore back into the room, grabbed the phone and alerted Consuela, she answered immediately.

"Hello Consuela," he shouted, "I've been tracked, it was in the jacket I got from M.I.5, check it out I'll be there as soon as I tell the Dave's."

"Shit, Christian, this is really shit, get the Daves to the escape door outside, I'll go through the front, contact Willoughby now, we also need the chopper now." The phone then went dead, Christian stared at it briefly then he called the Daves, they too answered quickly and within a couple of terse sentences they were on their way. Christian needed to be with Tsargrin too, but in his flurry of action, he realised that he didn't have a car, and his wait for a taxi was frustratingly long. He used this time to prepare himself for whatever, Rutherford, he reasoned, wouldn't know about the tunnel. His mind was now whirring, he strapped on his hi-tech body armour and stuck a loose shirt over it followed by his overcoat. Instinctively he reached around his side for the comfort of his gun, there wasn't one, his stomach began to rumble as he made his way down the stairs two at a time. After a furious bout of pacing, he leapt into the rear of the taxi when it came. Although he pleaded with the driver to make haste it seemed to fall on deaf ears, he pottered neatly along at 30 mph, stopped dutifully at red lights as he was legally obliged and politely waved other drivers into the road ahead. *If*, Christian thought, *he had his gun he would in all probability shoot the most infuriating driver in the world*. As they pulled into the Sycamore car park, the driver muttered to himself as he lost the signal to his phone/sat-nav.

"They are here," Christian said to nobody, "they are bloody here, it's a signal disruptor."

"Huh?" said the driver.

"Call the police," he said throwing a ten-pound note at him as he began his fifty-yard sprint toward Tsargrin's make-shift quarters. He had absolutely no idea as to what he should expect as he pushed open the old wooden door, which incidentally was always kept locked. Immediately he felt quite sick, the huge form of Tiny was sitting on the floor staring his way, a neat red gory hole oozed blood down from his forehead, a figure ducked below the counter, Christian's stomach was retching and he could feel his knees beginning to tighten. There was a black-clad man at the doorway to a room at the end of the narrow hallway, slowly almost in a dream, he could see the huge cylinder barrel of a silenced gun being raised up to meet him. He found himself dashing headlong toward the man to plough through his gun arm milliseconds before a champagne-like pop issued forth, he kept blindly going forward, his open overcoat flowing like a cape, oblivious to any conscious thought, through one doorway and then the other, another couple of pops followed as he skipped inside the room and instinctively leapt over a prone figure on the floor and crashed down the steep stairway. That prone figure was Consuela covering the entranceway, both Consuela and a man's voice uttered 'what the fuck!' almost simultaneously before she let loose another round in his direction. Her unsilenced shot was loud and alarming, Christian shouted back up to Consuela.

"Tiny is dead, two men, one on entry, the other at the doorway across from you." Consuela nodded grimly and slunk halfway down the stairs with her gun hand and steely eyes just visible above floor level. Christian was relieved to find Tsargrin well, he now had great faith in his body armour, but like Tsargrin, all he could think of doing was to watch the thick timber door to the tunnel slowly disintegrate. Tsargrin looked at him with open palms, he just stared dumbly back, he didn't know what to do, he had got to Tsargrin but he had no way of helping him, he clearly hadn't thought things through. Eventually, the door gave way and Christian overturned the big table to hide behind which unfortunately would offer little resistance to a bullet.

"Stay back or I shoot," he shouted to the splintering door, that comment alone bought him another second or two. Consuela though ducked down and fired a couple of shots toward the door before returning to her other job in hand with another round directed at the man above. Tsargrin then had the cunning plan to cut off the power which was good for him and Christian, but catastrophic for Consuela at the top of the stairs, hurriedly he turned it back on. A black kitted man now stood at the broken doorway, a light submachine gun in his hands, the voice he knew well, it was Rutherford, he was cool and comfortable with the situation. He aimed his gun at the stairs.

"Not today Consuela…" he said, as he raked the stairway from top to bottom with a long squeeze of the trigger, even silenced, the noise of the bullets slamming into everything in their way was deafening to Christian behind the table, she instantly dropped to the bottom with an uncontrolled clatter, Christian feared that she had been killed, a scuttling shadow alleviated his fears.

"Come and join us, Mr Throtestabler, if you don't then you are dead, c'mon, move it, you have no choice, and you Simpkins, you have been a complete pain in the arse." It now seemed a hopeless situation, Consuela was sitting in a corner with her gun pointing up the stairs. Time seemed to be crawling along but reality showed everything to be fast and furious. Back down the tunnel came the retort of a big powerful unsilenced weapon, Rutherford flinched and cursed as he sidled away from the door.

"Okay, death it is then." Again he squeezed the trigger, Christian flew back grabbing at his chest, his fall was cushioned by Tsargrin who now found himself underneath Christian's pained body, again the bullets came and Christian fell limp but they abated briefly as Rutherford reached for another magazine. Consuela picked her moment well, let off a shot up the stairs to keep them at bay then twisted and put a bullet in Rutherford's chest, but despite the impact, his body armour held up but the shock put him to his knees. There was now pandemonium in the tunnel, someone, probably a Dave was laying about him with an assault rifle, two men blundered into the room to escape the mayhem, another man quite limp and lifeless dropped down through the stairs, and another screamed but Rutherford was back on his feet, but now, without the distraction from above, Consuela focused and put a bullet, her final bullet through Rutherford's throat as he squeezed the trigger for the last time and bullets rained in her direction. She was pinned down behind a big pile of clothes in a box and wall at the bottom of the stairs, she was shaking her head whilst trying to give herself a physical. The situation had now dramatically changed, the cavalry had arrived. She glanced over to the door where another couple of very sad men in black stumbled through followed by big Dave in camouflaged greens, helmet, special goggles and big bulky body armour, he carried a big specially adapted American assault rifle that menaced everything that moved. Another green helmeted head appeared at the top of the stairs looking down. A deathly silence now enveloped the scene, outside a military helicopter hovered overhead.

"How's the old boy?" said the other Dave from the top of the stairs.

"He's moving a bit," said the big Dave, "you alright, Dave?"

"Yeah, I'm alright, you alright?"

"Yeah, I'm alright, Christian doesn't look so good though."

"Nah, but I think he has saved Throtestabler. He is right on top of him. Hey Consuela, what about you?"

"Not sure, Dave, something is very wrong. I should be dead or at least shot up a bit, I can't tell."

"Well, you clearly ain't dead, well not yet anyway, the medics will be here in a jiffy. Okay, Dave, I'm coming down, if any of those jokers even twitch, kill 'em for me will ya?"

"Can I kill them even if they don't twitch?"

"Nah, we'll get told off again." On his way down he looked at Consuela on her haunches in the corner, he swept aside the pile of old clothes to reveal a heavy old iron wood-burning stove. "There you go darlin' you were safe as houses where you were, let's get the old boy out of here, the backup is 'ere and the tunnel is covered, the chopper will find their boat, no worries." Consuela struggled to her feet, gave the old stove an affectionate pat and went down to where Christian lay. Sadly, she stooped down to check for a pulse in his neck, the pulse was strong, she then opened one of his eyes and checked for life, the signs were all there.

"Give him a bit of a slap, I think he's having you on a bit." Consuela did as was suggested and in an instant Christian snapped his eyes open, looked around briefly and clutched his chest in pain. Still somewhat perturbed, she ripped open his shirt to reveal the body armour. She looked up at big Dave who was sporting a big grin.

"Generation four body armour works don't it?" Christian, at last, found his voice.

"No, it bloody doesn't, I've been shot, get an ambulance."

"It's okay, Christian," she said softly, "you'll be fine, that armour will stop a bullet okay but the impact will always still be there I'm afraid, can't do anything about that."

"So I am not dying then?"

"No."

"Well, I bloody am, get off…please Christian just move, this is really not good for my back." Christian grunted something unintelligible and rolled off Tsargrin, allowing Consuela to help him to his feet and escort him up the stairs. All sorts of noises were percolating down from the floor above and outside in the dark, Police sirens, helicopter rotors chopping the damp air and a huge hullabaloo of voices, a group of what can only be described as soldiers appeared at the tunnel entrance allowing big Dave to drop his guard, a few more came down the steps. Then, to Christian's relief the medics came, they were very professional and very able, they checked out the wounded and gave Christian the once over. It appeared that he was at the bottom of the queue when it came to dishing out the first aid.

In due course and with some help he inched his way up the stairs, through the adjoining rooms, past the blanketed corpses and to the outside, the damp cool air for once was so very welcome. After that, it was about fifty tiny steps to the ambulance when the medic bearing his weight handed him over to the crew. Someone somewhere said 'It's Chris Simpkins, he's been shot'. He really hoped that it was one of the crew and not a member of the public. They then gave him some rather pleasant gas and whizzed him off to some unknown hospital. He got examined, he got scanned and then he got put to bed, comfortably drugged up and comfortably laid flat without a pillow.

In the morning a tad before midday, Consuela was the first to visit him, she looked shattered and spent, in Christian's mind she looked like she needed the bed more than he did.

"Hi," was all she could say as she sat down.

"Hell Consuela, that was a close one, don't take it personally but you look awful."

"Mmm…I know, I have been interrogated most of the night, I was supposed to be in the American embassy remember? They were absolutely livid that I had your gun, or even being in on the act at all."

"Well, if you weren't, none of us would be here now."

"Agreed, make sure that you impress that on them, Christian, do your best for me, please?"

"Who is them?"

"M.I.5 of course. George Willoughby is outside, he is waiting to speak with you, and while I have your attention what in heaven's name were you doing yesterday charging through an armed standoff like you did, I could have killed you."

"I know, I didn't really understand my body armour, there are never any instructions with this stuff you know. I realise now that when the guy shot at me, he missed, but I thought my armour just worked really well."

"Christ, I was so taken aback I aborted my shot, bloody idiot."

"Yeah, I know, but look at it this way, if I'd had known that it hurt so much, I wouldn't have shielded Tsargrin would I, huh?"

"You have a very strange outlook on life, your vest shows three impact marks, two on your chest and one on your right side. Your scan says two cracked ribs to the chest and two points of severe bruising, in short, you are lucky to be alive. I also had a narrow escape, I managed by pure fluke to find the only item in the whole place that was bulletproof, that old cast-iron stove. I am getting far too old for this Christian, too slow to react and too damn slow to move my ass if I have to."

"You looked quick enough to me, the way you jumped down the stairs and rolled over."

"That's the way it looked I suppose, but actually I just fell as soon as Rutherford opened up." Christian laughed and then twitched with pain.

"That is usually my tactic, I actually come out of things looking reasonably good but in reality, I'm just blundering around in the dark. I just can't fathom out why the Daves do this stuff?"

"It's their Job and thankfully they are very good at it, I guess that Norman must have allocated them and believe me, all those armed and trained men would have been crestfallen if they realised that they had to take on a couple of hard-assed Royal Marine Commandos armed to the teeth."

"Yes, I got the jitters just listening to them, what happens now?"

"Well, I am just really here to say goodbye, back to the US pretty quick." Christian fell silent, he had known her for a little over four years, lots of adventure and far too many near-death experiences. It dawned on him that he really didn't get to know her that well, he was thirty-two and she mid-forties and she was smarter, faster and sharper than he would ever be.

"You know, Consuela, I am sure that we shall meet again, the US is not exactly on the other side of the world is it?"

"Well Christian dear, it probably is. If you ever get the chance to look me up, please do, anyway I intend to monitor your meteoric progress, so stay alive will you?" He nodded and held out his hand as she stood, she brushed it aside and kissed him on the forehead before turning to leave.

"Consuela!"

"Huh," she said, arching one of her dark eyebrows.

"Thanks for…well, being you." She smiled gave him a nod and made her exit.

George Willoughby entered immediately afterwards.

"Ah…hello Christian, and good morning to you, how do you feel?"

"I've been shot but without all the holes."

"Yes, a bit sore, I'm sure."

"Yes, a bit, I think that there is something very amiss with your department though."

"Yes, very much so, both most recent incidents concerned you, first your gun had been tampered with, but we really have no real evidence on that besides your own statement, and secondly, this time, evidently you had been tracked, and this, of course, cannot be disputed. This Christian is a severely testing case."

"Yes, and I am not too enthralled with either of them."

"No, shouldn't imagine you are, we have interrogated Sean Holmes and the seamstress, and we have also taken the firearms people to task, we cannot find even the slightest lead."

"Have you found the locater thing, it was in the lining of my, or rather your jacket?"

"Of course, it is not one of our making, but easy enough to obtain in certain circles."

"Okay, so I got bugged, but that just tells them where I am, so how did they find the rear escape route, the tunnel, someone must have told them?"

"Not really, they are well kitted, they would just assign a drone, a small infantryman device, it would just home onto your signal, it wouldn't have been bigger than a small bird. It could watch your every move if outside. You can't get away from these things, Christian, that is why just one field operative needs a whole team to back him or her up." Christian laid back into his bed and drew a long deep breath, all his suppositions had now vanished into thin air.

"I don't think I am cut out for all this."

"No, you are not, it takes many years to train a field operative up to scratch, however, you do have a talent for asking yourself the right questions. It was you who worked out my whereabouts in the Cotswolds, but not your fault that we had been compromised. You were also right about the boat and it was you that worked out that Mr Throtestabler had somehow avoided the clutches of these murderous raiders, no one else took that tack."

"Well, actually, it was Consuela that found Mr Throtestabler, we worked together, I had nobody else I could trust."

"Yes, granted, but she would not have been looking otherwise would she? And while we are on the subject that woman has caused one almighty row between Whitehall and the C.I.A. You gave her your gun, for god's sake."

"She was staying at the hotel, incognito, she was the closest, she needed the gun."

"Listen, Christian, there are certain protocols to be observed, lots of them, and a big one is that your weapon is yours and yours alone."

"I made the right decision, Mr Willoughby, she saved the day, just long enough for the Daves to do their stuff."

"The Daves?"

"Yes, the Daves, the Commando guys that Norman assigned because they weren't attached to M.I.5."

"Mmm…curious, we have very little to do with this Norman man, he is a high ranking M.I.6 bod, that's all I know." Christian looked intently at Willoughby, but the man simply could not be read in any form or way much like the mysterious Norman.

"You know," said Christian in a matter-of-fact way, "your department or section is still compromised isn't it? You said that both Mr Holmes and the seamstress had been interviewed and they are denying everything, to me this means that you, all of you, have not got a shred of evidence to work with, otherwise you would not have interrogated them in the first place." Willoughby dipped his head slightly just enough for Christian to assume that he was right.

"Yes, some of these people could have been in place a long time, we believe that we are dealing with one very clever individual. However, I refuse to discuss internal matters with you."

"No, you are tidying up all the loose ends and I feel that I am one of them. What now?"

"Yes, very perceptive as usual. But seeing as you put it so candidly, yes, we are having a very careful clear out. I know that you have been very loyal and invaluable to the cause, but as an untrained amateur in the field, we must divorce you from any further proceedings. Your clearance rating from this day forward will be revoked and therefore your firearms permit also, although it must be said, heaven knows how you obtained it in the first place."

"Yes, something I often wondered myself. It also then means, if I have no clearance, I also lose my job at Ancillaries and Procurements."

"Don't be ridiculous, Sir Jeffery will find you a safe little place in a back office somewhere, I'm sure."

"How wonderful, I can't wait, where am I anyway?"

"Plymouth, under the exemplary care of the Royal Navy medical section."

"Navy base huh, when will I be allowed to leave?"

"Christian, you are not under arrest, but you are still bound by the Official Secrets Act, you can leave when you wish. You have, I must add, performed with outstanding skill, bravado and insight. Once all this has died down, a few years maybe, there will be a place for a man like you, someone who can think outside the box as it were. My department for one would be very interested, but as you know, I have been rather silly and very soon to be permanently laid off, but that is another story. For someone not attached to any one of the services, you have outperformed any operative I know, you have proved yourself in three different armed skirmishes in less than two months, not counting all your overseas adventures. Our field operatives, for example, are highly trained, fully kitted, with full backup and high-resolution up-to-date information, they wouldn't achieve that in six months or more. What I am saying, Christian, is when you feel ready, contact any of our security ministries and they will snap you up as an operations advisor. Physically, we can train people up for most things, mentally we can coach what we know. It is the mind you see, your mindset for example cannot be taught, it has a value and these people know it. Do you hear what I am saying?"

"I do Mr Willoughby, but I shouldn't be here in the first place, or anywhere like here. I was just minding my business doing my own risk-free unarmed job running a project in Wales."

"Fair enough, I get it, well I have had my say and my replacement whoever he or she may be will have your report, my section is due to be shut down for the foreseeable future, and I can clearly understand why. Good day to you, Mr Christian Simpkins, it really has been, shall we say, 'an experience' to have worked with you." Christian nodded, gave the old thumbs-up sign and cast his sight back to the ceiling above. He loitered around the naval hospital for a couple of days until he felt able to get up and go with some limited confidence. He was still very sore and every move seemed to jar the bones around his chest. He caught a train back to London and mulled over his fate up in his little flat.

Cleaning House

Back in Cornwall, Tsargrin was taking charge of his inventive self again. This proved to be a tough chore without the calming administration of Consuela at hand. The row with the Americans appeared to be abating, with their claims that it was their operative that saved the day and stopped the rot in M.I.5 plus of course saving Mr Throtestabler from certain death. This was also augmented by the fact that Tsargrin had been corresponding with the world's most eminent specialist in gravitational physics. This man, Mr Thorgril Skarphedinsen, an American of Scandinavian descent, had agreed to work with Tsargrin and to somehow create a mathematical formula to describe his concept. Somewhere along the line, it had become an important Anglo-American affair, thus the proverbial bun fight could now be put to bed.

On the M.I.5 front, Sean Holmes was still protesting his innocence, which meant that things were still not as they should be. George Willoughby was to stay on until the last spy had been identified. And until that time all operations had been passed on to other sections pending the closure of that department.

After a couple of weeks, Christian's body began to ease up a bit, he was able to move without saying 'ouch' too many times. He had a meeting with Sir Jeffery the following Monday and he had a very good idea as to what it was about, for with his clearance now rescinded, he wouldn't be a lot of good to Ancillaries or many other departments. The home office maybe or perhaps Work and Pensions might take him, they both had big staff turn-overs, and he well knew why, that old friend called 'tedium'. Monday soon came around and Christian prepared himself, the meeting was at twelve, so he timed his departure for eleven, that way he should find time to have a nice chat with Mie, he had missed a good few Wednesdays and looked forward to a nice but very gentle bout of passion to put a bit of colour into his fast becoming black and white life. When he arrived, he barely got the chance to use his dodgy charm on the beaming Mie before Sir Jeffery opened his office door and beckoned him inside.

"Ah Christian, nice and early for once, come on through." Christian had a quick glance around to check if anybody else bore that name, for he had always just been 'Simpkins'. This greeting sounded ominous.

"Hello, sir." Christian thought that maybe now that they were on first-name terms, he should call him 'Jeff', a thought that dissolved instantly when he sat down opposite him at the giant foreboding inlaid desk.

"I assume that you know why you are here?"

"Yes, my clearance has been rescinded, therefore, so has my job here, whatever it was."

"Good, nice to see that you are not too embittered."

"I'm not overly pleased and I would really like to avoid any more gun stuff."

"Course you would, goes without saying, but you are right there is very little here for you, you are far too well known and there is more to come, there has been an investigative journalist on your tail for some time."

"Yes, Anne Bottomley, bit of a pain."

"Yup, that's her, we've heard from certain circles that she has put together quite an exposé of you and your various exploits. Big stuff, but nothing that can't be found elsewhere, so we cannot stop her from going into print."

"Oh god, I knew she was doing something, this is going to be a bit of a bummer."

"Yes, couldn't have phrased it better. So in short, I have to terminate your employment, you have worked wonders for this department. For the first time, Procurements and Ancillaries are mentioned in discussions at a ministerial level. The department will be as generous as possible, I am advised that redundancy is the best option. You are still owed some holiday money, plus we will stick you on gardening leave for a few months. On top of that Christian, I shall personally lobby for some sort of pay-out for you."

"Thank you, most generous…possibly."

"On a high note, Christian, your advice and input into the tidal generator scheme in Wales has worked unbelievably well under Ms Reilly's guidance, the construction and installation are almost complete, on budget and on time, which is a first in itself. This is a huge feather in the cap for the department and word has it that it has been shortlisted for a conceptual engineering award, most prodigious. And for this, the department thanks you and will I hope be reflected in your termination pay-out. Going out on a high, couldn't be better, what!"

"Mmm…whatever."

"Now, a bit more business, you need to surrender your security pass to Mie on your way out, and may I remind you that you are still bound by the official secrets act, and of course, your firearm permit is now thankfully null and void, so that is the end of all this gun nonsense. Now lastly, Mr Throtestabler's facility in Cornwall. You are no longer permitted to venture there willy-nilly as before, now it is by request or invite, seconded by the security officer in charge, I think that you will find that things have been tightened up there. So thank you, Christian Simpkins, I'll shake you by the hand if I may, your efforts here will not be forgotten." Christian stood as Sir Jeffery did and lamely shook the outstretched hand. Closing the office door, he gave Mie his security pass. She smiled and mouthed the word 'Thursday' to him and Christian's slightly wretched expression burst into a smile. She handed him a neatly handwritten envelope and smiled her goodbye coupled with a favourable wink.

In one way Christian could understand his termination of the contract, every second person he met in those long corridors of power that was Whitehall either nodded enthusiastically or smiled at him. He had, by no real fault of his own, become one of those celebrities that he so avoided.

On the tube back to Camden and his little flat, he sat right to the rear to avoid recognition, he opened the envelope, he had been formally invited to attend a meeting with Tsargrin and others at his facility in Cornwall this coming Wednesday, this lifted him a little as he thought over Sir Jeffery's comments on the matter. The date on the letter was last Friday which meant that it was during the time of his employment, therefore, it was departmental business but he decided to go anyway, after all, what on earth could they say to him, he forgot to look at the date, he reminded himself.

That afternoon he reluctantly called Anne Bottomley. He didn't relish this call, but this morning's meeting jogged his memory. He had asked her for a favour in return for an interview, it was her that came up with the correct name of the ship 'Caravel 1' a deal had been struck and he felt obliged to honour his part. She was absolutely thrilled to hear from him as if she just assumed that he would renege on the deal (as so many others did). He was in turn absolutely thrilled when he found that he wouldn't have to do the interview, after all, she just needed him to collaborate on some data. It did intrigue him that she had already managed to speak to Sir Jeffery Pollock and also managed to extract some crucial information from Commander Ted in Belize, no mean feat in itself. Plus, unbelievably, she had also spoken to the police Superintendent in Plymouth. Whatever this woman had, she used it well to open an awful lot of doors. All he had to do was confirm a few dates, a few locations and some short run-ups to certain events. All of which he could do there and then on the phone. At the end of her bout of enquiries, she hit upon the most dreaded of questions.

"Tell me about Mr Throtestabler Christian?"

"Now that I cannot do, Anne, it is very restricted."

"Oh c'mon, he is category fifteen, he must be pretty special, surely?"

"Sorry Anne, you'll just have to guess."

"Yes, I think I can guess reasonably well, actually. His first name is Tsargrin, he's local to the Lizard Peninsular in Cornwall and has his own facility there, he is continually monitored and barred from leaving anywhere without an escort. He is insanely clever and has a penchant for real ale, am I getting close?"

"No, miles away."

"For the sake of anonymity, I am going to refer to him as Charlie Stable, maybe Charles, do you have a problem with any of that?"

"No, not at all, also this conversation did not exist either, did it?"

"Of course not, I will have it out in a few weeks, so anything you want to add, now is your chance."

"Nope, you seem to be better informed than I am. Unfortunately, I don't seem to recognise myself in any of this."

"Oh Christian, you will love it, you come out like a shining star, it is wonderful, your natural modesty knows no bounds. To me, it is like having a blank canvas." Christian let her harp on a bit regarding her much treasured, *Exposé,* he didn't really get where she was coming from, eventually, after another swathe of bluster, he managed to put the phone down and put a 'done' tick on that mental list of his.

Next on that list was the invite to Tsargrin's meeting on Wednesday, this, he was looking forward to, he had been moping around his little flat for three tiresome weeks, his chest still hurt and he was bored out of his tiny mind, he had now shaved off his trendy beard, got his hair cut really short and had taken to wearing dark glasses in November, coupled with a cheap baseball cap. He knew that he probably looked like a complete twat, but that was the way he felt at this moment in time. It could have been the effect of some sort of trauma from a host of near-death experiences, or maybe the dejection of being almost unemployable, or, quite simply boredom, loneliness perhaps, both, in all probability.

Tuesday threatened to be yet another dreary dull day. To brighten it up somewhat, he called Robyn Reilly about lunchtime, when he hoped that she wouldn't be so busy. Unfortunately, for some reason, she was disappointingly cold.

"Hi Robyn, it's Christian, just thought I'd give you a call, I got caught up in various bits of annoying stuff. How are you doing, how's it going in Wales, the tidal generators?"

"Well, nice of you to call I suppose, the generators are working better than expected, but I should imagine that you knew that."

"Erm…what, I'm sorry, I don't know what you mean?"

"No, you wouldn't would you?"

"Ahh, okay what's up? Something's biting you."

"You are, Christian, you are. You led me into this programme, this project, on a falsehood. You let me believe that its concept was the brainchild of Mr Throtestabler didn't

you, well I've been speaking to him, he says he had nothing to do with it, too busy, it was yours all along wasn't it?"

"Well, I think we have touched on this before, I hear what you are saying but does it really matter?"

"Yes, of course, it really matters, when you outlined the principal design, you gave me tonnage, joule capacities and tidal lift ratios, that takes a lot of doing, Christian, lots of research and endless hours of calculations, and you let me go ahead thinking that I'm working on one of Mr Throtestabler's projects. You even stated that it would all be accredited to me and it would be my name on it and not his because it wasn't his thing and so forth. Guess what though, where is your name Christian Simpkins, where is it? Nowhere, and I am getting all the praise, the write-ups, the publicity and I feel like one big fraud. It was you that gave me the stuff to work with. What the hell is wrong with you, couldn't you just be true to yourself, just once maybe." Christian didn't know where to start, he didn't even know how to calculate stuff, he just replicated, then divided the technical information from Tsargrin's water pump in Western Sahara, it was pretty much the same machine, but instead of pumping water, the pistons made power. The semisubmersible aspect was the same and it was clear that all the superstructure of the rig they used then, was unneeded.

"Well, Robyn, I cannot understand why you are so upset with me, you have worked wonders, on time and on budget and as for the calculations, I just—"

"Just stop it, Christian, for god's sake, if you downgrade yourself one more time I will fucking scream. Grow up and do something for yourself for once, go on, try it. You are clever, make yourself feel good. Jesus H Christ, everything you achieve you deny."

"Um…Well, sorry and all that, I guess it is just the way I am."

"Possibly yes, now I am rather busy, too busy, tell you what, give me a call when you feel like being truthful." Christian just stared at the handset before gingerly placing it back down, he had just experienced a thorough telling off, but for the life of him he couldn't work out what for. It was Tsargrin that was the ultra-modest one, not him. He tried to get on with his day, but her somewhat belligerent diatribe ranged through his brain. He had liked Robyn, but any hope there had now washed away into the ether. Tsargrin must have sensed his affection for her and had tried in his rather inept way to make him more credible, just a few tiny words that were well meant but truthfully unacceptable.

Tsargrin's Prognosis

Early Wednesday morning, he was clean and fresh by 6 am. He felt a little less sorry for himself now and looked forward to the day in Cornwall. He had no car but was quite used to the Train journey. He had packed his overnight bag with some forethought, he would travel incognito, baseball cap, dark glasses and a comfortable tracksuit. He would check into a different hotel under the name Gordon Knox, he still had the details of his alias. He hadn't as yet been asked to return it to that particular department and assumed that M.I.5 would demand the fictitious 'Gordon Knox' back when things returned to normal. The trip was uneventful as was his hotel check-in. It was a tiny inn type hotel, five rooms, nicely secluded with fine views of the sea.

When he turned up at the facility by taxi, he was back in his familiar pale grey suit. He put on a suitable smile and headed for the security gate and the familiar faces manning it.

"Hello Jack," he said by way of a greeting, "brought you in from the rear gate, huh?"

"Hi Chris, yep, makes a change, new regime here now, anyway, can I see your I.D. please?"

"Huh? But you know me, we've met dozens of times."

"I.D. please, you can't come in without it."

"C'mon Jack, you can't be serious?" Another man walked up, he nodded to Christian, he dipped his head and said 'hi Bob'.

"Any problem, Jack?" said Bob.

"Not really, it's Mr Simpkins here, he won't show his I.D."

"Sorry Christian, no I.D., no entry." The problem was that Christian's wallet now held the details of Gordon Knox. In a mischievous bout of rebellion, he handed over Knox's driving licence, the photo was of Christian and it was enough for the cursory glance of Jack to tick a certain box.

"There, that wasn't so hard, Christian, was it?"

"No, just me being stupid…"

"No problem, come through." As he was let in, he glanced back at the farcical situation behind with a bemused smirk. He followed a set of arrows that bypassed the old farmhouse and directed him to the side entrance of the canteen, the biggest room in the facility. It had been thoughtfully transformed with a raised rostrum and several rows of chairs, there was tea, good coffee and an array of biscuits, scones and little cup-cakes. There were a good few people already there including all the regular staff. He headed to the coffee point to load up with a large Americano, out of the corner of his eye he saw Robyn Reilly approaching, he visibly cringed and dumped some coffee on his trousers before turning toward her.

"Erm, hi," he said, a few octaves higher than usual. Robyn noted his discomfort and so came directly to the point to allay any further misery.

"Look Christian, I apologise for what I said yesterday, it was cruel and unneeded. I just wanted you to be recognised for what you really do. I don't mean the James Bond stuff, the other stuff, big stuff like bringing water to Western Sahara, peace to the troubled Belize border, the mighty Skyship and now a huge leap into green energy with the tidal generators. My tidal generators I am told, it is not mine, where is your name, where's Tsargrin's? It just saddens me, I got too frustrated yesterday, I am so sorry, Christian."

"It is okay Robyn, don't lose sleep over it, I'm just, well, kind of shy I suppose."

"Modest to the extreme maybe, I wish I had time to look inside that head of yours. Anyway, thanks for being so understanding. On another note, today should be really interesting, we all have so many questions. The upheaval over the last couple of months has distracted just about everyone from their chosen paths. I understand that there are a few replacements, between you and me, I have handed in my notice and Mr Throtestabler has gratefully let me go. It is the Welsh project you see, the tidal generators are going to be big business and I, little Robyn Reilly will be at the helm."

"There you go, I think I said that ages ago."

"Yes, you did, but at the time I put it down to confidence-building flattery."

"Ah-ha, so it worked then?"

"Let's not go there, Christian, come on now, let's get a good seat." Christian was feeling a lot better now as he sat down next to Robyn whilst acknowledging other people he knew with little nods and polite waves. Shortly, a man appeared upon the rostrum, one of Tsargrin's more senior people, he waited patiently until everyone found a seat and the murmurings of 'excuse me's' and 'hello's' abated.

"Thank you all for coming," he began, "I appreciate that it is short notice and I am aware that some of you have travelled far to get here. We thought it best to have this meeting sooner than later while it is still fresh in our minds. It is also an opportunity to thank many people for their loyalty and input to resolve the issues of the past events. Mr Throtestabler is keen to get things back as close as we can to what may be considered as normal here, whatever that is." A slight snigger rolled around the audience for a couple of seconds.

"Ladies and Gentlemen, before we go any further, there have unfortunately been several very sad fatalities. Notwithstanding their alliance or calling, it is real lives that have been extinguished all too soon. Please be upstanding for a minute of silence after which our cook Mrs Duggan will say a few words." The throng did as they were bid and hopefully drew some time for reflection after listening to Mrs Duggan's short sermon. The man then withdrew from the Rostrum and the portly frame of Tsargrin Throtestabler took his place, dislodging the mike as he did so.

"Ah…Oops, right, thanks everybody, um…sit down please, I have quite a bit to say but as most of you know I am not awfully great at speeches. Firstly, I want to try and alleviate any remaining fears because I realise that it has all been very traumatising for everyone. The new security regime in place is a bit harsh as many of you have so eloquently mentioned, but very soon, I am assured, a lot more gadgetry will be installed to cover the perimeters, and a hotline in the communications room is already in place. Also, to avoid unnecessary distractions our security people will not be permitted to enter either of the barns, a new portacabin arrangement will be assigned to them just west of the tennis court. I am sure that we, now more than ever, will appreciate their presence. Please give them a hand for their sterling work thus far." A polite bout of clapping echoed around the room, a thickset gentleman at the door dipped his head in some kind of salute. Christian knew Tsargrin well enough to target his moods and emotions, he was now beginning to become a little excitable.

"Now everyone, we have a few new names to join our team, first of all, we have to say goodbye to our young engineering whizz, Robyn Reilly." Robyn, as if prompted, stood briefly, gave a little wave and sat back down. "Robyn is off to Wales, the tidal generators are in place and she wants to put her time and considerable skills into following the system up. Robyn is to be replaced by Mr Keith Yearley, a specialist in innovative engineering methods." An amply built balding man stood up briefly to accept a polite applause. Another woman was introduced who bore a title that Christian could not understand and the new housekeeper made himself known, the pleasant young man named Christof. Next up was Tsargrin's surprise, Christian could tell that he was almost twitching as he made the announcement.

"It is my great pleasure to introduce a new position. I am fortunate enough to have a fully-fledged personal assistant, she has vast experience in most fields and I am very sure that you will make her most welcome. Please put your hands together for Mrs Lillian Smith." A figure emerged from a corner, with short dark hair and a print dress, some people began to applaud and then once upon the rostrum next to Tsargrin she looked up and faced the audience, to Christian's delight and a thunderous applause Consuela gave the tiniest of curtseys and a huge smile. Tsargrin added something about a new accord with the Americans and that Lillian Consuela

Smith was now a fully-fledged employee at the facility of her own free will.

Christian felt for her, it was clear, that like him, she had been dismissed from her position in the C.I.A. Tsargrin would have had to pull a few strings to bring her back to work with him. Without the burden of her rather loose covert activities, she could now work with Tsargrin without suspicion or distraction. He just hoped that the newly re-structured security protocol would have the sense to give her a Glock or something similar, but he very much doubted it. After another short bout of congratulations and a sort of pep talk to address any fears still remaining, Tsargrin drew up a chair onto the rostrum and then got the lectern removed as he couldn't see over it. He then informed everybody that there was to be an open discussion regarding the Fridge project, which as he rightly stated, was the source of all the recent troubles. It was suggested that everyone should take a break, grab some coffee and possibly a snack. It sounded to Christian that this was going to be a long haul, however, he too was rather enthralled. One thing bothered him though, he was no longer a valid partner of the facility anymore and neither was he aligned to a credible Whitehall department. He tracked down Consuela and had to wait for a little until she found time for him. He pulled her to one side and aired his little worry.

"God, I am glad that you are back though."

"Yes, better than ever now, I'm legit. This problem of yours, just keep quiet about it, for now, just play dumb if you get my meaning."

"Well, that shouldn't be too hard to do, okay, thanks for the tip, I'll fret about it later."

"Yes, you do that." Christian laughed at her 'so simple' way of dealing with it, he ambled off to grab a mug of sweet tea and a handful of chocolate biscuits before sitting back down next to Robyn. It dawned on him that she too was also now disconnected from the organisation, although, she like he, also had an invite. Annoyingly Christian's internal analytical mechanism began to stir.

Eventually, everybody had settled and Tsargrin was back in his seat clutching a bunch of badly folded paper, his notes. With a loud 'Ahem' he signalled the start of what he had to so importantly say. The security man at the door, the canteen staff and one or two others tactfully left the room.

"Now, pay the utmost attention please. The Fridge Project is the rather fickle name to my, or rather, our labours to research the feasibility of a gravity reaction motor system, it became one of those projects that started well, then faded away and then was taken back and so forth. It was probably about twenty years ago that I started tinkering around with gravity conundrums. I won't go on too long about it. The initial interest was kindled by a man from the water board of all things. He was here at the farmhouse and he was looking for the supply pipe which had long been covered over and badly documented, when he had run out of options to locate it, he made a call and shortly afterwards a man arrived on a scooter, he had two metal rods set into wooden handles so that they could turn. This man, of course, Ladies and Gentlemen was a dowser, a water diviner, and pretty good at it, he was. He zigzagged over the suspected area until he narrowed it down to a couple of feet, he then stuck a marker pennant in the centre and was on his way, or rather tried to until I stopped him, this man was so confident in his findings he didn't even wait for the men with shovels. I invited him in for a cup of tea and tried to make head or tail of his spurious art. He was dowsing for water, that was his job but he also told me that rods or the more traditional forked sticks could be used to source minerals, oil even. The scientific side of me said 'bollocks, it's unproven tosh' but my curiosity gene would have none of it. By the time he got back outside the men had exposed the pipe pretty well next to the marker, none of these people were awed by the talented dowser, he was just doing his job. Magic maybe, that is what the ancient's thought, devilry, it was termed in medieval times, and now, if you will excuse my English, dowsing is now described as 'bollocks' even by the learned few. I did a heap of research into the topic and I was convinced that something else was afoot. Gravity, ladies and gents, that was my conclusion, minerals are heavy, water is light, each density rippling the earth's gravity in minute rhythms, we all know that it is there, we all accept it as a fact, but as yet we cannot even describe it accurately. So…moving on from that point, maybe ten years later, I was looking into something called the Norton effect, this effect occurs when two contrary spinning rotors, one above the other, will tend to slow down at certain times, this 'Norton effect' was named after James Norton who noted it in his work as an aircraft designer, a helicopter in this case. At one time they made a machine with two sets of rotors, one above the other rotating opposite ways, it was thought that this would do without the need for a tail rotor. The helicopter was built and flown but never commercially taken up as at certain rotor ratios the Norton effect would kick in, possibly with some disastrous consequences. But what really mystified James Norton in the seventies was that when this effect manifested itself and slowed down the power, the input remained the same, therefore, where did this excess energy expend itself, this, he nor his team could find the answer. Now, this is where it gets interesting, for this flummoxed me for a while too, and I really do not like being flummoxed, it gives me headaches. So, I constructed a couple of rotary discs designed to invoke the Norton effect. It was most peculiar, the discs rattled and complained at first and then settled down to a slightly slower revolution speed than the input power suggested, although this effect lasted only a few seconds it was enough to have me scrabbling around for a cause, amongst other things I eventually strapped the thing to my bathroom scales, and that was it, when the effect kicked in, it weighed less and so I now had my grail to follow. So, here we go, something for all your hungry minds to chew on. Any energy expended will have to react upon something, heat normally, which includes motor generation, electricity etcetera, whatever, anything that demands a counter-reaction, the energy expended needs something to react upon and the only force remaining, in this case, is gravity itself. This theory has taken a good while to refine and define to its current level to get the excess expended energy to react upon gravity. Well, that is where we are at the moment and I have been labouring on with it ever since.

Now, what caused all the fuss was the Royal Air Force when a couple of jobs-worth types filed a complaint against us by claiming that we did not file for permission to launch an object into the stratosphere, the intercepting pilots said it looked something like a fridge spinning out of control at 40,000 feet. I would also like to point out that my gravity reaction motor looks nothing like a fridge, it looks more like a cabinet with a tapered circle at the bottom. At that time, I obviously denied having anything to do with that object in the sky, but they decided I did simply because it just happened to be in the vague vicinity of this place and so they filed a report. Now somehow the details of that report got aired and all the interest was unfortunately focused on me. In a way I can understand this interest as some people, maybe too many people, knew that I was messing around with this branch of physics.

At that time, I realised that gravity was a forever fluctuating force so I created something I termed as a compensator, this was a device to balance the machine as the gravitational pull forever changes, but, and this is important, I needed a point of reference to work to, effectively a benchmark, something to call zero. It is a bit like mean sea level so the Air Force chappies could work out where 40,000 feet, or the zero in a mathematical equation, something to base plus or minus on. All things need a reference point, it is vital for the math. To get this, I decided that Salisbury Plain was the best bet, it was the most stable place I could think of. Accordingly, we picked an area and plotted it out with a series of gravimeters and came up with a number we could call zero. We, or rather one of our engineers took the compensator there, started it up, entered the reading and brought it back here ensuring that it was still running. We fitted it to our gravity reaction motor, tweaked the settings and let it loose, but it rattled and bucked all over the place but never really got off the ground. A failure I am afraid and whatever they saw in the sky was not my doing. My physical understanding of gravity is perhaps deeply flawed.

Latterly, just a few weeks ago I contacted an old acquaintance, I do not normally beg for help but pure frustration drove me to call upon one of the world's most respected authorities on the matter of gravity, one Mr Thorgril Skarphedinsen, he is an American national and from his name, it is clear that he is of Scandinavian descent. I haven't personally seen him for many years, but now, courtesy of a bit of tech, I can see and speak to him on a regular basis." Tsargrin paused for a glass of water, Christian leaned over to Robyn.

"Do you think that if I got myself a really complicated weird name I'd be super clever too?"

"Nope, not a chance."

"Ah well, just a thought." Tsargrin scanned a couple of his notes.

"Right, so now we come to another problem, there are several schools of thought regarding gravity and what it actually is. Mr Skarphedinsen has one which is very well documented, which, I may add, makes excellent reading, whilst I have another. Very briefly put, it is err…I suppose, I'd better 'layman' it down a tad, so those not familiar with the science can get to grips with it." Christian emitted a slight sigh of relief and proffered a tiny thumbs-up sign, this small movement was picked up by Tsargrin.

"Mmm…I don't think I can dumb it down that much, Christian!" Again another polite ripple of laughter ran through the throng, but this time at Christian's expense, he tried to stop the blood rushing up to his cheeks but Robyn caught the moment and thought it was, as usual, priceless.

"Yes," continued Tsargrin, "my particular favourite prognosis on gravity runs a bit like this, rather than drift into particle physics, we shall for the sake of some clarity imagine a frequency of energy, this frequency can penetrate all known matter. Any mass, no matter how big or how small emits this frequency, the greater the mass, the greater the frequency. Everyone comfortable with that?" He looked around the room and continued.

"Now imagine that it worked a little like radar, the mass fires off the frequency in all directions until it hits something that it cannot penetrate, then it pings back to its source, that something can only be another equivalent frequency and when it returns back to itself, it drags the other frequency with it and eventually the smaller mass. That is it, I have managed to outline my preferred gravity prognosis in maybe fifty words. The thesis from which it stems runs into more than 300 pages, read it if you dare. We are not trying to stop gravity, we are merely trying to make it fluctuate in our favour, I am sure that in the future we will somehow master this. Mr Skarphedinsen is highly intrigued by my findings thus far and hopefully, in the new year we can get our heads together and we shall see if we can get something off the ground, er…figuratively speaking, of course, just my little joke."

Something was now bothering Christian, he couldn't quite put his finger on it, but he knew the feeling well. Tsargrin was now delving into the finer nuances of science to satisfy the other mighty minds in the room. Robyn, next to him, was alert and quite intense as she attempted to follow Tsargrin's train of thought. Christian possibly looked the same but his mind was now off on a far different tangent. Another bout of brief applause awoke him from his inner self. Tsargrin looked buoyant, almost pleased with himself.

"Right-ho," he said, placing his pile of notes down. "Any questions please?"

Robyn's hand was the first up. "Yes, Ms Reilly, go ahead."

"Well, Mr Throtestabler Sir. It is the compensator, I had a fair bit to do with it, but when you realised that you needed this, er…benchmark, you needed a place of gravitational stability, you decided on Salisbury plain and to be honest, you were right, very stable, how did you know, how could you possibly know? Without ever going there?"

"Excellent question, wonderful, simplicity itself. You see I didn't have to go, the ancient druids, the people who built Stonehenge, they liked their hallowed ground to be unsullied, pure, no graves, no old ruins, no running water, old mines and so forth. Therefore; back to the water divining, the dowser, the druids had them and used their respected arts to locate their places of worship. It is all just history now, but history is a fine tool for learning." Robyn accepted his explanation and although not embracing, she nodded politely but still remained slightly doubtful of this ancient art, something that tears at the very heart of an engineer's logic. Another man, the chief engineer, was at pains to find out what it actually was that the R.A.F pilots saw and what it was that the Americans pulled from the Irish Sea. It was falteringly described by Tsargrin as perhaps part of an aircraft or space debris falling back to earth and in the end just yet another unidentified flying object, as 'they happen'. When it was suggested that the pilots would have photographed the object tumbling around at forty thousand feet up in the sky, Tsargrin just shrugged in a matter-of-fact manner, and as far as he was concerned, the Americans didn't pull up anything from the sea, it was just a ruse at the time to divert attention from their C.I.A. operative in the facility.

"Until the object in question is identified it remains classified information for after all it could have been a spy drone of some type controlled by a foreign actor." The chief engineer wasn't overly happy with this explanation and before he could air a suitable response Tsargrin had taken another question regarding the integrity of their security forces. To this Tsargrin insisted that this was one for M.I.5 but it was believed that the one remaining spy that remained active was stationed outside the curtilage of the security services' normal boundaries. One of the last questions was from Christian himself. Tsargrin eyed him warily, he knew Christian well enough to know that his train of thought often differed from the norm, which of course made him who he was.

"Okay Christian, fire away, what have you got for me?"

"Well, er…Mr Throtestabler," he said to fit in with the occasion. "Just a thought, if there is still one infiltrator still unaccounted for, then why are we holding this rather open forum, it can't be helpful, can it?" Tsargrin stared back at him dumbly for a few moments for he did not have a ready answer. Christian noted his struggle and followed up with an easy rescue.

"I'm assuming then that you shouldn't have told us that one other insurgent remains." Tsargrin's eyes softened with Christian's prognosis.

"Erm…Yes, Christian, unfortunately, you are right, slight mishap on my part, however, I am glad you mentioned it. I am sure that the others here will share your concern and will be conscious of the sensitivity of what has been said here today." An agreeable mumble followed this sentiment. There were a few more questions proffered and these Tsargrin could answer without any bother. It had been a long talk for Tsargrin and he was as pleased as any to see it end. There was a fair bit of polite small talk afterwards, but Christian still had serious doubts about the content of Tsargrin's lengthy dialogue, it wasn't very like him to air his thoughts and failures thus. If something had to be said he would normally just get someone else to do it. It was almost like he had been coached to issue a denial of this new science, to admit to a good many people that he had failed and needed help to master gravity. Christian wisely decided to keep his thoughts to himself, for the time being, he didn't believe in UFOs and doubted if Tsargrin did either.

Outside, making some effort to say his goodbyes he managed to find himself alone with Robyn.

"Wow, what do you think?" She looked up at him, those big dark velvety eyes were a lot kinder than before.

"Not sure yet, Chris, I need to think things over, I guess that I am now obliged to read the full tome of his Preferred Gravity Prognosis just to correctly grasp his meaning."

"Why Robyn? Like me, you are not affiliated with his projects anymore are you?"

"Oh Christian, get a grip, please, we are all part of it wherever we are, whenever. We are hooked and will respond if called, I will anyway." He thought briefly, *she was undoubtedly right.*

"Yeah, I guess you are right." There was a short pause in their conversation as they crunched over the gravel drive, "Back to Wales?" he asked.

"Yep, I am a really busy girl these days, look, Chris, I have to go, but Monday week we have our opening ceremony, our tidal power goes live, try and come please, if you can. I'll email you an invite."

"Monday week huh, I am sure I'm available."

"Good, anyway, bye for now and try to keep out of trouble." She reached forward and gave him a peck on the cheek, turned and headed for the gate, a tall handsome looking man with a chiselled jaw swung it open, she hooked her arm through his and together they headed for a rather upmarket Range Rover. Christian was a little saddened by her new beau but hoped that she would be happy, he, Christian, had put her through a lot and although not by design it was still an awful lot. He put his collar up against the damp air as he waited for his taxi to arrive and take him back to the little Hotel. He briefly dwelt over Tsargrin's rather curious and uncharacteristic speech, his whirring mind appeared to have reached some kind of conclusion in that the whole thing was just staged. It was all simply a denial of facts for the benefit of the remaining spy and the other host of cohorts with their hungry minds on the concept. He preferred his own prognosis and smiled wryly to himself as the taxi arrived.

Loose Ends

He was glad to get home, the hotel was fine but the ensuing train journey was somewhat arduous as some railway union types had decided to 'work to rule' whatever that meant. A large brown envelope lay on his doormat as it was too big for his letterbox, he did have an inkling as to its content and he correctly reasoned that it was from Anne Bottomley, the journalist forever on his tail, it was the copy proof of her, *Expose* as promised, supposedly he was to comment or correct as he saw fit before publication. He very much had his doubts as to Anne's scruples but reading it he found it very much in his favour. The photos were exceptional, spanning several years from his first death-defying adventures in the Sahara, then Belize, with the Skyship on the Caribbean and finishing with his exploits here in England, of all places. She had filled in all the missing bits with a bit too much artistic licence. Christian found that he had somehow come across as cool and level-headed, without a mention of his rather nervous disposition or his uninspiring physical capabilities. He dreaded the thought of any forthcoming fame or excessive exposure. This so-called, *Expose*, he hoped, would be his swan song until he escaped from wherever it was that he should escape. He had a few little details he wanted Anne to change, just small inaccuracies.

Christian's rather short list of things to do included Mie, he sent her a text to see if they could meet as it was a Thursday although Wednesdays occasionally suited her just as well it seemed. Just dinner would be okay as far as he was concerned, anything, just some company. Shortly, even before he could get his hopes up, she messaged him with a sad tale of her being under the weather and consequently being unavailable for anything. With nothing much else to do, he called Anne Bottomley regarding the changes he suggested that she make, her secretary took the call and informed him that the *Expose*, had already gone to press. He was right about her scruples, she had no intention of making any changes whatsoever. He sent her a furious e-mail knowing very well that it wouldn't make the slightest difference, he then stomped off to take a long hot bath until he felt marginally better. Come the morning he was almost human again, with a clean shave, a decent breakfast and a freshly laundered flannel tracksuit to slop around in. A couple of days later, in a rare expression of vanity he picked up the brown envelope again and drew out the batch of photos, checking that the envelope was clear he noticed a smaller piece of paper, a compliments slip signed by Anne, a tiny footnote caught his eye, it was, *the Expose,* release date. At first, he just set it aside without a further thought until he glanced at his phone, for that date he now realised was this very day, this Sunday. Unaccustomedly galvanised, he tore down the stairs, crossed the street and charged into the newspaper shop, he grabbed a copy of the 'Sunday heavy', flicked through it and bought two more copies, Raj, the shop owner just looked at him as if he were mad, which at that moment, he probably was. Back in his little attic flat he just stared at himself looking back at him from the glossy Sunday supplement special, the photos were of him but the narrative was all about someone he didn't really know.

From that day on, his phone never stopped, interview requests, breakfast TV, publishers, ad-men and a host of unknown people that wanted to be his agent. When his phone eventually ran out of power, he couldn't be bothered to recharge it. The mail that week piled up also and he dared not go anywhere near the social media sites. He even avoided the TV, he just sat around in a darkened room listening to Dusty Springfield songs for company and dwelt upon a distant girl named Petunia. After a pretty grim ensuing week, he lightened up a little as if he thought some of the media hype had lessened and of course, if Mie were to call him, he would need his phone, this he charged up for better or worse, yet he would never answer it unless he knew the caller and these days it was a rare occasion.

One of these rare occasions was Thursday afternoon when a rather excitable Mie sort of demanded that she should come around that evening. Christian of course readily agreed, a friendly smiling face and a friend with proven benefits would be just the tonic he needed, sore ribs or not.

That Thursday night would prove to be a Thursday rarely forgotten. He had cleaned up the flat as best he could and put fresh sheets on the bed, he was washed preened and ready for when she arrived. She banged on his door bang on time and she threw him a huge crushing hug as they met. Although her embrace was full of passion, Christian sensed that she wasn't quite herself, a bit emotionally flat and he put it down to whatever ailment she had the previous week.

After a bout of fantastic sexual preambles, she sat astride him and produced her treasured pieces of silken rope. Relaxed, supine and compliant he let her do her stuff with the rope. That beautiful smile of hers, her golden-hued skin, her perfect teeth, she could do as she wished with the renowned Christian Simpkins. She then drew out another piece of rope, he widened his eyes questionably, she just laughed and put her finger to his lips, then fate came calling as it often did, the door buzzer sounded, she raised her eyes to the ceiling, donned his shirt and went down the hall to the front door.

"It is okay, Mie, it is the entry phone." He heard an electronic crackle and a few words that he couldn't make out from where he lay.

"You are wanted, Christian, what should I say?" He spluttered a bit and then started giggling.

"Tell them that I am a bit tied up at the moment and to come back later." Mie stuck her head around the door, beamed that big smile of hers and gave a thumbs-up.

Presently she returned, re-took her most satisfactory position again and grabbed the third piece of rope. She gave him a long kiss and looked at him in the eyes.

"Now Christian, you really have been a very naughty boy…"

"Oh, have I?" he replied with a grin on his face. Again fate took its cue, this time by an assertive bang on the door.

"Delivery…" a girl's voice sang from the other side of the door. This time Mie tutted loudly in frustration, hooked the shirt back around her and stomped down the hall to the front door. Christian barely heard the latch turn when there was an enormous crash as the door flew open. Immediately Christian tried pulling at his ropes, but to no avail, they were tight and strong. In the hallway he could hear some sort of combat in hand coupled with curses and loud karate style screams, he saw Mie flying backwards past his open door, but with a wily flick she was back on her feet, she had the stance of some type of fighter, low, almost crouching and slightly side on to her adversary. She delivered a powerful quick kick and then backed off slightly as the response came.

"Get out here, Christian," a voice yelled but it was not from Mie, he knew the voice, it was Consuela, she then appeared at the doorway, her combat stance was very different, upright, her feet rarely leaving the floor, shuffling this way and that like a boxer to avoid or fend off Mie's onslaught. She glanced into the room and did a double-take once she saw Christian in his restrained position. This falter was enough for Mie to counter her attack and launch herself at Consuela. Christian could hear the crump as Consuela hit the floor, then to his dismay, the two combatants tumbled in through his bedroom door. From his point of view as an unwilling spectator, Mie was getting the upper hand. Consuela was already favouring her left side but she still had a few tricks to play and neatly parried another rib smashing kick to her right side, Consuela caught the foot with her upswing, Mie spun backwards onto the bed and did a neat back roll over Christian and onto the floor the other side, as she grabbed the headboard to vault back over, Christian managed to grab a handful of her jet-black hair with his hand still tied at the wrist.

"Christian, don't," she screamed, "let go…" He tightened his grip and she retaliated with a swing from her far side, an upside-down fist impossibly hard to his face, he turned away struggling furiously with his bindings but not before another blow to his right eye and then another. Somewhere in his mind he saw the shadow of Consuela fly past him, she did something with her knee followed by a weird blow using the palm of her hand, Mie went limp, much like Christian himself, in an awkward way.

He could tell that Consuela was hurting as she twisted to one side to grab the third piece of rope, which she used to tie Mie's hands together behind her back cruelly tight. She stood upright, looked at Christian and shook her head sadly.

"Really?" was all she uttered before throwing some bedclothes over him and untying one of his hands, this piece of rope was used to bind her feet. She was already beginning to stir from her brief bout of unconsciousness. Christian hurriedly untied his other hand, donned his dressing gown and followed Consuela out to the other room. She was already on her phone snapping out Christian's address and other more unsavoury snippets of information. Christian meekly interrupted her.

"Um…Consuela, you don't really have to mention, you know, exactly what happened here, erm, do you?"

"I'm afraid so, dear, they, M.I.5 will have to know every little detail, you can tell them yourself, they will be here very shortly."

"Oh, God."

"Yes, quite, don't worry too much, they will have come across far more peculiar sights than someone just being tied to a bed. Christian, what is wrong with you, I have been phoning, texting, everything, why the hell didn't you pick up?"

"Oh yeah, that. It is that bloody article in the papers, my phone hasn't stopped, I've only been taking calls I know, I guess that you have a new number then?"

"I do and I suggest you get one too. Mie is the remaining spy, I had a chat with Norman and thanked him for the bit of help he gave you. He didn't help out, he wasn't even asked to, from there it was a simple matter of tracking it back, Sir Jeffery's secretary. It was her that tampered with your gun, Christian, and it was her that planted the locator in your jacket to disclose Tsargrin's whereabouts to Rutherford and God knows what else."

"Aah, no, it means that I was the source then, me?"

"Well, yes, as an unwilling proxy anyway, sort of. You didn't know and you didn't even put your mind to it, Christian, did you…that is the old 'Honey Trap' it diverts your conscience elsewhere."

"Hell, didn't it just, are you okay?"

"Not really, bust a rib or two I think, bit annoying, they take months to mend. My fault though, I am just getting too slow for all this, I was quite looking forward to my nice legitimate job down in Cornwall."

"What about, Mie, what happens to her now?"

"Not sure, depends on the security forces, anyway her name is not Mie, Mie Ng is at home looking after her young children up in Barnet. A neat bit of identity theft, the real Mie had never been abroad, she had no passport, so this other woman, the one in your bedroom, got enough paperwork to apply for one, Mie Ng's name with that woman's face on it. The rest was simple, ex-police officer, easily enough clearance for the Procurements and Ancillaries department and a real passport that could stand up to the checks. The real

Mie is Thai Chinese and our little Kung Fu queen here is, by the look of her, probably Cantonese, Hong Kong Chinese that is."

"God I feel so stupid!"

"Mmm…I thought you would have been used to that." She smiled a little at her trite remark and Christian smirked too.

"Tell you what, I'll put some coffee on, it's got to help, I think that it's going to be a long night."

"Good idea Christian, it would be nice if you could put some clothes on as well, er…please."

"I would, but she is in there, my bedroom I mean."

"Just get on with it, in fact, I'll get some stuff for you to wear, you carry on with the coffee, I need to check on her anyway." On her return she confirmed that everything was as it should be and handed him an armful of clothes, Christian looked at them dubiously and decided that Consuela had been a bit over-selective with her choice. Suit trousers and a garish Hawaiian shirt that he used for BBQ days, it was late November now and he was going to look like a complete twonk when the M.I.5 boys turned up. His face was really beginning to hurt now, it was swelling up and his lip stung when he tried to drink his coffee, his right eye was closing and his nose was impossibly tender, even his wrists pained him as he had stripped off the skin in his struggles. Consuela looked at his battered features.

"You did well, Christian, she was getting the better of me, you have been knocked around quite a bit, give it a couple of weeks and you will be fine, barely noticeable."

"Thanks…" he said whilst wincing at another sip, "I guess I know where that third rope was going, you came just in the nick of time Consuela, this must be about the tenth time that you have saved my skin over the years. So thanks yet again, I am out of this shit now, no more Sir Jeffery bloody Pollock and hopefully, very hopefully, no more near-death experiences, I'm really not cut out for this you know. I happen to keep saying that."

"Oh, I know, Christian dear, I know."

Presently the security bods arrived, four men in suits, two armed policemen and four others in uniform. Christian's little flat was filling up fast. He was asked to compile a long, drawn-out statement of events in front of the investigating officer, who, to Christian's dismay, was an attractive looking woman who demanded clarity to every little detail. Mie or whatever her name really was, was wrapped up and manhandled out of the flat. Christian turned his back on this moment, he didn't feel that he should let her see him.

Eventually, after what seemed many hours, everyone left, the investigating officer being the last.

"I have read your profile Christian and unfortunately you are in the public eye as we speak. I would strongly suggest that you do not mention this little episode to anyone, for the time being, we have a lot to follow up on. I would also remind you that you are still bound by the Official Secrets Act and therefore still duty-bound, understand?" Christian just nodded, he didn't want to talk about it ever, he said 'goodbye' and attempted to re-fit the front door back into its frame. His flat was a complete mess and the neighbours were shuffling around the stairway very much ill-at-ease.

He knew that someone somewhere would soon make a call and he would have even more unwanted attention if that was possible. In a rare act of foresight, he packed a bag, stuffed his laptop and a bunch of documents in a briefcase and made his door as secure as possible and then left. Despite it now being almost 6 am, he managed to check into one of those cheap little comfort hotels ten minutes' walk from his flat. He still had the I.D documents for Gordon Knox, his invented persona, which was enough for the sleepy-headed man on reception. Due to Mie's violent administration, he was unrecognisable as the man in the papers and surprisingly enough his Mr Knox's debit card still worked and so he now had a room incognito, courtesy of M.I.5. His room was tiny but clean and modern, there were very few facilities which thankfully reflected the cost which of course was funded by others, he knew Gordon Knox would be on borrowed time, but he didn't really dwell on this too long as by checking in as Mr Knox they would know exactly where he was, it all suddenly felt unimportant. Christian could see the rather comic irony of his escape, he was fleeing from himself. Today was Friday and today he would lick his wounds and sleep without any interruption.

Saturday morning as the pale sun arose Christian found that he could sleep no more, he was hungry and he was still hurting, the swelling was still there but the red bruises had now turned to a dark purple, and his lip was still overly fat but had ceased to bleed, his wrists were still very tender, it was the first time he had experience rope burns. All in all, he was a right mess but hoped it would fade before he went to Wales on Monday. He had promised to be there for the grand switching-on occasion of the tidal generators, a promise to Robyn, after all, that had happened, he just had to keep it. By Sunday night, he was feeling a lot better but his face was still as frightful as ever, the swelling to his lip had now gone down but it was now of the deepest blue, he could now see reasonably well out of his right eye but the swelling remained and it was badly blood-shot. He would have to leave early tomorrow, bad face or not. He had a pair of sunglasses and these coupled with an old baseball cap should, he thought, offer him some guise of normality along with his tracksuit. He could have done with more clothes but he was loath to go anywhere near his flat. He checked himself in the full-length mirror, he was not impressed, it was clear that black business shoes didn't work well with a tracksuit and then, he knew the area he was going to, and knew that he needed his coat, but a big overcoat over his already strained attire made him look like one of the many unfortunate homeless people about the streets of London, *maybe*, he thought, *there could be a chance to hook in some loose change on the way*. That night he burgled his own home, appropriated the right clothes and picked up some useful odds and ends. It was clear that someone else had been there, certain things weren't in the same place and his mail had been moved, which he also took with him. Strangely though, he wasn't even the slightest bit perturbed for it just didn't seem to matter anymore, nothing seemed to really matter now.

As luck would have it, the UK train network appeared to work properly and he made his connections without too much bother. He knew his way around the Welsh headland fairly well and he had about an hour to spare before things started. There were a good few dignitaries, representatives, key workers and to his dismay a TV crew and a few newspaper hacks bearing sophisticated looking cameras. He kept his distance as best he could and meandered off toward the seafront. From his elevated position, he had a good view of the tidal generation system. To the uninitiated, it looked like a giant biscuit tin with four big legs around it just poking up above the sea. It was positioned within the shelter of a natural rocky cove. Christian knew its weight, just over five thousand tons of concrete and steel. Five weeks ago, it was towed into position, anchored to the sea bed and fitted out with giant pistons and as Tsargrin would have put it, it would simply go up and down with the enormous tidal range, five thousand tons down and then five thousand tons up again, twice a day, the energy rate produced was apparently astonishing. Christian had worked on the project for almost a year mainly from the comfort of his desk in Ancillaries and Procurement in Whitehall, but it was Robyn who had put it together and made it work. He knew she had some misgivings over the origins of the initial concept when Tsargrin denied having any input, then she decided that it was Christian after all, but to make it even more confusing he too denied it as in reality it was just a bastardised version of Tsargrin's tide powered water pump in Western Sahara, years ago. Now Robyn understandably feels a little bit uncomfortable with her name featuring very high on every document so far drafted.

Out there with the bracing sea wind stinging the wounds on his face, he forced a smile and even a light laugh, something positive did after all emerge from all the past horrors. Robyn threw herself into this project with marshalled fury, she was the one that made it happen and she was the one that should correctly reap the benefits and he, Christian, despite being on the side-lines was happy for her. She was real and ironically, courtesy of Anne Bottomley, he was the one that felt like one big phoney now. Conversely in his mind, Tsargrin who was never a phoney had to pretend he was by denying that the fridge at forty thousand feet was not his doing. All nicely staged by someone to offset the hungry eye of the scientific world, Christian's point of view anyway.

He glanced at his watch, replaced his dark glasses, dipped down the peak of his cap and made his way over to a large marquee type arrangement that was open on one side so that the Tidal Generator could be seen in all its supposed glory, but with some cover as a precaution to the unpredictable elements. To Christian it was just a piece of pageantry, for the Tidal Generator would look exactly the same if the power was on or not. Nothing would change, no big gush of water, no roar of machinery, not even a comforting hum, just power. On entering, he handed over his invite and accepted a nice glass of Champagne, his fat lip didn't sting so much now. He could see Robyn up upon a raised dais along with other, presumably, important folk, he recognised a few faces there but kept his distance and manoeuvred himself into the far corner once he had secured his second glass of bubbly. He was there, just one among a hundred or so, he had kept his promise and all he had to do was hang around a bit, wait until the power was on, applaud accordingly and then sneak away back to obscurity. His invite was his calling card, she would know that he kept his promise.

Christian's rather lame assessment of the proceedings yet to come were poorly judged. He hadn't reckoned with the speeches or at least the length of them, especially from the local Mayor and the head of the environmental agency. Then there was the power company representative followed by the spokesman for the Welsh assembly and so forth. Two hours later and on his fourth glass of bubbly, he stayed in his corner and looked at his watch. Eventually, in the latter part of the afternoon a spokesperson from the 'Tidal Generator' consortium, the people that had put everything together over the last two years, unveiled a big red lever for the Mayor to ceremoniously turn on the power. There was a hush, the man looked about himself rather magnanimously, declared that the power should run and pushed down the lever. Christian knew that the lever was just a lever and someone at control would get a call to turn it on. To a resounding cheer a string of lights came on and a laser show mounted on the generator did its best to mark the occasion in the now fading light of late November. There were lots of people nodding heads among a good number of mumbled compliments abounding everywhere. This moment, Christian decided, was the best time to exit. It was getting cold and blustery now, he buttoned up his overcoat and removed his baseball cap lest the wind steal it from him and shuffled out for one last look at the tide and its awesome power.

"Ahaa, there you are Christian, I thought I saw you skulking around." It was Robyn's voice, he put on an upbeat smile and turned to face her. "Jesus Christian, what the hell?"

"Hi Robyn, don't worry about this face it'll get better, I am glad I came, big day for you, fantastic stuff."

"What have you been doing, you've been beaten to a pulp, what happened?"

"I know, I know, let's just say that the last spy is now safely locked up. Bit of a bruising but I'll be just fine." Out of the corner of his good eye, he saw a tall man approaching, the one with the chiselled jaw, he lowered his face.

"Erm…yes this is Mike—" Before she could finish Mike thrust his big hand out to Christian, he dutifully took it and found that the grip was unnecessarily hard.

"Yes, I'm Chris, nice to meet you," he said looking up, Mike flinched a little at his facial damage.

"Whoa, walked into the wrong guy huh."

"No," said Christian truthfully extracting his hand from the iron grip, Robyn looked down at the movement and drew in a sharp intake of breath. Mike was slightly taken back by his response but before he could collect himself Robyn firmed up the introduction.

"Mike here is my better half, Mike, meet Christian Simpkins." Upon hearing the name, he took a step back and emitted a tiny awkward laugh, his confidence on the verge of collapse.

"Christian Simpkins? Yes of course, um…yep, well, must go, I'll see you again, erm…Chris, we must talk some time, ciao!" As he turned away Robyn reached down and grabbed Christian's left arm, pulled his sleeve slightly upward and exposed the raw rope burn on his wrist; she had already glimpsed the one on his right.

"Hell Christian, you have been tied up, bound! You've been tortured, haven't you? You shouldn't be here, you should be in a hospital somewhere, therapy, anything, I don't know, you just have to get away from this shit, Christian, you are not cut out for this, nobody is."

"I will tell you all about it one day when I'm really drunk."

"You never get really drunk?"

"Mmm…Maybe that is where I am going wrong."

"Oh God, look, I really appreciate you coming all this way, it means a lot. Without you, this thing would have never got off the ground."

"Oh, let's not go there again please."

"Okay, okay, just a reality check, that's all."

"Look Robyn, I am going to go now, long trip ahead, I've got your email, I'll keep in touch, promise." Robyn looked at all the people milling around, she was the person, she was needed. All she could do was nod and give him a tiny peck on the cheek. Christian gave her a crooked smile, turned and left. He could feel his emotions getting the better of him, the stiff breeze drying out his watering eyes.

After several more hours on several more trains, Christian wandered back into his hotel room, he was both hungry and thirsty for an alcoholic whack, but he just couldn't be bothered, there seemed to be nothing worth bothering about. After a week there, he slunk back to his little flat, his facial wounds could now be described as light bruising, and his bank account wasn't looking too good either, enough to maybe get him to the new year for the money Sir Jeffery inferred he would get hadn't yet materialised. December and a sad and lonely Christmas loomed. He often thought about his lot and knew that he could improve himself just by calling Anne Bottomley. Her e-mails promised him a lot but the very thought of diving headfirst into the celebrity circuit made him cringe. He felt that if nothing else came his way then he would have no alternative but to make that dreadful call. He thought about Maria, the narcotics agent in Mexico and he thought, perhaps too much about Petunia in Bhutan and also, always also, Robyn Reilly in Wales. He knew that she would fare well, she was an excellent level headed engineer, she had a new industry at her fingertips and she had good ol' chiselled jaw Mike to make her world complete.

When he first got into his flat, he noted that someone had repaired his front door, in all probability the landlord. A handwritten envelope lay on the mat inside, this too was from his apparently hapless landlord. In an awfully nice way, the letter informed him that he must leave. It cited numerous breaches, from complaints by the neighbours, a stream of unwanted visitors and unacceptable damage to the flat. Again this was laid out exceedingly nicely, he knew the landlord, he was big and brash, it seemed that very few wanted to face the wrath of the renowned Christian Simpkins, *if only they really knew* he thought in despair. He had a couple of months to find somewhere else, but what self-respecting landlord would even entertain the thought of having someone like him as a tenant?

Christmas Cheer

Christmas could be a wonderful time for so many or it could just become a painful memory of all that had gone before, Christian this year, suspected the latter. He bought a little tree, got hold of a few fairy lights and hoped to make the best of it with a little help from the TV. It was just ten days to Christmas and he didn't even have a present that he could give to someone. He did get a very welcome call from Robyn inviting him for dinner when she came back to London in a few days. "A little bit of festive cheer," she said followed by, "come and join us." The 'us' bit deflated him a bit, but the thought was there and the down-town restaurant was pretty swanky. He would like to see her again even if it did mean sharing the moment with big Mike. He had been keeping tabs on her new enterprise via the internet and it was looking remarkably good, with heaps of positive interest from all quarters. The Tidal Generating Company seemed to be high on the agenda of any authority sporting a decent tidal range.

The restaurant, 'il Gusto', was attached to a large Park Lane hotel in London and from what he could gather, it was a bit of a haunt for the more refined celebrities, this, he knew, was Robyn's little way of making him feel a little less uncomfortable as other faces, more important than his, would undoubtedly take the heat off him.

In his best light grey suit, he entered via the hotel lobby and made his way to the restaurant facing the street. The Maître D' didn't ask for his name but politely indicated that he should go to the lounge in the first instance, this he did, he was on time he had shaved and had washed and he thought that he was ready for whatever the fickle hand of fate could throw at him now. 'They' turned out to be Robyn and her enormous little brother Billy, no sign of Mike. Robyn seemed genuinely thrilled to see Christian, Billy too, but he was overexcited and despite his size, he tried awfully hard to fit in. Robyn handed Christian some kind of cocktail and eyed her twitching brother with amusement.

"Go on then Bill," she said to him, "go on, ask, he won't bite." Christian looked up at him and gave him a little nod to encourage him.

"Well, er…Christian, I mean, Mr Simpkins?"

"Christian is fine, Billy, what is it?"

"It is just, well, you know, you see—" Robyn laughed and rescued her brother from his own bluster.

"Christian, in short, can Billy have a selfie with you, it appears that his car got into the papers and it is now more famous than he is, you used it on one of your exploits, he wants to let people know that he really knows you, that's all, please."

"Of course, Billy, no problem." Billy's face almost split in half with the widest smile ever. The selfie, as it happens was taken by Robyn, several snaps in several poses. Billy then said a few too many thank yous and then, despite his size, skipped out of the lounge, through the lobby and into the street, phone in hand.

"Thanks for doing that, Christian, it means a lot to him, really."

"No problem at all, Robyn, I like this place, nobody bats an eyelid."

"Exactly, that's why I booked it, now we are two, hungry?"

"Oh yeah." It seemed so natural when she hooked her arm through his as they made their way to the table. Christian was overjoyed with the way things were working out. He liked Robyn and suspected that it could be far more than just 'like' if the chance were there.

He wasn't very good at making romantic overtures, clumsy, even. She was very friendly and felt close, but he really didn't want to ruin things by emotionally pouncing on the poor girl, he would see how things pan out as the evening wore on. He glanced around the large dining area and espied a few well-known faces before focusing back on her. Although he had ordered some wonderful culinary delights, such as the moment, he had forgotten what.

"This is nice, Robyn, just the two of us and not a Cornish pasty in sight, and it makes it a little easier to be a little more candid if you know what I mean."

"Yes, I very much hope so, we so need to talk, and enjoy each other's company, we have been through an awful lot together. I really hope that this will be far more than just a dinner Christian. The Tidal Generating Company now has excellent funding and has appropriated an exceptional production area courtesy of the Welsh Assembly, and guess what? I have become the Chief Executive Officer."

"Yes," Christian cut in, "I have been following your progress, full order book as well I hear?"

"Yes, glad you have been paying attention, and yes, heaps of orders and a couple of new designs in the offing."

"Yours I trust?"

"This time Christian, yes, smaller versions for marinas, they often need the boardwalks to go up and down with the tide, so why not produce some energy while you are at it?"

"Wow, that is good, I'd love to see the drafts."

"Hopefully you will, because Christian, I would like to offer you a job."

"In Wales?" he queried.

"Of course, I want you to be in the thick of things, you have a lot of insight that is why your solutions are so successful."

"Mmm…I do need a job."

"Well, you had better take this one, I am counting on you for a number of things."

"Right, okay, I have given it some careful thought, and yes I would love to take the job thank you very much, when do I start?"

"Mmm…glad you have given it some careful deliberation Christian, at least two seconds I would say."

"Yeah, I don't like to rush these things." She laughed as did he.

"I'll have to find a place to live I suppose, it has to be cheaper than here in London."

"Everywhere is cheaper than London. I have a wonderful house in South Wales, old, woody and facing the sea, you must stay there."

"Uh...must huh? I don't think chiselled jawed Mike would be overly happy." Christian winced, he hadn't meant to slight her beau.

"What did you just call him?"

"Ahh sorry, he has a, well you know, kind of chiselled features...er..."

"You just called him chiselled jawed Mike, didn't you, that's hilarious." Robyn creased up with laughter and Christian, sensing the situation, joined her.

"Chiselled jawed Mike, I will never forget that, never, anyway 'chisel jaw' is history now, so, just me and you in that lovely old house, what do you reckon?" He tried to talk, say something witty perhaps, but all he could manage was a high pitched 'yes'. He took a healthy slug of exceedingly good wine to somehow slow down his metabolism, he fought hard for the right words.

"Dammit, Robyn Reilly, I so wish that I had made some sort of approach to you before now. I think about a lot of people but you are always way out front."

"Before I knew you better, I wondered about that and to be honest it is quite refreshing that you didn't, especially when I was so emotionally vulnerable. So many men take the slightest bit of attention as a green flag to make a move on you. You, Christian, were and are the perfect gent, up until you came into my life, I didn't know they existed, you are impossibly modest too and that is unusually nice as well."

"Oh dear, don't go too far, I can feel one of my wretched blushes creeping up on me."

"Oh good, wonderful even, I just love it, love you, when those cheeks of yours flush red, so, so sweet."

"Oh god," he muttered just before his face filled up with red blood, Robyn snorted into her glass of fine red wine. From then on, the conversation deteriorated into innuendos and slapstick humour.

As they emerged from the marbled hotel lobby hand-in-hand, a sparkling old-style BMW, low slung and with a gurgling exhaust pulled up for them, or rather her. Billy leapt out and opened the door for Robyn, she was going back to her family, he gave her a polite hug and a kiss on the cheek. Her big brown eyes held his greys in a pleasurable hypnotic moment then they parted, her to her family in Streatham, South London, and him to his lonely, tiny, shitty little flat in Camden Town. He couldn't wait to get back, close the door behind him and then whoop around the room to his heart's content.

He got the job, he got a nice roof over his head but most of all he got the girl and a marvellous one as well. Every day they spoke to each other, or texted, or maybe e-mailed. He would be up in beautiful South Wales before the New Year just after Christmas and happily, they would live forever after.